ENIGMA IN BLUE

ENIGMA IN BLUE

Klaus Bytzek

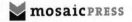

Library and Archives Canada Cataloguing in Publication

Bytzek, Klaus, 1937-, author
    Enigma in blue / Klaus Bytzek.

Issued in print and electronic formats.
ISBN 978-1-77161-007-0 (bound).--ISBN 978-1-77161-008-7 (pbk.).--
ISBN 978-1-77161-009-4 (html).--ISBN 978-1-77161-012-4 (pdf)

    I. Title.

PS8603.Y89E55 2013   C813'.6   C2013-907592-5
                                           C2013-907593-3

No part of this book may be reproduced or transmitted in any form, by any means, electronic or mechanical, including photocopying and recording, information storage and retrieval systems, without permission in writing from the publisher, except by a reviewer who may quote brief passages in a review.

Pubished by Mosaic Press, Oakville, Ontario, Canada, 2014.
Distributed in the United States by Bookmasters (www.bookmasters.com).
Distributed in the U.K. by Gazelle Book Services (www.gazellebookservices.co.uk).

MOSAIC PRESS, Publishers
Copyright © 2014, Klaus Bytzek
Cover design and book layout by Eric Normann
Cover art by Klaus Bytzek

Printed and Bound in Canada.
ISBN Hardcover 978-1-77161-007-0
    Paperback 978-1-77161-008-7
        Epub 978-1-77161-009-4
        ePDF 978-1-77161-012-4

MOSAIC PRESS
1252 Speers Road, Units 1 & 2
Oakville, Ontario L6L 5N9
phone: (905) 825-2130

info@mosaic-press.com

www.mosaic-press.com

ACKNOWLEDGMENTS

I wish to thank Maggie Levy for her endless patience, I appreciate Hugh Cook's early constructive guidance and I am most grateful for Howard Aster's encouragement.

My thanks also to all who read the manuscript and helped by providing feedback.

This is a work of fiction. All characters, human or otherwise and all events, plausible or not, are interchangeable composites and the product of the authors imagination.

For B.B. and Kat and family

− 1 −

Down the driveway yet another time—he can't relax. Of all the days for her to be late. She doesn't go away that often, so why did it have to be today.

The early part of the morning had been much like others without Kate. Blue had gone on his usual exploratory round. Only this time he'd headed more towards the north and wound up near the small patch of forest by the lake.

He had first sensed it and then he found it and Kate will be the only one he takes there and he will wait outside, freezing rain or not, no matter how long it takes. Blue feels himself shaking.

When he had first seen the two coyotes at a distance, they had been nervously circling a small area and not noticed him. Even after they started to dig and claw furiously at the ground and finally did become aware of him, they had halted only for a moment to glare at him and expose their fangs. Coyotes...? In the daytime?

Neither the gathering dark clouds, distant thunder nor onset of cold rain had disturbed the invaders. It had disturbed Blue. And when he made out that large figure with what looked like a pick axe over the shoulder appear on the horizon, he had moved away, trembling.

*** * * ***

Kate Walter is driving faster than she should. She's tense and late. She normally enjoys the occasional, almost two-hour drive home from Mississauga to the farm, especially during the Canadian fall. But today...! Never that eager to go into town in connection with the family business, she feels that the meeting had started out well enough for her. She lets go of the steering wheel and brushes the hair from her forehead, sighing.

Sam needn't have been that persistent and hadn't she had misgivings from the beginning when her father had asked her again to cover for him at the company's weekly engineering meeting? She accepted that his health and age were a factor, but deep down she knew that his real motive had more to do with his desire to see her get out more into the world. Live more, as it were.

The most benign of little strokes and the possible onset of Alzheimer's disease he had self-diagnosed for his benefit not that long ago. So convenient. That he didn't enjoy exercising his authority, except in a defensive position, she knew well. But what would make him think that she did in his place? Not fair. He was trying to set himself up to where he didn't have to make sense anymore at all; or talk, for that matter. Only if he felt like it. As he did a couple of days ago when the subject had been of interest to him. He had not seemed that confused then.

No matter how kind and considerate he generally seemed to be towards everyone—albeit one at a time—he was not a real comfortable member of the family of men. He loved her and Serafina—not people. Others before...individually...two simultaneously at the most, but not people.

He had tried to take advantage of her doubts. This he had done by eagerly agreeing with her observation, not at issue for the first time in her writings, that leadership positions are not generally sought by those most suited for them nor driven by noble motives.

"How very astute of you," he had said with special emphasis on the word 'astute.' "People are foolish for wanting to be led in the first place by anybody—and more so when they get together en masse towards that end." His speech had been clear enough at that point.

"And finding satisfaction in being at the head of such a parade of weak fools!" he had gone on. "Well, it's self-evident."

What was self-evident was that Leo had tried extra hard to sound reasonable and thoughtful; she had remembered another conversation about the same subject when the words 'lead buffoon' and 'village idiots' had been bandied about.

Lucid though! A little convoluted, but lucid. In line really with her own conclusion that leaders, when necessary, should be drafted for a most temporary period from among the qualified and reluctant. In the interest of fairness, the overly eager should be provided with ample opportunities to be noticed and to shine in other ways— Leo had suggested—such as being shot out of giant air cannons with much fanfare and in full view of everyone. Safely, of course, and in costumes of their own design. He had also seemed to enthusiastically support her suggestion that such individuals should also be supplied with free and colorful bobble-heads of themselves for distribution to their friends.

But shooting an imaginary, overly ambitious wannabe out of a cannon was one thing. What was he proposing for her? Take his place at the head of a fools' parade, get married in her spare time, but still manage somehow to avoid being expelled from the business end of a big gun?

She had given him a long look and he seemed to have realized that he had been selective in applying his standards; his speech pattern had suddenly deteriorated.

Words would be in order with Leo about his ideas. His real name being Leopold, she normally called him Dad, Leo occasionally, but Leopold whenever she was upset with him. Leopold it would be tonight.

He had asked her to observe for the most part and try to pick up on anything noteworthy at the meeting, but had urged her to be specific regarding one technical matter. There had been five of the development engineers, two of them women, and Sam Randolph, the department head at the conference table. Kate had worked with this team some time ago for two months, so she knew all of them well, especially Neja. They were all on a first name basis, except Sam Randolph, who would address her as Miss Walter. A sign of respect? Not. Was it just because she might occasionally confuse the actions of her children's book characters with the business at hand? Couldn't he ever tell? The others seemed to. She really didn't want to be there in the first place; she would have been quite happy spending the day with Blue and working on her notes, thank you very much.

There was general agreement that the tri-directional Azimuth technology for the propulsion, steering and stabilization of motor yachts continued to show good promise and that progress had been made towards the net energy efficiency issue. Kate was very familiar with that subject. A bump on the head would do that. Slid right across the deck she had in moderate seas. So Leo decided to do something about it, starting with their own boat.

Adding stability capability to the propulsion and steering means, if it could be done, would make sense. The economic issues might in the end not be the deciding factor to the success or failure of the concept; a motor-yacht typically was a rich man's toy anyway.

Sam Randolph had excused himself for a time over what he termed "a pressing matter" requiring his attention near mid-day and she had enjoyed lunch sitting with Neja. Hadn't Kate learned first-hand how difficult it was to obtain an engineering degree? Not only did Neja have a degree, but she had gained ever more respect among the other engineers and from Dad for her ability to merge what was analytical and inventive.

ENIGMA IN BLUE

To take a spring and make it function counter to the direction that it had been wound is an absolute no-no. One doesn't even have to look at textbooks. You don't do that—except Neja did. The result had been of substantial benefit economically, and also had greatly reduced the size of the package for which the spring had been intended. No hookups required, durability proven and verified thoroughly over millions of cycles. Simple, fundamental and effective; Leo really appreciated this kind of thinking in anybody.

But that was not the main reason Kate liked Neja's company. The resemblance to Louise was uncanny. Older yes, at a little more than thirty and Kate knew she was originally from Sri Lanka; but with her inquisitive mind, that intelligent narrow face and those pigtails, wasn't she just the spitting image of Louise? A sweet child, Louise, and definitely one of her primary book characters, although at times she could drive you to distraction.

Louise was a good example of someone being drafted into a leadership role by a substantial faction of Kate's characters consisting of Flying Puppies and Children.

Kate, to be sure, felt so much better now that she was consulting with her characters more, trying to reach consensus before committing them to action. Not always done without difficulty and present, more often than not, would be the fine hand of Louise.

Kate was well aware that she herself had increasingly steered away from much introspection and analysis when it came to interpersonal relationships. She had shifted their focus more in the direction of action, adventure, daily chores and basic survival with plenty of play mixed in. Fundamentals. Crawling around the minds and insides of others? Especially without permission. To find out in great detail what motivated them to do what they did? No. More frequently now people, when caught doing very bad things, were ever more comfortable blaming their deeds on relationships gone wrong with, say, distant cousins, then volunteering to undergo spiritual restoration and forgiving themselves, usually followed by accepting the kind understanding of all others with a view towards a comeback and a profitable book.

Louise and her disciples felt different from Kate, about... everything. Vehemently.

"Just look at the great literature of the world," Louise had lectured her in front of everyone. "Or read up on Carl Jung." Age six, fond of quoting the fathers of psychology. Frequently. "It's all about inter-relationships and how we are what we are as a result of what everyone else is and does."

Could I be wrong? Kate worried. I think not, but I must stay open-minded. If I put something in writing, I'd better be sure. It's a great responsibility. Everything in print seems to assume a mantle of truthfulness and a level of dignity it may not deserve.

"Miss Walter?"

And Louise and Neja are highly intelligent...

"Miss Walter...?"

"Sorry."

The discussion had briefly turned to a potential recall situation and then moved on to the need for finding more creative engineers. From England, most of them agreed, Poland perhaps, not Germany with all due respect. They knew how to execute over the long haul; but quick, clever creativity?

Kate's mind had wandered again, she couldn't deny that. A hot bath. And she wouldn't mind an ice cream cone and should she use the name "Next" or "Truly" for the new puppy in the story? Truly? Truly Misty Blue... yeah.

Sam Randolph alone seemed to take note that she had become distracted once more. He had been Leo's right-hand man for a long time when it came to all matters technical, in addition to being a Senior Director, and had known Kate for so many of her twenty-six years. And he had always been aware that she was adopted and of

ENIGMA IN BLUE

Afro-Asian blood. She caught him studying her. He used to call her Katie. What had changed?

She didn't have to bring up the subject that Dad had asked her to deal with—Sam Randolph did. Near the end of the meeting, already organizing his notes: "You may want to tell your father that there has been some progress with respect to the electronics package for the equilibrium garage door lifting device. Joe here..." Sam had paused with a broad grin and pointed at some substantial holes in the young man's sweater, "has made some real progress over the last eight days or so."

Joe Vinter, scruffy as usual, had looked pleased even as he was trying in vain to cover up what Kate was already so familiar with.

"Actually, Sam, Leo asked me to bring up the matter—"

"Oh."

Kate could tell; he probably still liked her a little bit—maybe—but didn't really want to discuss this complex issue with her. He worked with women all the time? Or was it because he saw himself...? No, he was "the" man behind Leo. It's Leopold! Didn't Sam begin to change when Leopold first started to encourage...push her to become more active in his absence?

"Leo reminded me that he did authorize Joe to pursue this design even though he has always had—that's what he says—reservations about artificial intelligence controlling this equilibrium in motion." Somebody give me a break, please.

"Miss Walter, we are eighty-five percent there." Sam had stood up at that point.

"I know I didn't do that well with my engineering degree." Yes, she had tried to sound apologetic. "But I think I understand why Leo is so adamant. My car is loaded with electronics and it's not that often they all work in unison; and talk about computers..."

"Miss Walter...."

She had summoned the courage. "Leo says that if you're not there now, he wants the project halted, and he doesn't want it pursued again unless you find a way to include that mechanical control means which you have apparently talked about. I don't know what that is about, but presumably you do."

Sam wouldn't give up. "Miss Walter, are you certain that you didn't misunderstand? Are those the actual words Leo used?"

Oh god no. She had felt her bottom lip beginning to quiver. "No Sam," she had said, "his exact words were: tell them that in spite of my misgivings from the very beginning I've given them every opportunity to make it work and then tell them to..." Kate had stopped there—she couldn't do it. She knew she had stared at an empty space on a wall before trying one other tack. "Sam, Leo was getting frustrated, even with me—"

"Miss Walter, this is engineering. Precision is important."

She had grimaced. Sam? There had been that flashback to when, as a child, she had rubbed her face in a vain attempt at change. She's been biting her bottom lip to steady it as she became self-conscious of her body while contemplating the color of her skin.

"Miss Walter?"

Very well then. "He said: tell them to do now what I fucking say."

When she left, feeling pain near the roots of her hair and sick to her stomach, she had gone over to Joe and shaken his hand. She figured it was the right thing to do.

She doesn't have to drive through the village. If she doesn't, it's a long way past the conservation area. Around here there are mostly gentleman farmers. Heavily forested and undulating, the land is not much good for crops or livestock. A couple of the farmers try to scratch out a living and a few of the gentleman farmers put their acreage to some use primarily for Canadian tax reasons. Their own place they primarily use for training their own standard-bred horses. It has a very nice lake at the back and there's a large corporate retreat across the water, owned by Americans.

ENIGMA IN BLUE

It joins up with their property on the east side. And to the west lies the conservation area. It's not used often, but they have held dog-sled races there in the winter. There used to be a target range and you could hear the gunfire. Something must have changed; she hasn't heard any guns lately. In the middle of it, only a couple of miles from their farm, the village of Good Hope. Hardly even a village.

Good Hope is little more than a collection of buildings at a road crossing. A handful of private homes. Modest for the most part, two of them rather substantial. A church and a tiny bank. A gas station and an adjoining tack shop that she's heard is about to close. Word is, they cannot compete with Tim Hanson's General Store, usually the busiest place in the village. And then there's Mrs. Aubrey's. How she gets by, heaven only knows. Her husband passed away recently and she now runs the little guest house by herself. Nobody ever seems to be staying there, but she's known for her good country cooking and especially for her pies. Leo and she stop by there occasionally. That's about all there is to Good Hope—if you don't count the departed at rest in the tiny graveyard, that is. What of their status? They probably all once were, even if not so much now, viable participants in the life of the village. Mr. Jack Aubrey, the most recent addition, certainly was.

Almost home. She will definitely have words with Leopold. Others are probably right at that; he is faking the onset of Alzheimer's disease. She will have that long, hot bath tonight and a special treat of some kind after her walk. With luck the drizzle will have ended by then. Might not be before dark. She slows way down when she's almost at the garage at the end of the quarter-mile driveway, thinking that this might even be freezing rain and wonders why, as she closes the overhead door, she has not seen Blue. Normally, weather wouldn't deter him. Walking to the house, she has a look down the driveway. She must have driven right past him!

The small, distant figure starts to trot her way. Hesitant at first, then ever faster.

"Blue, my boy." She ruffles the top of his head, then nuzzles his wet coat. "We better get you dried off. Come on."

Blue squats in front of her—his drooping wet ears tight at the side of his head—and he is trembling.

"What is it?" There must have been thunder and lightning around here. That's about the only thing that might rattle him so much. He gets up now, all the while looking at her and actually tries to lead her north, away from the house. "Oh boy!" It's not until she gets a hold of him by the fur at the back of his neck that he follows her to the door—slowly.

− 2 −

"And with that, ladies and gentlemen, friends, I give you the birthday boy himself, Marshal Curtis."

John Martins is smiling as he adjusts his spectacles and remains standing when he acknowledges Marshal. There's enthusiastic applause and somebody shouts, "Speech, speech."

John was recruited by and has worked for Marshal—a more appropriate description lately might be worked with—ever since he finished his education at the University of Washington. Marshal, at forty-six today, barely looking thirtyish. He is the senior managing partner of D.R.T. United with all the benefits that go with partly owning and running one of the—even if no longer the preferred model for growth oriented corporations—more successful privately owned American diversified conglomerates in recent years. Not among those benefits unfortunately is one Marshal would probably appreciate the most. Assured everlasting fame. Though what's left is not too shabby: prestige, power and wealth—a lot of it. Additionally, there is that virtual mane of well groomed, wavy brown hair complementing a bright smile and matching well with the ever-present tan. The crisp white shirt under the double-breasted grey suit blends well with the purple tie and hankie. On this day John feels good ... for himself, yes, but especially so for his friend.

The timing couldn't be any better. It isn't often that someone so young would receive, as Marshal just has, an honorary Doctorate for contributions made to anything. This one in the field of Science primarily earned for advancements made in understanding and improving energy efficiencies of commercial structures in the northern hemisphere.

It was John's idea to combine Marshal's birthday with a previously contemplated gathering of some of the New York-based principals of the publishing arm of D.R.T. United. He had first considered holding an event at the company's Canadian lakeside retreat. Marshal liked to work out there in that relative isolation at least three times a year, schedule permitting, and they had spent a good part of their time in Canada over the last three weeks; Marshal in endless meetings and John at times bored while clinging to a fading hope that Marshal would not really go through with and drag him along on his ill-conceived political adventure. Unfortunately he already knew there would be a return trip soon. In the end, especially after it became clear that Vincent D'Groth as the chairman was never going to attend, no matter where the event would take place, John thought the logistics to be a bit complex with all the Publications people and had decided on New York.

Publishing, while representing only some four percent of the nine-plus billion total annual revenue, was becoming of great interest to Marshal and John did want to see him happy if at all possible.

Marshal had a large number of acquaintances and friends, but no family that he knew of. A bit odd, but something that Marshal would never talk of and everyone gave up asking about.

When John told Marshal about the concept of combining the occasion with business, he had first seemed indifferent, pretended not to be interested in whether Vincent was going to be there, and had then given his blessing. John too would have been pleased, but more than a little surprised, had Vincent D'Groth accepted his invitation. John had extended it more as a courtesy than with any real expectation. While D'Groth did hold the controlling majority interest in D.R.T., it had become only one of his numerous worldwide activities. The recent negative press he has been getting over his perceived misguided effort to influence the rare earth metal market—although on a very limited scale, to John's knowledge—was likely keeping him busy enough as well. But the people betting against him might do well to remember his determination and his well-documented ability to smell out opportunity. Still, it might have been educational to observe him during this period of stress, to see how he handled his latest pressure point.

* * * *

Marshal rises amid enthusiastic, prolonged applause as John scans the room one other time. The staff has done an excellent job—with the capable help provided by the management of this relatively new Lower Manhattan boutique hotel—of organizing the event. They have rented two of the floors, including this small ballroom. From his position at the head table he makes eye contact again with as many as he can, specifically acknowledging one or the other. About ninety people. He knows almost all of them. Well, he has at least seen most of them before except for a couple of reporters. Earlier, he had been introduced to one of them. Everyone here is either friend, staff or from the press.

ENIGMA IN BLUE

"I'm so very pleased to be able to share with all of you this special evening." Marshal pauses for a moment. "My word, this is just so much better than my usual routine of picking up pizza and sticking candles on it."

There's laughter and more applause.

"Seriously, though, I doubt it is very often that so many handsome and clever people are gathered in one room. And to paraphrase Hugo"—he glances off to the side—"behold what four million years of evolution have wrought."

John can see it. Not everyone in the room is entirely comfortable with the remark. Some appear to think it a bit over the top while others seem to realize that it can be interpreted in at least two different ways. Most are still beaming, including a few who perhaps shouldn't be.

"Thank you all for your kind wishes and in return I will not bore you with a long speech. I must take a moment, however, to address all of you here representing D.R.T. Publications." Marshal pauses again. "Bravo. I am sure you are all aware that our novel, *The Blood of Abel*, is about to become another bestseller, probably within the week. And I am particularly excited about our series of articles about *The Origin and Destiny of our Universe for Everyone*. Bravo indeed."

He smiles broadly and directly addresses Hugo Roselle. Greyhaired, middle-aged and very relaxed looking tonight when happily pondering a wine glass at the far left end of the head table.

"Hugo, I cannot begin to tell you how much I admire both the concept and the execution of your effort. Vincent D'Groth, unfortunately, cannot be here today, but I am certain he would want to join me in this sentiment. Familiar as I am with the uplifting style by now, reading any installment, I can never escape the feeling that I am walking alongside God, followed by humanity, during the creation. I have absolutely no doubt that due to you and your collaborators' unique style millions of people, who may have never been interested in the nature of our universe, will become so now. I note with pleasure the inclusion of my little contribution, Hugo. To perfection have you captured my sympathy and concern for future generations. Along with all the benefits of the exploding information technologies and knowledge come burdens that I, for one, as a boy, did not have to deal with. There is a clear difference between looking at the moon as a permanent and romantic fixture in the sky, however erroneous that might be, and knowing for sure that it is slowly receding and will eventually lose its stabilizing effect on our world with disastrous consequences. I am so very proud and comforted to have all of you alongside me on this journey as we do our part to demonstrate the way to the fulfillment of mankind's destiny by example."

"Hear, hear."

"No, no, please. But I dare say that never before in the annals of modern civilization has a business entity succeeded so well in blending the accumulation of capital with this level of social fairness and moral fortitude. Keep up the good work, everyone. Finally, a few words for my dear friend, Dr. Surtees. Matthew, you will agree, is without peer among ethicists. Not all of you may know this, but our friend has been battling a severe case of pneumonia contracted while combating demons in a foreign land on our behalf. I am so happy to report that, even as I speak, our dear Matthew is high above the Atlantic on one of our jets, no doubt smiling at the thought of his proximity to God and thinking about..."

Marshal continues to speak while John is becoming increasingly aware of the developing flirtatious interplay between Marshal and the one person in the room John doesn't know. Not that young really. Icy blonde type. Hair straight back in a bun. The large black earrings a very good touch. Full lips. She maintains eye contact comfortably with Marshal and John senses it: bold and deliber-

ENIGMA IN BLUE

ate, probably shameless in a flash. He can see Marshal thinking about it.

* * * *

On his way to the conference room John wonders whether it would be wise to point out to Marshal the possible conflict in his speech. The use of the motivational aspect for the purpose of demonstrating that permanence is an illusion he gets, though there may be better examples than the receding moon. Isn't it an inch a year and good for tens of billions more? But the ambivalent references to creation and evolution? Just in case he wants to use it again. Knowing Marshal, probably not. He might be referring to that conveniently modern concept of creation having set the stage for evolution. Maybe he'll ask him. He doesn't expect the discussion to take long and suspects that Sharon is over-reacting, but she and her lap-top have just brushed past him in the hallway where she had chuckled. "Marvelous baloney, getting better all the time, right John."

It had been prearranged at her request that after dinner, at the end of the formal part of the gathering, they would have a short business meeting about a specific problem.

He knows the two people who have joined Marshal and him well. Sharon Epstein is another senior and highly-regarded personal assistant to Marshal, and Robert Sato, not always at his most gracious when beating John at tennis, is from Finance. Sharon has dressed for the occasion. It's a nice blue cocktail dress, but it doesn't really help. She still looks like a school-marm. A very decisive and aggressive school-marm who starts out by bluntly explaining that they have been caught off-guard. They have invested a great deal of time in the effort to purchase the German magazine and it was thought to have been a done deal.

"I think you all know that in Germany a managing director, even without owning any part of anything, has a great deal of power while holding office. This man either doesn't want the deal to go through at all or is trying to delay as much as possible for his own personal reasons, whatever they might be."

"I was not aware there was an issue with that fellow at all and when you say delay, how long are you talking about?" Marshal is tapping the arm of his chair.

"Here is the dilemma," she says with a quick glance at Sato. "We are set to go and the owners are eager to close anytime, but his signature is also required on the documents and he can probably stall it another three or four days, maybe a week."

Marshal Curtis shifts from the Blackberry in his hand to look at Sato. "And that would not be good because...?"

Robert Sato stands up and starts to pace about the room. "It may become a real problem," he says. "We know they'll be looking at the latest financials within a couple of days and our research shows it will be something quite different than they have become used to seeing. They may start to rethink the whole deal."

"I think we should consider—" Sharon is cut short by Marshal's gesture when he abruptly gets up and walks towards the door where he stops to stare at John. "This doesn't require me. When are you people going to learn? I'm trying to navigate uncharted waters for all of us, and you would have me scrub the deck. Have a heart and try to stay with me. Handle it."

With that he walks out.

Well yes John can handle it. He has already figured out how. There isn't anything that unique about the situation. This is precisely why you never put yourself at the mercy of a single individual. "We're going to wake up some people in Germany," he says and can't help grinning when he sees Sharon already opening her laptop.

Still, this is about publishing...? It's Marshal's latest passion, if you ignore politics for the moment. It has given John cause for concern once before and is doing so now. Marshal Curtis would not walk away lightly from anything important to him. Does he have that much confidence in him? He doesn't want to think it, but think it he does. Plausible deniability.

− 3 −

"He's been acting like a kid heading for some etiquette boot camp," Kate said of Blue and heard Leo add, "hosted by one hundred mischievous talking heads." Blue's been picky about his food too, keeping her in sight whenever possible. He does know there will still be a walk with her, but today his drooping ears and eyes seem to wonder—when?

There had been a little leftover dinner, everyone for themselves; the kind Leo liked so much. There's just something about an accomplished, mature man carefully distributing goose fat on a slice of dark bread and meticulously salting it.

Leo had not asked about the meeting and she had not been eager to bring it up either...at least not yet. Still sitting at the kitchen table, she can just barely hear the muffled sound of music coming from his study. There are voices, so it must be opera. He, as he often does, helps to tidy up before they move into the living room. It's unusually large but they've been able to—sort of—maintain that comfortable lived-in look with the exception of the T.V. in the corner and the computer on the desk opposite the windows. There are some leather pieces and a couple of flame-stitch wingbacks. A large antique chest, some oriental carpets and the many paintings really make the room more than anything else. The recent addition of the card-table and the accompanying chairs help fill a previous void and for now they have proudly agreed with one another that further additions would be optional.

Most of the paintings are collectible Canadian art, although one of the landscapes is Leo's own effort and, to Kate's eye, not that awful. Surprisingly so, because she remembers it having started out in a rather conventional way with the water of a lake in the foreground, a tree line to the left and above, followed by a narrow strip of the sky roughed in.

She had been there when he, nodding with determination, had taken a hold of the canvas and decisively turned it upside down and continued to cover it with expensive Windsor products, turning water into sky and trees into clouds.

"You should've gone to the races, Kate. You can still go, you know. Didn't Lisa and that friend of hers say they'll be there?"

"Yes, but not tonight." The nerve. She decides to give Leopold just a little heads-up about what's still to come. "I've had an interesting day as it is."

He ignores it. "Post time's not 'til eight-thirty and it would be dark by the time you take Blue out." He keeps right on going.

"You can see yourself how Blue's been," says Kate. "I'm taking him out in a bit and that is final. But if you have been morphing into Mr. Sociable without me noticing, why don't you go to the track. Blue and I will manage." Things got quiet for some moments after that.

They occasionally go to different race-tracks to see their pacers win if lucky and lose mostly, but more often than not they will watch them on television. She's heading for the computer when she hears him clear his throat. "Uh, uh." He's going to say something of importance—to him.

"Yes, Kate, and to think that before he composed it there just wasn't anything there."

"It wasn't there?"

ENIGMA IN BLUE

"Those thoughtful opening bars to Beethoven's *Fourth Piano Concerto*. It sounds as though the piano is asking a question of the orchestra. And as if that's not inventive enough. At the time, you were expected to start a piano concerto with the orchestra leading the piano to the opening bars—everyone knew that—and he does the reverse." His voice drifts off.

She knows well how much he admires all things brilliant and inventive, matched only by his disdain for everything mundane which he, sometimes even successfully, tries to conceal. But where does this come from? He isn't even listening to Beethoven. Nevertheless: Gauguin, Beethoven, Einstein and the like should count their lucky stars. Leopold is not generally tolerant of men who do not plant potatoes or make chairs. The diminishing need for all men to start with the obligation to look after themselves and provide for dependents—in his mind—is an even greater threat to the way things have always been and should be than the decline of the conventional family unit. To compose a sonata after rotating the soil would be a good thing, but...

Kate rubs her forehead. Wouldn't this kind of thinking put into serious jeopardy many of today's people, prevalent on the airwaves in those reality shows, joyfully celebrating their very existence, trying to be appreciated for what they already are instead of what they have grown? Not to mention actors, politicians and reporters. Luckily, all of us women are excepted from most burdens. Childbearing and childrearing are noble and sufficient.

When he gets up to walk slowly towards his study, she notices him hesitate before he gets there and slowly turn around. He has that helpless, sheepish look on his face again. He's forgotten what he was going there for.

Confused or not, at least he's found his study. Casual in his customary track suit, his short hair mostly white now. Bright, grey eyes. Lines in his face that speak of things he has felt and thought. Kate even knows the specific origins of some of them. There are the ones that, according to Sam, first took hold when he used to work fifty hours straight with no rest. Others she recognises as having evolved along with his interest in metaphysics, biology and late nights with young women. Although he claims to have been misunderstood and that he had really been engaged in the study of the meaning of everything and the very nature of excellence—yes.

Far too many of the lines were the result of occasional panic attacks he would suffer when confronted with wasteful inefficiencies, such as having to circle a block for a second time, because the street he had intended to take would turn out to be one-way or he had driven to a store only to find it closed.

Leo seems to remember now. He was going to get the racing form.

The filly did well, then struggled a bit, coming home to finish third. When Kate gets up, Blue clearly knows.

Now snug in her sheepskin coat, long rubber boots protruding from below, she checks her pockets. It's all there: little notepad, pencil and a small flashlight.

"I'll be talking to Serafina," Leo says when he opens the door for them, "anything from you?"

Serafina...? "Aha, we're supposed to go to the movies later this week. Tell her to be on time for a change or else. We'll see you in a while."

Serafina had become part of their lives almost four years ago when she, along with her friend Manuel, had come to the farm where he had applied for a job.

Kate hadn't been there, but apparently Serafina had driven him and Leo had taken a shine to her. Both of them were immigrants from Colombia and had known one another back home. Over time, she has become very important to Leo and is now also her best friend despite being twelve years her senior. She loves Serafina dearly and would love her better still, if only she would be a little more punctual.

ENIGMA IN BLUE

It's night, but the sky is cloudless now and there's bright moonlight. She sees Manuel by the barn, working on the harrows near the rear of the tractor. She gives him a little wave and starts out on the usual route down the driveway. "Come on, Blue, stop dragging your feet." He doesn't stop dragging his feet. "What's wrong with you?"

She loses sight of him and when she turns around, he is just sitting there, looking up at her. She moves towards him, stretching out her hand, but he gets up and moves the other way. If he really wants to start out in that direction so bad for a change, that's okay too. But why?

She knows the trails that lead north towards the lake, but they are overgrown and there is quite a bit of brush to go through. Blue has perked up now, ahead of her and occasionally looking back. Hmm?

The freezing rain earlier has mostly melted and not been enough to muddy the fields and pathways. She can hear the fallen leaves rustle beneath her feet and even with only moonlight she can see the colorful remaining foliage on some of the trees. Ontario, at this time of year, is a good place to be. There are sure to be animals around, but she isn't worried about that. Blue is a kind dog, but she knows Great Pyrenees to have taken on mountain lions when pressed. There might be the occasional bear or a very rare wolf in the area. Mostly, there are coyotes and, she isn't sure, packs of wild dogs. When they are in the neighborhood you would know it. They make an awful racket, howling relentlessly. Blue, and Misty before him, had occasionally joined in, but had never given any sign of wanting to join up with the pack. They would howl in the direction of the pack as if they were wolves themselves and she would have liked to know what the nature of their communication was.

Blue is checking out something near a large fallen branch and she pauses for a moment to take out her notepad. She doesn't need the flashlight when she scribbles: "and he boldly proclaims to all his intention to run for 'Top Dog' at the Puppy convention."

They've been out now for over an hour and are coming close to the end of the property. She has already caught a glimpse of the lake. There is a stand of old white pines near the edge of the lake. Looking through the nearly branchless lower stems of the trees, she can see the moonlight dancing on the water. Not hard to see where some of the inspiration for the Canadian Impressionists came from. Leo never painted anything he saw, but this view would appeal to him, she's sure. There, just about at the end of their property now. They will go around the trees and then turn back.

That wasn't quite true about Leopold's painting. He once did paint Serafina. Not Serafina exactly, Serafina's blouse inadvertently. Her favorite blouse. She had come too close and paid the price. She had not been too pleased and got him back for that.

Having caught the tail end of something he was saying about no longer being interested in minutiae, she had sharply turned to him. "And who is Minutiae?"

"I said I am not into minutiae," Dad had answered back.

"So you've been into Minutiae?"

He hadn't caught on and in exasperation had asked. "What are you going on about, woman?"

"Oh no," she had laughed. "I misunderstood. You mean minutiae. I thought you were talking about one of your old girlfriends!" Serafina had not been so very far off the mark and Kate will remind her about the fun some of them had with that conversation when next she sees her.

Leopold and Serafina Gomez? Kate's had her suspicions for a while about the two of them sitting around at times like two old ladies, worrying and talking about her happiness, or the lack thereof, behind her back. That is funny, them worrying about her. Not so much in Serafina's case, she seems balanced and content. She likes her job at the newspaper and has, so she says, an active social life apart from the time she spends with her and Leo. And she has lately become quite dedicated to her journalism studies.

ENIGMA IN BLUE

For Kate, there are barely enough hours in the day as is. Horses need a great deal of care. For company, she has Blue. And interacting with—at times—dozens of willful, juvenile partners, while rewarding for the most part, is not always easy. Today aside, Blue is usually calm and relaxed. That leaves her—Kate—having to worry, time permitting in her schedule, about...yes, Leopold.

He's the one in need of understanding and support, insisting, as he does so often, on living in the far too distant past. Surely, not all the fine actors during the 'fifties were that unlike most of their counterparts of today and shyly grateful for their good looks or their pleasant voices and their talent. Nor could Kate get herself to accept, as Leo claims, that virtually all of them absolutely knew the difference between being extraordinary and cleverly pretending to be so.

Neither does it seem plausible to her that, as little as sixty years ago, most people saw themselves as but a blessed part of the universe rather than the masters of all on earth. That would be more like six hundred years back, wouldn't it?

Too isolated is he. Has he ever had a real male friend? She knows of none. He interacts well with Manuel, but that is probably because Manuel talks little, uses sign language and for the most part ignores him.

She should have another look at that painting he just won't give up on. It's large and there's always been that wide expanse of pure, undulating snow with a single tree at the center. There used to be two, but only a ghostly shadow of the second still remains as he doesn't seem able to get it painted out. Perhaps he is conflicted about it. He has the weapons to get the job done, if he really wants to.

Kate is rounding the group of trees now and it is then she sees what Blue must have been trying to show her all along. There's a darker area about four feet in diameter that looks a bit like an irregular crater. Did animals dig around here? Did something fall? Did somebody try to bury something here? She hopes not and has a quick look around. Blue sits and stares at the site, but doesn't go near it.

She is close enough now to make out some detail of the dark shape near the center. Like black coal with some tiny blue specks and there are some dark terra cotta sparkles as well. A rock or a meteorite with precious stones embedded in it? Hmm... But why would a rock disturb Blue? Or has Manuel been digging around here for some reason?

Bending down, Kate spots what looks like a fragment of that same material about two inches long and half that size in width. Might Manuel know about this? Maybe he should come back here and fence it off just in case it does attract animals. They would have to make sure about the property line, it's awfully close. Too bad the old cedar rails appear to be gone, but in daylight this may all look very different.

Now that Blue has shown her his find, he seems content to trot along with her back towards the house.

"And maybe," she smiles to herself, looking at the fragment in her hand, "we have found an enormous treasure and shall tell no one." Although with her book characters she would certainly be safe. Wait till they find out! What an adventure this could turn into.

She hasn't realized that it's close to eleven when she gets back to the house. Leo is just fussing about aimlessly, not yet ready to call it a day it would seem. "Or else what, Serafina wants to know." He doesn't seem to be expecting an answer. "I see Blue has settled down... has he? You were out there a long time." Leo had gotten a towel and is eyeing with suspicion some mud at the side of Blue's coat; he had jumped on to the chesterfield in the living room.

"Yes Leopold," she says and has him look up instantly from his chore of drying off Blue, "for some reason he dragged me all the way north as far as we could go and now he seems content and I'm exhausted." She's definitely not going to share the good news of their found treasure tonight.

ENIGMA IN BLUE

"Well Kate, tomorrow is another day. Yeah, it'll have to be another day if it's tomorrow, right?" He nods slightly and she gives him the tiniest smile. "I'll be downstairs in the workshop for a bit," Leo says when he gets up. "Are we all right—I mean ...?"

"Right ... Dad, and we're going to have a snack before we turn in."

"Goodnight then, Kate, sleep well." He is moving so very slowly. "And you too, Blue."

"Yes, Goodnight, Dad."

Leopold Walter has arrived at the stairwell leading downstairs.

Blue is diligently eyeing his usual night-time doughnut while she toasts a waffle, covers it with syrup and a sprinkling of cinnamon-sugar. Finally, a glass of chocolate milk is recruited to join the party heading upstairs. And it is there she finds the sheet of paper on her night table, a little poem in Leo's handwriting:

>Day's near done,
>Down goes the sun.
>Cat to the shed,
>House to the mouse,
>Dogs inside;
>Scrub that child!

>Thoughts slowing now, neatly filing away,
>A little dilemma for some other day.
>A last check of old hearts,
>Are they still beating?
>Is anything left undone?
>A word spoken softly,
>A faint little whisper;
>Still now, this day is truly done.

He must have known what might happen at that meeting. Or else he has inside spies who have already briefed him. What is she to do now? Have words with Leopold?

— 4 —

Having had a couple of days to examine her new-found treasure, reviewing old textbooks on metallurgy and consulting with two of her more practical book characters, Kate had concluded that she definitely had no clue what it was. Talking on the phone with Serafina about a dark, coal-like lump had drawn no reaction at first. Not until bright, gem-like sparkles were mentioned.

"Let me check something and call you back, Kate."

She did, the next morning. "Yes, Kate, I know a university student who could meet with us even today at the restaurant. He thinks he can help."

"We need help with eating lunch?"

"Funny. He knows about rocks and says one of his teachers might support him, if necessary. But he did ask a lot of questions about where you found it."

"And you told him?"

"Well yes, you said yourself you weren't all that sure about the fence line of your property. That teacher he talked about appears to know something of your family anyway. Don't forget to bring our precious along."

She will. Maybe it really was a piece of a hundred-pound diamond originating in outer space. When earlier she had mentioned to Leo her possible afternoon with Serafina, he had said there was a chance he might see them in Oakville, but not to wait for him or change their plans. There was something in the area he was going to try and take care of and if he could make it, he would. Since that "something" had motivated him enough to go on a hunt for his missing striped red and black tie, she half expected that he would join them. Oakville is a small place and if they weren't already at the movies he would know where and how to find them.

She likes the town. They all do. It's about halfway between the factory in Mississauga and the offices of *The Sun* in Burlington where Serafina works as a secretary and translator. Unfortunately, it's also a long two hours from their farm near Orangeville, but you can take some of the country roads and make the drive interesting.

Oakville is, in some ways, a unique small town on the outskirts of Toronto. They have nicknamed it Pleasantville and usually call it that. It's both a prosperous and industrialized community with substantial suburbs and a wealthy community mostly along the shore of Lake Ontario that has come to be known as Canada's gold coast. While only a handful of the five-plus acre estates remain, even the now smaller, redeveloped homes are impressive. Some of the historically significant properties have been gifted to the township. They have become parks, tourist sites and art galleries. There's a quaint old harbor with a history of its own near the town center. The main strip and some of the side streets of Oakville, along Lakeshore Road, while only five or six blocks long, are...well, pleasant. Flower shops and bookstores; not Chapters, mind you, second-hand bookstores. A custom jeweler. Three or four art galleries. An importer of oriental rugs. A photo studio. Some very selective small furniture and interior design stores. An ice cream parlor along with several coffee shops and a number of very nice, small restaurants from which they have chosen their favorite long ago.

And the characterization of Pleasantville for several reasons, other than the overall small town atmosphere. A disproportionate number of women you might encounter on the streets will be well manicured, smartly dressed, fit and blonde. And so many of the men seem to wear those large-rimmed hats and down-filled vests that identify them as successful Canadians. At least that is the impression they make on Kate with their relaxed and calm demeanor. To no one's surprise, Serafina has a slightly different take. She insists that, if you flip around the words women and men, the descriptions become even more appropriate.

And while it really isn't so, every second person on Lakeshore seems to be walking a dog or pushing a baby stroller. Both, quite often.

Kate once personally encountered the wrath of an outraged Pleasantvillian when she had inadvertently stepped out of line. Near the town center you can always comfortably turn your car onto a street, even cross a main road. Everyone seems patient and courteous and ready to accommodate everyone else. She realized at the time that she had turned left onto Lakeshore a little too quickly and too close to a woman pedestrian crossing the road. Glancing back in the mirror she had seen the woman standing in the middle of the street, angrily shaking her fist at her. Worse yet, the woman seemed doubly distraught over the danger Kate had visited upon two short, future Pleasantvillians at the hands of still another woman nearby. She kept gesticulating at the toddlers with the hand not otherwise occupied.

Kate had gotten the point, but it really hadn't been that close.

Dad had once been troubled outwardly that, if some of the people passing him on the street would find out what he was thinking, they might put him in jail, perhaps tar and feather him. And then with his usual self-effacing reversal followed up by saying, "On the other hand, do I know they're not all thinking the same thing?"

Entering the Black Orchid, Kate is pleased when the maitre d' recognizes her and addresses her as Miss Walters and she chooses to ignore the misplaced 's' at the end of Walter. Serafina is already at one of the very nice tables by the window, but she is with another man; well, a boy. Serafina gives her a kiss on the cheek and introduces the young man as Stephan Podorski, "the student I mentioned to you this morning."

ENIGMA IN BLUE

He must be only about twenty, barely old enough to drink, she wonders when they shake hands. His brown turtleneck sweater, shoulder-length straight hair, prominent nose and diamond earring all add up to give him a casual touch—Kate is having difficulty visualizing him picking up rocks. Serafina looks good. You could put that woman into the proverbial potato sack and she would look good. Black hair, straight back, light brown complexion with those big brown eyes and that ever-present smirky smile. Today, it's her tight-fitting black pantsuit with a white blouse, a little too much gold earring and of course too much shoe.

"Dad said he might stop by if he gets a chance later on. I think he will."

"He mentioned it last night. And do be generous," Serafina adds as the waiter fills their glasses with wine from the decanter already on the table.

Kate and Serafina have a pretty good idea what they are going to eat, but Stephan studies the menu carefully.

Serafina will have the broiled salmon. Kate knows she is going to enjoy the lobster thermidor, and Stephan keeps glancing back and forth between the waiter and the place on the menu where the house specialties are listed.

"The beef stroganoff," he asks, "do you recommend it?"

"Definitely, it is one of our specialties." Good heavens no, not the stroganoff—Kate can just see the waiter thinking—what does he expect me to say?

"But the vegetarian Pad Thai also looks interesting," Stephan says. "Dear me."

Agonizing for another moment, glancing at the waiter again, and making his decision with a decisive nod. "I'll stick with the stroganoff then." He really seems to be enjoying his moment in the company of older women.

"Show Stephan what you found," Serafina says, putting her hand on his arm, "maybe he can tell straight away whether it's a pure diamond or something even better."

Stephan leans forward. "I didn't say I would know right away. But whatever it is, it shouldn't be that hard to tell if we get it into the lab."

"If?" Serafina is pouting.

He is holding the fragment in his hand, studying it, moving his hand up and down as if he's weighing it. "I agree. It looks unusual. It's too heavy to be a plain rock. But if it's made of..." He's dragging out his moment. "No," he says, "a diamond it is not." He is having trouble hiding a big grin. "At least not yet, it isn't."

Serafina exaggerates her frown. "But you definitely will have it analyzed, right?"

"Give me a couple of days, it's not gonna be that difficult. As I said, I did already ask one of my professors. Mercier seemed surprisingly interested when I told him where it was found and said he would let me know." Stephan energetically flings aside some of the long hair that Kate had not seen.

Having finished their lunch, Serafina's and Stephan's focus has shifted to the remainder of the wine and being silly, well away from Kate's focal point. Stephan has not offered to leave and—now having accepted the assignment to at least begin to organize the research—doesn't appear to be in a particular hurry to do so anytime soon.

"Did I hear you say Mercier earlier on, Stephan?" Kate asks.

He nods.

"I remember a teacher by that name, Professor Jerome Mercier. They used to call him Jovial Jerome."

"I can see why," Stephan nods again, "you have the right professor. If you want me to, I'll tell him you call him that."

"Do that," Serafina says, "but be sure to wait until after the lab tests are completed."

Stephan manages to appear contemplative when he looks at Kate while swirling his glass and spilling very little of the wine. "So be it then. He seemed to recall your family right away when I told him where you found the fragment. Said you are farmers and have horses, near a conservation area."

"Dear, it better not be just a lump of coal then," Kate says, looking at her watch, "and we can forget about the movie now. Leo might..."

"Not might, he's across the street." Serafina waves, trying to get his attention. "He's not alone."

Entering the restaurant, Leo, striped tie and all, looks a little lost—being surrounded by so many... people. The neat, greying Pleasantvillian couple at his side only serves to enhance his appearance of a visitor from somewhere else. The mature, decidedly handsome man with him is Barry Endsman, the associate editor at *The Sun*, whom Kate knows, and the woman, she was to find out, his wife, Roda. Leo explains he had run into the Endsmans on the street. When he learned they were heading for the same place, he couldn't just walk away. He didn't actually say it—Kate knew that. They were only going to have coffee and a piece of pastry.

Leo does spend the better part of fifteen minutes in an apparent state of confused concern over Stephan's function at this gathering, his connection to other people and his very reason for existence. Stephan in turn, having been looked over by Leo, has become quiet and respectful. They both react good-naturedly to Serafina's teasing with respect to five years being a long time to consider becoming a vegetarian—as in the case of Stephan—and reminding Leo about his incomplete, ill-conceived economic impact study of using for human consumption only those animals that were terminally ill or had died of natural causes; it doesn't deter him from claiming that this day had been a productive one.

Leo must have picked up on the searching glances Mrs. Endsman is directing at Serafina. Why else would Leo of all people—albeit after much hesitation—allow himself to be drawn into a conversation by Barry Endsman and admittedly to a lesser extent Roda about standards of tolerance throughout history. Somebody is going to regret this.

"I've always had difficulties with this," Leo finally says to himself rather than anyone in particular. "There have been so many different beliefs, convictions, moral standards, doctrines, lifestyles, ethical codes—not to mention legal standards. In Africa, women still have babies today at the age of twelve and the average life expectancy used to be thirty-five years. Some men have had hundreds of wives, others married their sisters..."

Leo seems to have lost his train of thought and Mrs. Endsman is becoming alarmed. Kate reluctantly decides to try and intervene—gently—while hopefully remaining constructive. "There were also periods in history when human sacrifices were totally acceptable, at times brought on by little more than possible overreaction to excessive pontification and why don't you go outside for a smoke, Dad?"

"Because I haven't completed my—"

"I think you have, Dad. Go have your cigarette, okay? If need be, we know where you're heading..."

"A smoke it is then." Leo walks out slowly after some additional reluctant fumbling for something.

"Where was he going with this?" Roda asks.

"I've heard his speech before too," a laughing Serafina says, "let me try. To what he has already said, he would almost certainly add that homosexuality has been both celebrated and condemned. People have been tortured and killed for their convictions and their actions, while others have been elevated to a state of godliness for similar practices. Cannibalism has not always been frowned upon." She's directing too much of her recital at Roda, worries Kate, including her summary. "He just doesn't think that human moral codes at any particular point in time could possibly be relevant."

Roda Endsman doesn't look impressed. "This is really delving deeper than I had anticipated." She too laughs—haltingly. "I'm really just here for coffee and cake. How about you, Stephan," she teases, "do you have strong opinions on the subject?"

ENIGMA IN BLUE

"Goodness no, but I really do have to leave now." Kate is glad to see him tapping the pocket of his trousers where he had earlier put the fragment as if to indicate that he had not forgotten about the reason for his being here. "A friend is driving me. Wish I didn't have to... go I mean."

Walking down the street of Pleasantville, Serafina and Leo are laughing. First at themselves and then at one another before finally Kate joins in.

"Your Stephan friend, Kate, we may have frightened him away," says Leo. "He came out when I was having my cigarette and couldn't say goodbye fast enough."

"He is the sentient, artsy type," Serafina says. "I wasn't surprised."

"No, he said geology."

"Well yes, that too. And he'll help to make your daughter very rich and maybe famous with her find."

"How much wine did Gomez have?" asks a confused Leo.

— 5 —

"Are you no longer in need of the support you are receiving from D.R.T. United, young man? I am not missing something here, am I?"

Jerome Mercier is staring grim-faced at Stephan, who is nervously rubbing his upper arms, trying to avoid the professor's eyes.

"I asked you a question, young man."

"No, Sir," he answers, "I think you know very well about my needs and the problems I have—"

"I went out of my way to accommodate you," Professor Mercier interrupts, "and you wind up trashing the lab."

"It's the spectrometer malfunctioning," says Barbara Sauter.

"Would you repeat that," says the professor.

"It's the spectrometer—"

"Barbara..." Stephan is beginning to breathe hard.

Barbara Sauter, a classmate Stephan has become friends with, had agreed to help after he got permission to use the lab. The first result had clearly been wrong, showing no more than a trace of carbon which just couldn't be. They had extracted another sample from the fragment, being very careful not to contaminate it, and had run the experiment again. Worse yet, no indication of carbon content or silica. An electronic glitch?

They had tried to make sense of it—without success. Barbara had become nervous and they finally agreed they would face the consequences and contact Professor Mercier, who took not more than a few minutes to appear.

"You know I overstepped my authority here." Mercier is now measuring Barbara and some of the blond hair that has escaped from her beehive and is making its way out from below the hairnet. "It is not going to be helpful to the remainder of my career at this institution, having to get maintenance involved. Let us pray that between you and your... farmer patrons there are sufficient financial resources to take care of this massive damage. I do not expect Mr. Curtis will be too pleased. You had better tidy up and leave."

"That's not fair," Stephan protests, "Barbara had nothing to do with—"

"Do we not know that." Mercier fixes his gaze on Stephan. "What we have here is a case of overactive hormones clouding your judgement. Kate Walter once attended my classes, I will have you know, and I remember well that shy, charming smile."

"I didn't—"

"Most assuredly not made for the sciences or engineering," Mercier interrupts. "She has drawn you into her fantasy world. Take care. She is not as helpless as she will have you believe. Even then her difficulty with separating reality from her make-believe flights of fancy was a concern to those around her, though not always convincing to me."

The professor starts to walk towards the door, but stops and turns around. He is already a dour-looking man and downright frightens them when he raises his exceedingly long arms up to the sides of his disproportionately small head, two fingers extended on each hand, putting his head and what he is about to say into a quote: "Of course there may be another outcome. There is still the possibility that you have not actually destroyed our very fine laboratory and will receive a Nobel Prize instead for your effort. The total absence of carbon and silica, do you not know, can only mean that what you have discovered cannot be...from our known universe."

He drops his hands, but keeps staring at them.

"Better still, do not touch anything anymore. I am going to try and put things right myself. I wish you a good afternoon." Professor Mercier indicates the location of the exit.

When they are in the hallway, Barbara slows her steps to whisper. "I don't think he meant that, do you?"

"Highly unlikely," says Stephan, pinching his left arm hard. "Perhaps I should call Serafina or Kate. What if it is a fragment of a meteorite with no trace of carbon or silica?....I'd just better call Kate and Serafina...and somebody at the Nobel Prize committee." Stephan grimaces and then adds. "Ha ha."

— 6 —

The driver has the limo moving north at a fair clip and John Martins motions a second time for him to slow down. They have picked up Marshal Curtis's mother at the Toronto airport and are heading in the direction of Orangeville to the retreat. Having smiled an appropriate amount of time, John decides to equivocate—a lot.

"Marshal asked me to tell you how very sorry he is that he couldn't personally pick you up. We've been trying to sort out an unusual situation around here. And I know he had an unavoidable meeting set up with a Professor Mercier following which he absolutely has to attend a prearranged video conference with some people in Europe."

The woman in the limousine next to him leans his way, slides the spectacles down her nose to study him. She doesn't say anything; she doesn't have to. Her expression is unmistakable: 'Naturally he does; it's Sunday afternoon. Doesn't everybody?' To be fair, Marshal had warned him. Whatever my mother is, a fool she's not.

It had caught some people off guard, including John. Not the fact that Marshal would take a run at politics, but that he would do it so soon. Although in recent times, John is aware, everyone successful at anything seems to feel emboldened to take the bull by the horns without delay and try to tell everyone else what to do and how to do it. So why not Marshal? On this score alone he certainly qualifies. John himself has never been able to develop an interest in politics, but he had become, he believes, Marshal's closest confidant and would do what he could to help him achieve his objectives. Little choice, really; his efforts to persuade him otherwise have clearly failed so far.

But the kind of help Marshal was looking for was not what he had expected. Marshal had other people in mind for the organizational aspect, was comfortable himself in dealing with party insiders and was confident about being successful whether he ran for Congress or made a run straight for the Senate. John could not really visualize Marshal as a failure and was well aware of overtures that had been made by party officials. And the reason for the confidence—John had learned during their extended stays at the retreat, even though he wasn't supposed to—resulted from the fact that Marshal and the politicos around him weren't really focused on your everyday, unpredictable sort of election. Oh no. And that was likely the reason why U.S. politics were being discussed in Canada. They were eyeing two specific scenarios. A potential opportunity involving a sudden retirement which was to be followed by an appointment. And there was another less likely, but possible by-election prospect coming up.

"Absolute discretion is key if I tell you what it's about," Marshal had emphasized. "This whole effort may be a waste of time if we can't solve this particular problem." And what it's about—John takes off his glasses and rubs his eyes—is the fact that the woman next to him is vulnerable to discovery over past, at minimum, unethical activities. Marshal's actual words. She is a silent partner in the company that holds Marshal's interest in D.R.T. by virtue of having provided most of the seed money. A re-examination and any resulting publicity concerning the sale of his mother's introduction service business, albeit years ago, along with the resurfacing of a paper trail of the inconclusive investigation involving enabling practices would, in Marshal's opinion, stop him cold as far as any political ambitions are concerned, either now or sometime in the future. John's task is to make it all go away.

"Marshal tells me you'll probably go along to Newfoundland on his hunting trip, Mrs. Curtis."

"Should I? Would it be safe?" the woman asks, peeking over her glasses again.

Good, thinks John. That will make it easier. A sense of humor.

"Safe for whom, Mrs. Curtis?"

"Look, John, if you're going to try and take advantage of me, you'd better start calling me Monica. I think I know what you want and, who knows, you might get it. If you don't turn this into a marathon Kabuki dance, we might get along."

Even better. A sense of humor and direct. He reaches over and shakes her hand for a second time. "Very well, Monica."

He doesn't find it all that easy. She might be in her mid sixties. Tall and almost muscular. There are strands of grey in her hair and he cannot detect a trace of makeup on her face. She has noticeably high cheekbones and green, slightly uneven eyes and John finds himself wondering what your usual average, unethical enabler should look like.

"You may be lucky with your timing anyway. I've been thinking about moving to Europe permanently. That might well involve re-arranging my finances anyway."

She's testing him. It's not going to be that easy. "If Marshal moves ahead, he's going to have to put all his holdings into a blind trust. He wants everything to be a neat and tidy package." Damn. He shouldn't have used the words neat and tidy. He knows it instantly.

"I understand," is Monica's answer and idiot should be my middle name, thinks John. Not a good start and now I've got to play catch-up.

He's beginning to think that getting Monica to sell her interest may be the easier task; getting other commitments might be a whole different story. Marshal had been adamant. "My mother's word would be good enough. But I must have it. And I can't do it—I think you understand that—it has to be you."

"Say John," Monica whispers, nodding in the direction of the driver, "will there be more muscle up there or are you going to be the only ones working me over?"

He playfully punches the palm of his left hand with his right fist. "I'll be the only one. We've been here off and on for weeks and there have been a lot of people—mostly political types from the States, but everyone has gone now except for some extra staff." John lowers the dividing window. "You know the place, Ely. It's coming up. Where's your partner today…Aholl?"

"His pet worm died."

"Say what?"

"His pet worm died."

"He's grieving?"

"His pet worm died."

John raises the dividing window.

Monica had wanted to stop somewhere along the way, which suited John just fine; the more time he had with her alone, he figured, the better. Though he wouldn't be too surprised to find that she is on the same strategy. When inside the Coffee-shop she looks around and slings the small overnight bag over her shoulder. "I'll just be a couple of minutes. Will you get me a cup of tea, John?"

While the place is not that busy, the coffee is fresh. A couple of teenage girls in the far corner are giggling at nothing in particular, it would seem, as they are not talking, just giggling. A squat, native-looking man standing near the counter is looking up at the prominently displayed menus. When he lowers his head, John's eyes follow his to the dark grey pickup outside with the young woman and the big dog playing nearby it. The dog looks like a St. Bernard. Big! It's white with gold and dark brown markings around the head and the ears. The young woman is playfully running around with the dog, encouraging him to put his paws right up on her shoulder; that way the dog is taller than she is. At one point he gets close to the open window of the limo and Ely, but is steered off to the side by the girl.

What a nice full face, made to look darker than it really is by the gleaming white toque with that little bit of red trim she's wearing.

The girl stops playing and comes to the door where she motions the dog to sit and partially opens the second door, trying to get the attention of the squat-looking man still standing by the counter. When she does, she points back to the dog and puts one hand to her mouth, making a chewing motion. The man nods. "Yes, Miss Kate." Kate.

When Monica Curtis comes back, now sporting slacks and wearing what looks to John like a stylish safari jacket, she must have seen him look outside to where the young woman along with the man and the dog are getting into the truck. "That's a nice Pyrenees," she says.

"Not a St. Bernard?"

Monica shakes her head. "No, a Great Pyrenees, a blaireau with those markings. I once had one myself—a long time ago. Attractive girl. Thanks for my tea."

"I assume we could agree that Marshal would make an effective politician," he says as he sees the truck pull out of sight. A little gun-shy now, he is meaning to probe without making it sound like an interview.

"Absolutely." Monica seems enthusiastic. "He's so not pragmatic by nature, but can be and knows how to play a game when he has to. Perfect for politics. Has he decided which party he's going to run for?"

As she's being cynical again, he laughs openly without answering that question. "Don't take me to be naive," he says, "I know it's not Marshal's ambition to be a congressman serving the people for any length of time. It's a stepping stone."

She surprises him with the intensity of her suddenly stern look. "Maybe you don't really understand Marshal as well as you think you do. There is the ego factor, I know, but beyond that he is a true progressive believer. He really thinks he can and will make the world better...for all." She has relaxed again. "You look skeptical, John."

"Well yes, 'better' is a hard to define and moving target, but I have no reason to doubt Marshal's good intentions. I just have trouble relating to the concept of doing good for distant others."

"You won't one day when you have children of your own."

"Yes Mother," John says, nodding with a smile.

"What I don't get," Monica says, taking a sip of her tea, "is...what's in it for you? You're young, but your resumé must be pretty impressive by now."

"I've been with Marshal for—"

"That's what I mean. You don't even have an official title, do you, yet you virtually run United in Marshal's absence." She looks at him, waiting for an answer.

"Well, I do my part," he is slow to react.

"Oh, come on, John, I'm a silent partner, not a dumb partner. You just haven't figured it out yet."

"Haven't figured out...?"

"You will one day."

"Will what?"

"Jesus, wake up, John. Look around you. Tell me, who are the most senior people at D.R.T. United next to you?"

"That's easy. There are dozens of them. We couldn't possibly have—"

"I don't mean medium-level management types," she says, shaking her head. "I mean top senior participants. I know what happened with Roger Cardell, but Irene La...La...what was her name?"

"Langdon."

"Yes, that was odd."

"Not odd at all. You don't know? She's cleaning up on the Chicago Mercantile."

"There, you see what I'm saying; she's cleaning the Chicago Mercantile."

"Monica!"

He has never thought of this, but now that he does he has to admit that there has been somewhat of a history of a handful of people rising very close to the top and then for one reason or another fading away. Some have departed abruptly. Usually much better off than they had been arriving, but gone nevertheless.

She's trying to distract you, he tells himself. Focus on the job.

When John sees the apprehension on Monica's face as they approach the massive—contemporarily stylized—totem-pole gateposts at the entrance to the retreat, he tries to be reassuring. "Don't worry, there really is a log house." He feels a little sheepish. "It's over twenty-thousand square feet, but otherwise it's much like the two little cabins over there by the boat-house." John is pointing at the opening in the forest that allows a quick view of the lake on the left about halfway down the long winding flagstone driveway.

"That is a pleasant view," Monica says. "Doesn't exactly match up with the entrance. Can one get down there ...?"

"Oh yeah, there are some nice trails by the water, you'll see. Enough to get lost..."

"Then that must be the main house," Monica says, looking ahead.

"The upper storey," John says as they start to round the final corner and the whole cabin comes into view. At the front entrance stands Marshal Curtis in short sleeves despite the cold.

"Good to see you, Mother." They barely touch when they hug. "Must be two years or so."

"How are you, Marshie?"

Monica Curtis takes a couple of steps back to look at her son.

– 7 –

When Kate last spoke to Serafina, she had not been too complimentary towards Stephan's contribution to date in their quest for fame and fortune. In her opinion, he is showing substantial signs of divided loyalties. Serafina did, she claimed, fully appreciate the scientific aspect of the increasing interest at the University over the nature of the mysterious rock, but...

"But what?"

That is a problem with academia, Serafina had complained; just not greedy enough. How else can you explain this level of apparent disinterest in the value of diamonds or other fabulous riches? And—she couldn't go into details just yet—she was initiating a back-up option to Stephan's effort that unfortunately also involved smart people; one of them a professor in Florida, a Professor Reeling. Whatever all that means.

In truth, Kate herself has become quite curious and interested in gaining a complete understanding about the nature of the fragment. But that largely to the exclusion of others so far. And there is the problem. She is ever more worried about being too preoccupied with her find and not paying enough attention to, or including her characters. Still, to try and rectify that situation in the way she was contemplating had been a difficult decision. A regularly scheduled meeting was one thing; an extraordinary meeting quite another—intimidating before you even start. Extraordinary meeting. They would probably worry straight away. They'd be upset if she didn't let them know what it was about and probably more so if she did.

Their regularly scheduled meetings had become an almost pleasant routine. She had come to realize some time ago that she just didn't feel good about making any of the characters in her books do or be anything they didn't want to do or be.

Too often had there been tears and anger and sadness. Jealousy, frequently, and a lot of ego issues. She couldn't really say that everything was hunky-dory now, but things had gotten so much better ever since she initiated the meetings and the opportunity for resolving difficulties.

She has also learned to appreciate the degree to which she had benefited in other ways. Many good ideas had evolved as a result of these gatherings from sometimes unexpected sources.

But fur will be ruffled, she'd thought. Some of the current principal characters might wind up taking a back seat in the new venture, although that might be offset by others who would see new opportunities for themselves. And Blue too had a stake in a possible change of direction.

Except for Louise, she wasn't that concerned about the Children. They tended to be more happy-go-lucky, flexible and ready to go along with anything. The Flying Puppies could, at times, be the more deliberate and serious bunch. Well, Kate had realized, democracy in action. But she had made herself a mental note. She had better think about this. Was it really—democratic? After all, she was so much more mature than all the rest. Was it truly fair then to call it democracy in action?

There is a very good reason why they had chosen this particular location above others and have used it for all their meetings so far. On this side of the mountain the rock candy is especially sweet and there's a soda-pop spring right around the corner.

Kate can see the eager anticipation and apprehension on many of the faces. "As you know," she explains, "I'm generally well pleased with the progress of our latest venture. I feel it's going well, don't you?" From the expression on their faces she surmises that they do. "Blue," she continues, "will be able to verify the truthfulness of what I am about to tell you. Something strange and unusual has occurred and has made me think about the possibility of delaying or halting our current project and start looking at something entirely new and different. I trust you know me well enough by now to believe, when I tell you, that I have not come to these crossroads lightly and would not pursue this without reaching some consensus among all of us."

There is some unrest in the crowd, a murmur and quite a few ears are flapping. From the very back to her left comes an impatient voice that Kate knows to be from a certain schnauzer.

"Get on with it already, Miss Kate."

ENIGMA IN BLUE

She takes another moment and measures her team. She might as well come out with it. "Blue and I," she says, acknowledging Blue, "have come across some possible evidence that our world, our whole universe, may not be quite what we think it is and that the answers to what we are and where we came from may be somewhere far, far away. Much farther than anyone ever thought. Others—grown-up teams—may start looking as well and the search for those answers could turn into a great adventure. So my question to you is this. Do we want to shelve our current project in favor of this new challenge?"

"How far?" Herman asks. Herman is a German shepherd.

"Yes, is it near the mountain?" one of the Flying Children wants to know as well. "Definitely not near the mountain," Kate says. This is going to be difficult. Let me try it this way. "To the very end of time and space."

"We'd better pack some lunch then," says Goro, a pudgy Rottweiler, who gets a sideways look from Herbie for his foresight.

Benji, a well-liked, multi-talented puppy of unknown ancestry, plays a major role in the current undertaking and seems to have a real concern. "Could we not do both, Miss Kate? We're not all gonna go, are we?"

That's another possibility she hadn't thought of. That's why you have meetings, flush out all the options.

"I will seriously consider that," she promises as it becomes immediately obvious—that would be the preferred solution all around.

Louise, during all this time, has been uncharacteristically silent, although she has been taking notes furiously and Kate is pleased when she raises her pencil.

"Yes, Louise."

"It's Jacob who wants to say something." She uses her pencil to point to her left.

"Of course, Jacob," says Kate, happy to have been able to stimulate additional input, particularly from Jacob about whom she has been curious ever since his recent arrival. Even for a basset hound his ears are particularly long and tend to drag on the floor as he often seems to be in a contemplative mood with his head hanging down. In flight, clearly, his ears are very useful. The other thing you cannot help but notice about him is that, for a puppy so young, he has wise and thoughtful eyes. Even now he doesn't really raise his head and is barely audible when Kate hears him say, "Blah—blah—rah—blah—rah."

She looks a bit helplessly at Louise, who takes charge. "You're going to have to help Miss Kate, Jacob. Can you speak up and get closer, please?"

It is obvious to Kate that he doesn't really want to do that and she appreciates it all the more when he does. "I would caution against blindly accepting everything that the grown-ups say about distances and time," he says. Kate waits for more, but there isn't any.

"Can you elaborate a little, Jacob?" she asks.

His demeanor has definitely changed. He is standing erect now, alert, in stark contrast to Goro who has gone to sleep.

"There is still so much that is not known and might surprise, even help us," says Jacob without any of the previous hesitation in his voice. "Time-warps and worm-holes to begin with."

"Precisely," Kate agrees. She looks up at the sun and stands when she sees Louise point to a whole section of her crowd that has apparently followed Goro's lead and fallen asleep now.

Jacob gets it just right and she's sure she can see an unexpected level of confidence when he summarizes everything well, suddenly sounding almost authoritative. "We agree then that we must all stay open-minded." What a science officer he would make!

Louise nods thoughtfully and makes another entry in her notepad and Kate couldn't be more pleased with the level of participation.

"Very productive meeting," she commends everyone not sleeping. "And keep this in mind. It would absolutely have to be an all-volunteer effort. What say you? Shall we all think then and meet again in a couple of days?"

Hoping that she had been sufficiently persuasive, Kate reaches for her last tea biscuit and is about to make her final entry when she looks into the bright eyes of Louise. "Miss Kate, Jacob says he...he has noticed and I...I agree that you seem, oh, preoccupied and worried about something. We could both stay a while and...you know...only if you want." Kate puts down her pencil and keeps alternately glancing at Jacob and Louise—who curtsies while looking down—and decides to postpone her final entry as it will no doubt change in tone and substance now.

– 8 –

I think I will go...over there, John decides. Stand by that window for awhile. He's been trying out all the different seating arrangements in the great room of the retreat. It can be comfortable whenever there's a crowd. All by himself, he finds it damn overwhelming. Even the roaring fire doesn't change that. He's waiting for the fellow from the University who is to meet with Marshal and him. Why the student, who appears to have only a peripheral involvement with that probable space debris, isn't clear to John. He would have preferred to talk with Professor Mercier, but for some reason Marshal wants to handle that himself.

Awkward anyway, the whole thing. Vague indicators and nothing specific. Not the way John likes to operate. Tell me what you want and even if I don't believe in it, I will probably get you there. But my way.

He hasn't seen anything of Marshal in the last few hours. No wonder. Things couldn't have gone any worse than they did with his mother.

He has gotten to like Monica Curtis and her blunt, humorous way and he'd developed a gut feeling that things would turn out well. The deal part of it had become almost a non-issue and, knowing Marshal as he did, money certainly wasn't going to be a show stopper. Monica had even joked at one point that if things were to turn around the other way it wouldn't be all that bad. Perhaps she should buy him out. He had come to believe her too when she said she would never knowingly do anything to impede Marshal, no matter what their differences. They had managed to get through almost a twenty-four hour period without any unpleasantness and, to the best of John's knowledge, Marshal and his mother had not spent any extended periods of time alone. That seemed to have been his plan all along.

That's why he had been so surprised when he saw Monica walk briskly out of Marshal's office without even acknowledging him and had gone to her suite. John hadn't known what to do and had stayed around until Marshal came out. He could see immediately, though it didn't seem possible or clear whether it was as a result of some regret or frustration—Marshal seemed choked up. "That woman…" He stopped there and swallowed hard. "I didn't expect this, John." Stomping off with a dismissive gesture and barely audible when saying something about her leaving—he would not look at John.

No, not again he had thought when his mind jumped back to the time the two girls at the orphanage had come close to seriously harm, if not actually kill him. That only because he had tried to mediate between them a dispute over a boy they both liked and he didn't even know. He clearly did not learn enough of a lesson as he had promised himself he would at the time. Be that as it may, at this moment John strains to suppress a smile when he recalls the ultimate—definitely unexpected—pay-off involving one of the two feisty orphans that resulted from his initially misguided act of chivalry.

Monica had refused to take the limo back to the airport, but had finally accepted, after much insistence, his offer to drive her back in one of the small cars. They had both been silent for quite a while, but he needed to know and persisted in spite of her reluctance. It turned out that Marshal had made the mistake of offering to visit her whenever he could on his trips to Europe and she had taken it as a sign, no doubt correctly, that she was to be banished from the Americas as well as selling her business interests and giving assurance of total discretion. It had been too much.

"But for what it's worth, John my boy," she had said, "I have absolutely no intentions of embarrassing him. Why would I? He doesn't have to change his plans on my account."

He felt like a little kid when at the airport she hugged him to say, "You take care of yourself, John, you're going to learn a hard lesson, but you'll probably be better off for it." And then with a sad smile, followed by a little chuckle. "A bit over the top, but true."

On the way back he had driven past the doughnut shop, but the grey truck hadn't been there.

John doesn't mind having his vigil by the window interrupted by the appearance of Marshal with the student.

"This is Stephan Po... Podatski... Podorski," Marshal says. "Meet John Martins. Stephan is attending university here in Canada on a United scholarship. Geology, isn't it, Stephan?"

"Yes, Sir."

"And you're doing well, even without family support, away from home?"

"Canada is a very nice country and I do love it here." Stephan is stroking his right arm nervously.

"That's great, you know, because one day we may just call on your expertise and send you to the heart of Africa."

"I hope you will, Sir. I really do." Stephan is stroking his left arm nervously.

"Right, Stephan." Marshal is blinking at John, trying to draw him into the conversation. "I understand you were involved in that lab mishap where you got that false positive; or should I say false negative, isn't that right?"

"Yes I was, Sir."

"But we've heard," John says, "it may not be a false anything. All attempts so far have failed to explain the result, true?"

"Well, they're still trying to make sense of it, but I'm not part of that anymore. The latest theory is that it must be man-made. But if it is, it really just raises other unanswerable questions; nobody can figure out how. Because if it's not..." He looks confused and John finishes his sentence. "It cannot be from our known universe, right?"

"That's what people are talking about, right Sir. Many think it all a big joke, but that number is dwindling."

"And the people who found it," John says, "they live right around here, yes? You know them well?"

"Not well, Sir."

Sir, Sir! It's like extracting teeth. "Stephan, I know you're a student, but don't you have an opinion yourself and are those people certain they took it off their own land?" John waits for the answer, but gets disappointed again. "It's what I hear and nobody—"

"I heard differently," Marshal interrupts. "I heard that it actually comes from our property. You know we own some six hundred acres right up to the lake where it was found."

"I wouldn't know about that," Stephan says, desperately uncomfortable now; John thinks it unlikely that at the moment Stephan has another reason for having crossed both his arms and simultaneously rubbing them.

"No, how could you," says Marshal, surprising John with his sudden shift, seemingly having given up and trying to put Stephan at ease for some reason. "And in any event, I'm sure that a plausible explanation is coming. Give my regards to Professor Mercier and do keep us informed, will you? We are counting on you. And Stephan, as you have somehow wound up right at the center of all this, I'm sure I don't have to remind you of the importance of discretion, do I? We'll talk again soon, I'm sure."

With that Stephan is dismissed—rather abruptly. Disturbed likely, confused possibly, scared shitless probably and John is left to wonder why Marshal, if his intention all along had been to recruit Stephan, could not just have left that to him. This level of personal involvement on Marshal's part, not at his best to begin with these days, is uncommon and, by the looks of it, unproductive. Can it really be that it irks him so much to have a discovery made right at his doorstep without him being involved? Would he try to suppress knowledge because it interferes with his publication? Doesn't he have enough on his plate at the moment as is?

"He'll be of no use unless he gets smart and starts to think for himself. Let him steam for a couple of days and then we'll have another go at him. I'll have one more talk with Mer..." Marshal halts with a grin. "It's almost comical. We're explaining to our readers all over the world the nature of our universe, beginning with the Big Bang, and these presumptuous hicks around here are trying to prove us all wrong." Now he laughs, but it is forced and John can see how stressed he is.

There are a few silent moments while Marshal Curtis is pacing about, looking down and then at John. "I'm going back to Seattle, John. But I want you to stay around here for a few days. Something is going to break, I can feel it. I'll speak with Ely too, but I will probably see you again before I leave. Let's get a handle on this situation, John. You understand?"

"No, not really. I can see why you would be bitter at the moment. Shouldn't that be all the more reason for at least one of us to concentrate on making... fucking money?"

"John, sometimes you worry me so." Marshal has turned towards the fireplace. "Fucking money, as you put it, is well in our rear-view mirror. Together, John, we can...no, we will begin to change the way business, nations and theology interact. Mark my words."

Foolish me. John is biting his lips as he heads for the door. What made me think I was doing good?

– 9 –

Now that the morning fog has lifted, there are smiles all around. Frank Bartoli is casually leaning against the race-car in the pit-lane of the race track, winking at Kate, urging her. "Yes? I said...if I buy your Dad's car, you'll come out and watch me kick butt?"

Serafina seems unable to resist the urge when Kate hesitates. "Sure, why don't you?"

"I haven't thought of that." Kate fidgets with her stopwatch. "Next week is a long way off. How do we know—"

"Come on, it'll be fun. You know some of the people and the racing scene around here."

Well yes, at least she used to.

They've had some real luck with the weather. Late fall, an unusually warm Indian summer day. Sunny and probably fifteen degrees. Leo had said they would need at least twelve degrees to get sufficient heat into the tires to develop any kind of speed.

Frank Bartoli had been clear and clever about his approach, according to Leo. Knowing that Leo hadn't done any competitive racing in recent years, he had made an offer for one of his race cars and, because Leo had two nearly identical cars, Frank wanted to be certain he got a good package. It was an expensive grand touring car and he had made the deal conditional on a satisfactory test session where both he and Leo would drive it. He had the data to know what the car should be capable of in Leo's hands and some notion of what he thought it should do in his own. He had rented Mosport International Raceway for the day and planned to stay in the Toronto area for the week to race a late event for this season, if everything went okay. Serafina had gotten in on it and suggested they could make a picnic of it and Kate agreed that it would do Leo, who had first been reluctant, some good to spend a day not worrying about potatoes; or continue stressing that he might have to take to his grave lingering concerns about having possibly embarrassed Roda Endsman, upset Stephan and three or four unidentified others.

Kate has to admit... that Frank is a handsome man. A little on the cocky, confident side, looking smart in his driving suit. So does Dad, but not as smart. Also, Frank doesn't walk with a limp... yet.

"Say Frank," says Leo, "don't do what I say, but I would listen to Alfred here." He motions Alfred to come over.

Dirty hands or not, Alfred Brewer is a professorial, almost elegant-looking, tall man. He is said to be of partial Native American ancestry and a former—highly regarded—math teacher. Likely all true, Kate believes, because the one who has made these claims is Alfred Brewer.

"He's been looking after me for years. Without him... well, what he doesn't know about car preparation... you know the saying." Leo pads Alfred on the shoulders. "If this man would apply his brain and what he knows to things other than preparing race cars, we'd all be working for him."

"You are. You just don't know it." Alfred laughs and nods at Frank. "You don't need me to tell you, but for what it's worth, it's a turbo; at the peak you have some seven hundred horsepower. There's still a bit of lag and it'll come on fast... and look out for fallen leaves on the racing line. If you don't get heat in the tires first, you will spin, especially Turn Ten." He points to the last turn on the track. "You break the rear loose, the car will start aiming towards the inside. There's not much room. The tires may hook up again and you won't just spin, you're gonna go straight into the wall. Don't believe me, ask Leo; he's done it."

Leo's grinning at Frank. "You can go anytime. The transmission is warmed up."

"I think you should go. You haven't had the car out in about four months, right? See what it feels like to you, the way you think it should handle."

"I'll go if you really want me to, Frank. But I don't need to just because I brought my suet. I trust you with the car and you wouldn't want me to smash it up now; I'm not the driver I used to be."

"Na, we can allow for that. Let's stay with the plan."

"That's fine." Leo reaches for his helmet and starts to climb in and Kate sees he has a little trouble with that, courtesy of his introduction to the Turn Ten wall and the resulting steel rod in his left leg some five years back. It's never been much of a problem, except for that slight limp. When he is about to pull out, Serafina knocks on his helmet to get his attention. "We'll be over on the bank; Kate says you know the spot, Turn One."

He nods and drives off.

"Who's your friend, Kate?" shouts the older of the two ambulance attendants as they make their way across the bridge to the grassy area near the turn while Leo is slowly circling the track.

Kate waves. "Why, Randy, you want a picture for your wife?"

"Ha ha."

"I guess Leo doesn't mind Stephan coming out here?" Serafina asks, looking back at the car approaching from the final turn.

"No, just the opposite. He thinks he's my date, or a lead-in to other dates."

"Aha...? That Frank, he's hot, don't you think?"

"Well, yes," Kate agrees, but quickly turns the conversation back to Stephan. "He's already backing off again, isn't he? I'm not sure he is ever going to shed any light on our diamond. Why come all the way out here to tell us in detail what he doesn't know?"

"No no. He knows a bit about car racing, he said, and it's a treat for him. But he thinks we should be aware. There are some people asking all kinds of questions...exactly where it was found and by whom. He says there's something intimidating about them. He suggested that it might be safer to only talk about this in person from now on."

"What?"

"I'm not kidding, he seemed real nervous, even more than before."

"This is getting silly. How is this all getting to be more about people than substance? Well, let's keep Dad out of this, at least until he's done driving."

"Don't know why, but okay. Guess we'll learn more later on." Serafina points to the pits.

Leo has stopped and is out of the car. He talks to Frank while Alfred takes off the rear bodywork, makes an adjustment in the area of the sway bar and checks the tire pressures. The bodywork goes back on, Leo climbs in and drives off.

This time with authority.

* * * *

Mosport is a daunting place and known to be one of the most challenging racetracks in the world. But Leo has been around here thousands of times and knows what to expect.

He does two more moderate laps about three seconds off his usual pace, deliberately spinning the tires in a couple of places to feel out the grip-level. Time to go. On the back straight he can feel the car getting light cresting the hill. Climbing again before plunging into the blind, sweeping left-hand Turn Two, he feeds the power early and the car responds willingly and takes him to the right-hander approaching Turn Four. Down the fast left-hander among the trees to the double-apex tight Corner Five. That familiar feeling is coming back.

His dash has a read-out to tell him how fast he is lapping. He doesn't have to look. He can tell by the sound of the engine, the timing of the shift lights and the feel of the steering wheel.

Alone in his screaming cocoon, flirting confidently with potential disaster that is Turn Eight; just steel and concrete and his own limitations. Leo is happy. Right up to the point he becomes aware that he is, and then the thoughts come rushing in. He slaps himself hard at the side of the helmet. Too late, his old problem once again: that Stephan—nice fellow; but gee, he's too young for Kate, isn't he? And why were Serafina and Kate whispering about him and trouble with diamonds? And Serafina ought to do her part to get Kate out more.

The engine rpm start to drop coming off the turns and he knows: that's it for the day. He's not that unhappy about it. It's always been like that for him. It's been a kick though. Approaching the pits, he turns his radio back on and thinks of that old debate among drivers as to what is better—driving a race car at your limit or sex. Tough call.

* * * *

"Bet you, Leo had his radio turned off—at least in the beginning," Kate says. "We shouldn't have told him where we would be...Oh well. Where is our Rock-man anyway?"

"Late, I guess," Serafina says. "Oh well...what?"

"It's all about not thinking too much. You would know about that."

"Huh?" Serafina says, not laughing, "I'll have to...there's Stephan."

He waves at them from a distance. "Mind if I go across first? I want to look at the car up close," he shouts.

They see him walk across the bridge towards the car where he shakes everyone's hand. Frank Bartoli is getting in now while Alfred leans over and checks his belts. The engine comes to life and Frank makes his way slowly down pit lane. It doesn't take him long. A couple of slow laps similar to what Leo had done and then his confidence starts to show. Kate can tell—he is fast right off the bat. His lines are not as consistent as Leo's, but she can see it coming. After only eight laps he is faster than Leo has been, the last lap he barely lifts going down Turn One. There's a guard rail there and a steep bank.

Serafina looks impressed. "That guy is good, no?"

"Yes," Kate agrees, "he's never driven this kind of a car before; low-powered formula cars, yes. It sure didn't take him long."

"Even better," Serafina nudges her arm. "He likes you."

"Oh, I don't know."

"Jesus, Kate, you keep this up, you'll die an old maid."

"Well, I don't have to fall in love with every Frank I meet, do I?"

"No, but you don't even give it a chance."

"I'm happy the way things are. If I wasn't, I would change something. Like people do."

Serafina is frowning. "Leo is worried about you too, you know. You can't live your life for others and he's not looking for you to be like him."

"He said that?"

"Yes. Not in that way... but yes. You two couldn't be closer, but you're not his... well, you know about genes. He can't get himself to believe that you just happen to be like him."

"What's that supposed to mean—just like him?"

"He's a... Leopold, you're not. And you shouldn't try to be. I would be willing to bet that most women your age spend their Friday evenings mingling, perhaps worrying about the exact location of their boyfriends or wondering what their children are up to. Don't think I don't know you've been encouraging, even helping Leo with his search for those—what's that word you sometimes use—discombobulated atoms."

"It's a philosophical exercise."

"Particles that interact at a distance in multiple ways, simultaneously being part of alternate realities? He's had you looking for those rascals on a Saturday night, wondering what they're getting into."

"He can't have it both ways." She's getting frustrated. "He has always encouraged me to be self-reliant and independent. Now I should hang out in bars and marry the first man who asks me?"

"Don't get silly now," Serafina says. "The first man, no. The first Frank? Maybe." She just won't leave it alone. "You really should come out here on the weekend and spend the day with Frank."

They get up and Serafina gives her a long look. "You do know," she says, "no matter what, I mean well."

"I must write this down...yes. I still don't see how everyone would know what makes me happy."

"You're missing the point, Kate. It's not about this minute, it's your life. Listen to me, look what shhh...you made me say now. Here they come anyway. Let's drop it for now so I can keep annoying you later."

Of the three men coming back, Stephan seems the most excited. He's nodding to himself. "What a machine! A beast!"

Frank is alternating between grinning at Leo and smiling at Kate. "You're on for the weekend, if you want to be. You want to be? Say yes, Kate."

"I don't know yet, but we'll be in touch anyway, if that's okay? We've got a week."

"Kate!" Frank steps up closer to put one hand on her shoulder and reach around with the other to rub the back of her neck momentarily. "Do try, Kate, okay? It'll be great." He turns to Leo. "You gonna miss your toy, Leo?"

Leo shakes his head. "Nah, I've had my share of fun. So damn lucky that I've been able to afford this kind of equipment...and him." Leo is nodding in the direction of Alfred. "How about some lunch, Alfred?"

* * * *

With just one exception, they had generously shared the imaginative and well-balanced contents of Serafina's picnic basket. Stephan, it had turned out, has a particular weakness for poppy seed strudel. The revelation had led to a discussion that for a while seemed to have the potential for serious disagreement. "Never, absolutely not," Leo had insisted. "Raisins in any kind of strudel is just so wrong," he said while Stephan kept shaking his head and repeating over and over again that his mother always put in raisins and why was Frank grinning at everybody as if he could possibly know anything about strudel and that it didn't seem appropriate to him—Stephan—that Alfred in particular should act as if he was above the whole subject and that Serafina, being from central America—not exactly strudel country—might in the future be well advised to research her subject before taking such a definitive stand.

Frank is the first to become restless. Kate has to suppress a smile as she sees him alternating his attention between her and his new Baby. "Aren't you going to do some more laps today, Frank," she helps out.

"What do you think, Alfred?" When Alfred nods, Frank gets up. He says his goodbyes, but lingers in front of Kate. "Remember, Leo has my number."

"Alright. I will call and you keep safe."

"Be good to our car," mumbles Leo.

"Well, Stephan"—Serafina is closing the picnic basket—"what's the latest now?"

"They still don't have an answer." Stephan is no longer so giddy.

"I know. You told us that. You said there were some people asking questions. What else do you know about this?"

"Well, it's like I said. They're wondering who found it and where it was found, that's a fact. There now seems to be more focus on that than on what it actually is."

Kate can see Serafina becoming real impatient and herself real angry as it's readily apparent how uncomfortable Stephan is when it comes to her treasure. Something has changed—more than a little. He's become unresponsive to the point of being annoying. Leo seems oblivious to what is going on, apparently reliving his moment of glory in the car. She thinks it best to drop the subject for the moment and winks at Serafina who frowns but appears to understand—perhaps Stephan will be more forthcoming another time, and perhaps not. But now she will definitely ask Serafina for more details about her back-up plan.

During the drive home Leo finally seems to realize something and asks Serafina sitting next to him. "You were talking about that rock Kate found?"

"You know we were."

"I wasn't sure. I wasn't paying attention."

"You never do, Leo." Kate says. "What else would we have been talking about?"

"They're still saying that it can't be man-made?" He glances at Serafina.

"That's right."

"And because it has zero carbon content, it can't be from our universe?"

"You got it," answers Serafina, "and that yellow sign with black squiggles on it means there's going to be a left turn."

"And you found it on our property, Kate?"

"Right on the edge of it, Blue and I did, where the fence used to be by the water."

"Can you keep me informed from now on?" Leo is becoming animated. "Wouldn't this be something? Even if all it did is bring everyone just a little closer to a less finite, I really mean less presumptuous understanding of the universe."

"Watch the road, Dad!" She sees him getting too excited. "Maybe we'd better stop somewhere for another coffee."

"Right, let's do that," Leo says and twists his head quickly again to give her an approving look of sorts. "My daughter! That's the conclusion we came to years ago, remember? You said it well; not a limited Big-Bang Bubble, more like the ever changing center of a rolling wave in a limitless ocean."

"Yeah yeah," says Serafina, "can we stop soon?"—and no no, thinks Kate, I didn't say that, you did.

– 10 –

Apples are what John is thinking about and the splashing sound the oars of the dilapidated old rowboat had made when they hit the water. It is the childhood memory that comes back to him most often ... rowing across his uncle's small pond to get his bounty. He could easily have walked, but it wouldn't have been the same. The wild old apple tree on the other side would produce only every other year, but if you timed it right and with a bit of luck—there it would be! A perfect apple, for free. You wouldn't have to buy it and you wouldn't have to steal it. He had often thought about that tree later in life and it had given him comfort and had strengthened his sometimes ambiguous belief in a higher power. Who but a good God would create and place that perfect apple there for him to find?

John puts his glasses back on and picks up the book about Darwin's dangerous ideas when he sees the two men. They come out of the woods and head towards the side-porch of the retreat where he has been trying to read. Lucky that he doesn't want to anyway, but he can't get himself to be comfortable with either of the two. Ely Greguric is a tough-looking Balkan and doubles as Marshal's sometimes chauffeur and bodyguard. If he has good reasons for his constant arrogant demeanor, he hides them well. John isn't sure what exactly the function of the new, wiry small man is supposed to be—family tragedy excepting, you never see one without the other. Ely calls him Aholl sometimes and other things often and Aholl hardly ever speaks.

"You've been hunting?" John asks Ely when he sees the crossbow at his side.

"Just fooling around ... target practice," says Ely.

The small man has a wire sling attached to a wooden stick in his hand. It makes John hesitate momentarily before he points to it. "What's that, you're trying to fix something?"

"Snare," Aholl says.

"Is that legal around here?" John wonders. "I wouldn't want to get caught up in one of those."

The man just shrugs his shoulders, looking down at his feet.

"Goodness, be careful with that. Christ."

Aholl still doesn't react and it has John direct his attention back to Ely. "You know that wooded area by the lake? There're some tall pine trees where our property ends. There's a farm past there—a horse farm."

"I haven't been there."

"You sure? It doesn't matter. You'll find it, it's in that corner. You can ... no, don't take a boat, go through the woods, but I want you to go there and map out the area."

"What for?"

John cringes when Ely asks what is not really a bad question while the little guy keeps twirling his snare.

"It doesn't matter why." That damn insolent smirk is getting on his nerves. "I just want you to go there and look around. Focus on anything unusual and let me know about it. Make some notes about the fences, a drawing of their location."

"Unusual, like...?"

"Anything out of the ordinary; any sign of activity. Do I have to spell it out? We need to know if other people have been messing around back there...if anybody is doing anything now. Don't get caught on the neighbor's property. In fact, don't let yourself be seen. You got that?" Maybe I'm getting so pissed off because I don't fucking know why I'm screwing around like this to begin with. I don't want to. I want to get back to my book...or go and wash my hair.

"If that's what you say," says Ely.

John looks over at the housekeeper who is motioning to him. "There's a Sharon Epstein on the phone," she shouts.

"I'll be right there, give me a second. What?"

"That's it?" A lingering Ely seems disappointed.

"That's it." He keeps looking at the two men as they walk towards the guest cabin they're using. That long grey coat makes Ely look even bigger than he already is and out of place here—a quality coat in the middle of the woods?

"Sharon, how are you? They said you were in a meeting."

"No trouble. What's up?"

"I need you to get me some information. I don't want to be asking too many questions around here."

"Well, shoot."

"I need to get a feeling for real estate values of large parcels around here."

"That's all?"

"No. I also need you to find out who the owners of that horse farm south of us are. You see where I'm going? Have Research start to put together a dossier and get a phone number for them, they're not listed. Leopold Walter. W-A-L-T-E-R. You've got to do it discreetly."

"Discreetly? That's my middle name! Didn't you know? Name, dossier code?"

"Ah...area...area seven. What else is going on in Seattle?" John asks to be polite, not really expecting an answer but getting one.

"Well, you know the director of that German magazine we bought? He's not there anymore. He quit."

John can't help but chuckle. "Surprise, surprise. Guess he didn't like being only one of two managing directors with shared signing authority. Too smart for his own good. Sharon, let me know as soon as you can. If you don't, I know where your children live...hang on, hang on. Find out who's the best real estate type we have in the organization and have him or her give me a call. We probably don't have one, but whoever is the most savvy when it comes to real estate transactions. I've lost track of that action. Make sure they know it's not for an acquisition at home. Canada. Okay?"

"Roger," says Sharon.

When John gets back out to the porch, he sees Ely and the small man standing there again, looking at him. "Something else?" he asks.

"Phones," Ely says, pointing in the general direction of the neighbor's property.

"Phones?"

"Phones. You want us to do something?"

"Like...?"

"You wanna know what they're talking about over there?"

He hadn't considered that and thinks for a moment. "Can you do that?"

"Yeah. We can do that."

"Without trouble?"

"You don't wanna worry about that. We'll handle it."

John doesn't say yes and he doesn't say no—and he isn't proud of it—and he no longer feels like reading.

— 11 —

Serafina has never been in a professor's home office before, but from what she has seen in the movies and read about in books it looks about right. It's cluttered.

Professor Mercier directs her to a chair, but he remains standing. "I really think it is premature to get the press involved in this. *The Sun*, did you say?"

She's uncomfortable sitting when the professor is not. She gets up. "There may be a misunderstanding, Professor Mercier."

"How so, Miss Gomez?"

"I take it Stephan didn't make it clear. I work for *The Sun* as a secretary. I'm not here on behalf of the paper, just trying to help out some friends."

The professor groans. Serafina can't tell whether he is relieved or disappointed and she smiles at him nervously. "You see, now that we know it's not a diamond, the family is still curious just what it is."

"Well, so am I. But there is the question of whether it might not be a health hazard. Where exactly was it found?" The professor feigns a yawn and steps away momentarily in a transparent effort to project only marginal interest. "Was it not right on the property line of that company retreat?"

"I know approximately, not exactly," she answers, trying to avoid direct eye-contact. What is he really getting at?

He has finally made himself comfortable behind his desk. She's about to sit down as well when, no, he's up again.

"I think it would be prudent," he says slowly, "for you to stay away from that location until we complete additional testing. Radiometric dating is already scheduled."

"Actually, that's what I want to talk to you about. Do you know a Professor Reeling at Florida State University?"

"I do... well, wait." Mercier appears to be thinking. "I do not know him personally, but if it is the same man, I know of him by reputation."

"The owner of *The Sun*, Mrs. Eller—"

"We do know who Mrs. Eller is, Miss Gomez."

"Mrs. Eller is beginning to take a bit of an interest as well. She's friends with Professor Reeling, has spoken with him and is pretty insistent on—"

"Spoken to him of...?"

"About doing additional testing in Florida. Maximize the potential for a speedy resolution. And in time, who knows, some good-will on the part of the press might be useful. It couldn't hurt, could it?"

"Well, no, of course not." The professor doesn't appear really enthusiastic. "It just seems to me we are rushing things here unnecessarily."

"The people who found it are quite prepared to absorb the costs that might be incurred," Serafina says, relieved to see Professor Mercier finally sitting still even if she's not. "The family also has an interest in astrophysics."

"That would be Leopold Walter and Miss Kate."

"Yes, how do you know?" asks Serafina, knowing the answer.

"Well," he hesitates for a good long moment, "Stephan Podorski told me. And I was once a teacher to your, shall we say, tenacious friend, Miss Kate. But you already know that, I suspect, do you not?"

In spite of his manner of speaking, the professor suddenly seems quite at ease. "I was a bit hard on the young man, Miss Gomez." He gets up and gives a friendly tap to the back of the chair she's still not sitting in. "Why would I not make us a cup of coffee and together we shall endeavor to devise a master plan to share the glory for the discovery of the century. Well, decidedly the discovery of the century. And there are logistics to be considered, do you not know."

Serafina is walking towards her car slowly, not yet certain about the remainder of her day, trying to picture Mercier in an exotic setting. Turns out the professor can be quite an engaging man. Very agreeable, in fact. But the vision of him singing karaoke in that Singapore bar?

Stephan, whom she had tried to contact earlier while in the area, has not returned her call. She'll wait a bit longer this one more time to see if he has anything new before she tries to phone Leo and Kate.

It would be a long drive, well out of her way, but it being Wednesday, she would know where to hook up with those Colombian crazies for a bite to eat and a drink. They, not surprisingly, don't admit to being insane; they claim to be "dedicated expatriates." She really likes the crowd, but has continuing misgivings about their motives. They'd better be joking about their ambitions for the future of Central America. Are they trying to have fun at her expense? If so, she can think of ways to turn it around on them. Maybe she should do that; tell them that she has the connections for the supply of the heavy weapons required. And an effective way to launder drug money on an appropriately big scale.

– 12 –

It's been going on for hours. The horse, being a yearling, had apparently decided that he did not want his hooves trimmed on this day, or have anything to do with anyone connected in any way with the Walter horse training activity. He had been successful in avoiding capture in the large paddock by a number of ambitious volunteers under the direction of the head-trainer Bill Wilton and seemed downright proud for it.

Leo is glad these days for his past patience, as Bill has developed into a good trainer of standard-breds for his age and relative inexperience, though he can be a bit of a con man. He is fat and claims to be so deliberately. "It's good for the horse's legs—pulling the extra weight and they like it." Horses don't talk that much, so that's hard to prove. But yes, Bill Wilton can train them all right...once he gets a hold of them. He, along with the blacksmith and the groom, carrying buckets of oats, cornered the horse more than once only to have him bolt away. The visiting blacksmith, armed with a lasso and riding one of the retired pacers, had come closest, but...

Much of the time Leo has been amused and felt himself pulling for the horse. But it will soon start to get dark. There are some hard, icy patches in the paddock and the groom Lisa agrees that the horse is favoring his left hind some. Leo knows that failure will just make him feel foolish, but he has waited long enough and doesn't see a better choice.

"Let me try and don't interfere. What we got to lose?"

Lisa has her back to him, but he makes out her little giggle.

"I heard that."

Bill moves his eyes from the grinning blacksmith to him. "Old man, Leo, gonna get hurt." Leo reaches for one of the small buckets of oats and starts to walk out towards the paddock.

"Mr. Walter, Kate's on the line," he hears Lisa shout and turns back.

"Put her on the speaker."

"Dad, there's a John Martins on the phone, says he represents one of our neighbors and it's important. He wants to stop by."

"We don't know any John Martins, Kate."

"He does make it seem urgent. He says he's only here for—"

"You handle it, Kate, okay?"

"All right. Serafina's here now making dinner. Don't be too long."

"Don't interfere," he reminds them as he walks out of the comfortable barn with what he thinks is a good plan, hoping to make it impossible for them to say "we told you so!" The horse is halfway down the paddock on the right, eyeing him. Leo moves slowly away in a diagonal towards the large shade tree on the left without acknowledging the horse. McArthur, a nick-name given the horse by Lisa, becomes curious after about ten minutes and starts to canter along the fence line ever closer to him. He in turn walks slowly away. They repeat this ritual at an ever-decreasing distance some six times until McArthur is close enough and actually touches the bucket with his nose. Still, Leo resists the temptation. Somehow the horse has lost its halter. What to hang on to? Now the horse has his nose in the bucket and Leo slides his free hand gently up his neck and pulls back yet again. Three more steps away. Sliding his hand, he feels the mane, moves the bucket away slowly, then grasps the mane with a gentle tug. The horse grunts and raises his head. McArthur suddenly seems relieved and relaxed. They have connected.

When Leo rounds the corner into the barn, leading a horse by the mane, he feels good.

Walking towards the main house, now with Blue at his side, he feels very good.

Opening the front door, does he ever feel good.

— 13 —

Leo had clearly been too excited about something to properly clean up and had instead lingered about in the kitchen. At dinner too, he is attentively interacting with Blue as if the two of them know of something no one else does. They're feeling smug! Hopefully with some justification. That grinning and smiling doesn't really suit them, individually or in combination—they will hurt themselves.

"What?" Kate asks.

"Nothing."

Glancing at Serafina, even Blue for support and then back at Leo. "What?"

"I told you."

"Hmm."

Leo has been generous with respect to the size of his portions and continues the trend as they are finishing up with the crème brûlée that Serafina has made at home and brought along. There had been roasted potatoes and aromatic fried rice along with some very tender stewed beef, a little like goulash, but not as woodsy, or with that burnt taste, rather spicy and tomatoey—very good, tasty indeed. There had also been a garden salad and that yeasty, salty Cuban bread that no one, other than Serafina, seems to have access to. It's her big secret. With tea or coffee still to come, tea for a change Kate decides and is not at all surprised when out of nowhere, after eyeing both of them, Serafina giggles uncontrollably. Kate turns her face into a question mark.

"What a collection! Would you look at us," Serafina says matter-of-factly. They do that for a few moments with varying degrees of intensity but without coming to any actionable conclusions.

That's Serafina. What was it—given these frequent, at times annoyingly acute bouts of cynicism—that made her likeable anyway?

They both cared about Leo. Well...? Her sense of humor? Truth be told, Kate didn't really know why. Maybe just as well and probably the way it should be.

Yet with all of that penchant for lighthearted giddiness and passion for all things gay, she sensed an inner strength and another side to Serafina that was hard to pin down. Maybe Manuel had given them a hint. He was really the only person they ever met who knew anything about her life in Colombia. In response to a casual question from Dad he had once said in his halting English something like, "You ask... about mountain camps." Then he immediately tightened up and turned away as if he had said something he shouldn't.

She did not really spend that much time with Serafina alone. Usually it was the three of them. And, yes, it was Dad who had introduced them and, no, she did not fully understand the relationship between them; not completely. After all, Serafina was a handsome woman in her late thirties and Dad was sixty-six. A youngish sixty-six, but sixty-six nevertheless. Was she gay? Definitely gay, but not sexually gay, Kate is certain. She was more likely to respond in a flirtatious way to a handsome waiter at one of their infrequent lunches—or kindly take the time to rebuke a forward young man in a movie lineup without really meaning it—than Kate was.

Serafina had once tried to comfort her in the strangest way. She had grasped her upper arm to the point that it hurt, staring her in the face and harshly shaking her over and over again. All this while she was explaining with uncharacteristic patience the need for everything old to die. Like that was going to make her feel so much better. But it somehow did.

Kate had thought that Misty, Blue's mother, had become ill. She had battled for weeks trying to nurse her back to health. When Misty became too weak to climb up the stairs with her to the bedroom, she had set up a cot down in the laundry room, placed a comfortable mat by its side and slept there next to Misty while Blue lay at the laundry room door. It took nearly a month and she finally accepted that Misty really wasn't sick, but dying of old age. Not that it was any comfort, but she was twelve years old, which was a pretty good age for a great Pyrenees. Kate herself lost nearly fifteen pounds during that time. A good part of that possibly due to Serafina's at times misguided efforts to be helpful; five pounds probably. And when the end finally came, Kate was inconsolable. She just couldn't forget the very moment she knew that Misty was taking her last breath while she cradled her head. Misty had been a good friend and Serafina should do so well.

Dad is smoking again. She can see them on the porch through the kitchen window. He has his right hand on Serafina's shoulder, looking at her with squinted eyes while talking and she punches his left arm with a grin.

"Barry Endsman is the new editor at *The Sun*, did you know?" Serafina asks when they come back in.

"Oh yes?"

"He asked me if you would be interested in having some little excerpt from your latest effort publicized, along with an interview. He did say little and amusing, you hear me, Kate?"

"That's really not possible, I don't even think I have anything suitable at the moment."

"How about the interview," Leo says.

Kate purses her lips. "No, this really isn't good timing, but maybe sometime in the future. Anyway, has there been a response from the University in Florida yet?"

"I wasn't going to forget. There was." Serafina speaks more loudly now. Leo has moved through the open door into his study and Kate can see him staring at his latest unfinished painting as if it were a stubborn enemy to be defeated. "That Professor Reeling sent an email to Mrs. Eller. I haven't seen it myself, but in a nutshell I can tell, even though he reportedly didn't use words like dumb or idiots; he thinks this is a lot of nonsense and a waste of time. But he indicated that as a scientific challenge they may be willing to do something and it'll be discussed at the next department meeting."

Leo comes back into the living room, mumbling to himself. "You see. I don't understand why people are always so reluctant to at least consider, after all the lessons learned throughout history, what seems reasonable, even if not necessarily plausible. Uh-uh. You've really made me think all this through again with that find." He stops to look for his cigarettes. "Early man thought the earth to be the center of the universe, followed by the idea—for which people were imprisoned, by the way—that it had to be the sun."

He is still struggling to shift some credit for his pontifications. He has found his cigarettes, but where is the lighter? "Then, no, it was our galaxy. Not so fast, there are many galaxies. So it must have been the Big Bang at the beginning of all."

Kate worries that he might go on and on. True, he hardly ever talks for long, but equally true that he tends to belabor unduly a point that really captures his imagination. On those occasions he usually has little regard for the level of interest shown by others.

"But, Leo," she says quietly, only half pretending to be exasperated, "that debate is long over."

He nods. "I accept the evidence that the Big Bang did happen, but I believe—no, we believe, Kate—that it was only a local event in an incomprehensible forever."

Forever, whatever. It's written all over Serafina's face that she doesn't care that much one way or the other. She probably cannot relate to the importance of the age of the universe when there are things like the ever-increasing price of coffee beans and pre-Christmas jewelry sales to worry about. She even sounds a little impatient. "That Reeling also pointed out that there may be issues of jurisdiction and contamination and to be careful," and in the same breath, "are we going to play or are we still upset about the last time?"

It will no doubt please her to beat them at poker again and Kate starts to take out the cards but is interrupted when Manuel calls from the barn. "John Martins here. He say… called before."

Oh dear, she'd forgotten all about it. She hadn't wanted to be rude when the word "neighbor" was mentioned and she had said "yes."

She's glancing at Leo with a grimace. "Send him over, Manuel."

"He not alone."

"Well, send them over then."

The younger of the two men appears to be startled when he first sees her and his eyes wander back and forth between Leo and her before he introduces the older man with him as a lawyer acting for D.R.T. United and himself as a personal assistant to Marshal Curtis. A melodic, pleasant voice and those brown eyes behind the round goo goo glasses. A bit over-dressed for the country, thinks Kate, in that grey business suit. She feels as if she has seen him before, which really couldn't be, but there is something about him that makes her feel comfortable. Blue, however, as is his custom when there are strangers in the house, moves over from the living room and parks himself by the front door.

Leo interrupts John Martins when he tries to address him directly. "You won't mind, I prefer you deal with my daughter. I'll be around, if I'm needed." He starts to move towards his study and Kate knows; Leopold is at it again—except this time she doesn't mind.

Martins, looking puzzled, turns to her. "I apologize for disturbing you on such short notice, Miss Walter, but Mr. Curtis and D.R.T. United do have an option that is about to expire on some land around here and have authorized us to pursue another possibility that would suit them much better."

"Who's Mr. Curtis?"

"I'm sorry, I thought you knew. Mr. Curtis manages United and they own the large parcel north of you, on the other side of the lake. It adjoins your property on the east side. He's very interested in increasing the size of their retreat and, as I said, has a potential deal, but would much prefer to..." he hesitates and glances in the direction of Leo, who is standing near his desk, looking down at something important, no doubt, "buy your property."

"But our home is not for sale," says Kate after another quick glance in the direction of the study. That Martins fellow begins to look just so unhappy to her.

"I know that," Martins says. "You have a beautiful farm here and I think you can see where it would blend more, well, naturally and seamlessly into Marshal Curtis's property."

So far the lawyer hasn't said a word.

Mr. Curtis's property? None of them knew much about it and even less as to whom the north property belonged to. It did have the air of a substantial, somewhat impersonal retreat. It had been resold some six years back, Kate remembers. United? There is a privately held conglomerate with a name like that, based in the U.S. Maybe it's the same company.

Leo had waved Serafina into his office and whispered something to her. When she comes back, she turns to the lawyer to ask. "Does this Curtis fellow control—what did you say—United?"

The lawyer tries, but John Martins answers instead. "No, Vincent D'Groth controls D.R.T. United. But be assured, Mr. Curtis has complete authority to act."

Kate feels herself becoming nervous. She still likes the man who has been given this impossible task. How to be kind? "But my father and I have lived here, well, I've lived here most of my life, and my father before me. I don't remember us ever considering or discussing a possible sale."

Martins looks more and more distressed. For the moment he even seems lost for words as Kate adds. "Didn't you notice on the way in that this is a working farm? We train horses here." She stands to look down at Martins. "We also grow some produce. This farm is not for sale."

Kate again looks in the direction of the study where a seemingly content Leopold is busy carefully rearranging boxes of paperclips on his desk.

— 14 —

Serafina has become increasingly alarmed and wonders to herself—am I the only one who knows these United people are lying? And Leo? He is overdoing his act, well-intentioned as it might be. Somebody had better be prepared, in case Kate needs help.

She's seen a stretch limo parked on the circular drive at the front near the floodlight. She's ever more curious. One man had been leaning against the closed driver's door. She needs an excuse. She gets up and goes to the kitchen where she makes a mug of instant coffee, takes the side entrance from the kitchen and walks towards the limo. The big man by the car is still slouching against it, his long dark coat touching the ground, looking at some device in his hands. He straightens up when he sees her coming, and when he raises his head to look directly at her from below his hat with the brim turned down, Serafina just knows.

"It's getting awfully chilly out here. I thought you might like some coffee to warm you up."

"Nice of you, Miss, but you shouldn't have troubled."

She can't see into the back of the car, but she does notice a small figure sitting on the passenger side, staring straight out the front window.

"Perhaps your ... friend—?"

He interrupts. "No, Miss, really, we're fine."

"Well, all right then." Not very good at disguising his temper. A hard face. Security? Could be. Police, possibly. In a stretch limo, no. Bodyguard, maybe. All of the above, or worse. It's not as if she has never seen this type before. She hadn't planned on it, but she decides right there and then to stay over for tonight. "You have a good evening then."

The man touches the brim of his hat without saying anything.

Coming back into the house she is surprised to find Kate and John Martins sitting on the sofa, close to one another, looking at a photo album. Terrific! Kate tells her that they have stumbled onto the fact that they both know a great deal about yachting and have spent time in the waters near Aruba and in Aruba itself. Apparently John Martins' uncle owned or had chartered, it wasn't clear, a motor yacht from time to time. She sees Kate point with some pride at a picture showing Leo and her and a fish. "Dubious pedigree," Kate explains with a happy smile.

Isn't this great. That Martins fellow, for the moment, seems no less exuberant.

"Have you ever been on top deck on a cloudless night in the middle of the ocean and looked up at the stars?" he asks and continues without waiting for an answer, "and at first seen a few of the bright stars and then ever more and more. And if you keep looking without losing focus, the whole sky lights up as if..." He stops himself, seemingly worried he might be beginning to bore them. Not Kate, by the looks of it.

He suddenly feels for his belt and, glancing down nervously, stands up. "I wonder if you would excuse me for a moment. There's something I have to attend to." A beeper, probably, that they hadn't heard. Likely a signal from the goons outside.

Blue doesn't move, but neither does he take his eyes off the man walking past him and out the front door.

"You've been very kind to give us your time."

So it does speak. The lawyer, whose name neither Serafina nor anyone else seems to have caught when he had been introduced, gets up from his chair and tries to capture the attention of Leo, who doesn't respond and keeps on puttering about in his study. The man turns back reluctantly to Kate. "You know, John doesn't want to say this, but Marshal Curtis can be an exceedingly generous man. You may be surprised to learn just how determined he can be and how much he would be willing to pay for your land."

Serafina doesn't really want to participate in the conversation unless totally on her terms, but she has seen the discomfort in Kate. "I thought you had already covered that, Mister?"

The lawyer ignores her. "Mr. Curtis is a man of many interests and his motives cannot always be understood by others. You may not realize this, but—"

Leo, after first sticking his head around the corner, has finally come out of his hideaway to stand in front of the lawyer. "You say Mr. Curtis is a what?"

The man seems just a little apprehensive now. "Mr. Curtis is a well-known—"

"Ah yes. That's what I thought you said," Leo interrupts and keeps measuring with apparent dismay the lawyer, who must be very brave, arrogant, or both. "I happen to know something about who D'Groth is and find it unlikely that you are acting in accordance with what he would want. I've about had it with your—"

"You might be well advised to consider," the still determined, now visibly annoyed lawyer persists rapidly, "that a deal would avoid any unpleasantness or even legal action with regard to the dispute over the property line and the actual location of the discovery site. I think it would be so much more in everyone's interest,"—the front door opens and John Martins walks back in—"if this issue could be resolved in not only a profitable but pleasant way for you. Marshal Curtis has plans—"

"Enough," Leo shouts. The man takes a step back as Blue, alert and stiff, comes to stand alongside him in front of the lawyer.

John Martins seems totally confused for a moment and then, apparently realizing the direction the conversation has taken, he looks at Leo before refocusing on Kate with his back to the lawyer, showing him the palm of his hand at the side of his body in a motion designed to silence him. "I'm so very sorry. This is absolutely not—"

Leo won't let him finish. "You'd better just leave... now."

"Sir..."

"Now."

How could they have known—or should they have known? It had been about the discovery site all along.

– 15 –

Go to sleep? Not likely for a long time. "And get off my notes, Blue."

Kate is sitting cross-legged on the bed, Blue up against her. "Will you please get off my pad." She winds up with a little tear through her poem outline when she pulls it out from under him. "See what you did."

> 'Herman tried hard on the planet Odest
> To have all be more cautious on this dangerous quest.
> Still the puppies would do what puppies did best,
> They'd play, eat and sleep, interrupted by rest.'

"And interrupted by a tear," Kate laughs. It needs work anyway. She decides to shelve this subject for another day, puts down the pencil and hears herself sigh.

Leo is on the track now and she can see the lights of the tractor when he starts to round the corner at the far end and comes back towards the house.

So gentle a voice, that John—something just doesn't add up. He had at one point made a reference to an orphanage and spoken of an Uncle, but no other family. Is he out there on his own, without a connection to a "tribe" other than that United gang? Might this be an opportune time for her to finally follow through with that idea about exploring the downside of what inexplicably for most of the civilized world cannot come soon enough: a future unrestricted by the traditionally slow pace of progress and evolution? Start out with an essay anyway. It would make it the third active project, but what would be the harm in organizing some of the elements; she wouldn't necessarily have to bring it to a conclusion anytime soon.

With this subject, she wouldn't mind others also taking it seriously—just this one time, pretty please. Hopefully the process itself wouldn't turn her into another Leo. She thinks she knows this: he feels obligated to understand everything and resolve every issue. Must be driving him nuts.

Call it families, units, tribes...she's sure her thoughts are relevant, even if only to this one other person.

Something is alarming Blue. He sits up on the bed, head erect and his ears have stiffened. She too has heard it—a faint moan? Could only be Serafina. Blue jumps off the bed to follow as she rushes down the hallway to knock on her door. Nothing. "Serafina!" There is no answer. She opens the door to see Serafina sitting up on the bed even in the relative darkness. She looks disoriented and is wiping her forehead with the bed cover.

"What's wrong, what happened?" Kate turns on the light.

"Nothing. I must have had a dream. I felt I was...never mind, it's nothing."

Yes, easy to see that everything is just peachy. "That's not fair; how can it be nothing?"

"No. It's a nightmare. I've had them before, don't worry...don't fuss. Believe me. It doesn't help me—I mean, Jesus—reliving ancient history just because you want to hear about—"

"I would have thought that depends on your ancient...well, past." Kate is trying a giggle while straightening the bedcover when Serafina is lying back again. "Can't you come up with memories that don't give you nightmares? Can I get you something? Want me to stay a while? I don't just want to leave you like this. Want me to tell you one of my children's bedtime stories?"

"No Kate, please no. Get some sleep and let me try too. I'll see you at breakfast, right?" She manages a smile now when she asks. "Is Leo still on the track?"

"Uh huh. But I'm just down the hall, if anything, you hear...?"

Kate leaves her door partly open when she gets to her room. Back on the bed, she's just too wound up to even try to sleep. She'd better get focused, though. Bring logic to all this. She is a Walter, isn't she, and Leo is doing what needs to be done—she has just seen the tractor lights again in the distance.

"You think making some notes would be helpful?" she asks and takes Blue's silence to mean that at the least he doesn't have a real problem with it. Isn't it possible that John Martins is under some kind of duress? Maybe that outfit, the other people; could they have something on him? Something bad enough to make him do things he doesn't really want to be involved with. No, he would likely be too clever to get himself trapped like that. Could you even manipulate someone over a shoebox full of unpaid parking tickets?

This is getting more confusing, not clearer, Kate thinks. I better reset and start over. One quick decision before she starts. For one of her efforts she will use the title: Of Flying Children.

— 16 —

Leo had agreed with Manuel that he would, as he sometimes did, take the first shift of grading the training track to keep it from freezing.

"You'd best get some sleep," he had urged Kate before getting ready to go over to the barn.

"I will. There's coffee in the thermos in the kitchen. Make sure you stay awake, Dad."

He had watched her as she had gone up the stairs, Blue at her side. He felt, as he has more often lately, that little touch of sadness, worrying about whether she's as content as she says she is.

"Sleep well, Kate."

Without turning around and not saying anything she had acknowledged him with a little wave of her hand.

* * * *

Leo keeps circling the half mile track. It's monotonous, but he doesn't mind. A good place to be smoking and to listen to some music on his boom box, even so it's not that easy to hear over the noise of the tractor and the harrows grinding away at the stone dust. He doesn't like to use earphones. Something upbeat when he feels down—and more serious when he feels up. A Mozart concerto, contrasted by Wagner or Mahler. Today something in between. Bruch's *Violin Concerto* will do.

Kate seemed to have been so upset after the United people left.

They had spent some time talking about the site. The location was not really that close to the property line, was it? Too bad it wasn't properly fenced off. And the sooner additional testing of that fragment could prove things one way or another, the better. Maybe.

No subject could cheer Kate up and she stayed close to Blue all along.

When Serafina had come into his study to say goodnight, she had been insistent. "There is more to come, Leo. I know the man by the car. I mean, I don't know him, but I know him, and I'm staying over and you may want to think about hiring some security around here for a while."

Hadn't she looked different? The corners of her mouth had dropped and her usually large, shiny, brown eyes had narrowed. Tough! Leo had found himself wondering—what had her life really been like in Colombia?

He can feel and hear it. It's getting colder and the top of the track is beginning to freeze in places.

He increases his speed slightly to cover more of the area at the north end. If he can't keep the top layer of stone dust moving, there will be no training tomorrow. They've learned from experience that using salt is not a good alternative. Messy, hazardous and not good for the horses or the adjoining growth. A quick correction of the steering wheel; he had almost gone off the track in the turn near the steep bank. It had happened to him before and the tractor had nearly turned over.

Not like the old racing days and that sense of absolute control and comfort and the confidence he had all too occasionally experienced when he knew that nothing could possibly go wrong. This is not like that.

Odd.

The lights of a car appear on the main road, moving slowly and then stopping. There's never really any traffic over there and especially not at this time of the night. He slows down, then stops the tractor and turns off the lights and the boom box. On any other night he would have assumed that somebody had gotten lost, possibly kids parking. Not tonight.

He stays in the tractor for some four or five minutes; the car's lights never move. He finally decides to start up again, drives off the track and heads along the driveway towards the main road. When he's about halfway down towards the entrance, the car drives off. The track is now a write-off and there will be no training miles tomorrow. He will have breakfast with Kate and Serafina. He knows that because he isn't going to be sleeping tonight at all.

– 17 –

Things have changed since last night and Kate Walter feels marvelous. Why wouldn't she? It's five-thirty in the morning and she has barely rested during the night. Serafina had woken up from a nightmare and Dad hadn't slept at all. There is a sense of purpose in the kitchen that even Blue seems to share. It's almost too perfect. Leo is frying bacon and eggs, Serafina helps by buttering the toast and Kate pours herself a second cup of coffee while putting into place the final pieces of her logical jigsaw puzzle.

It's all so simple and she shouldn't even have needed most of the night to sort it all out. Not your usual wishful thinking or false hope. When it comes to matters like this, her father is really never wrong.

"If it looks easy, it will turn out to be hard and when everyone thinks it's impossible, it's probably not." She can just hear him say it. "When everybody says it's the right thing to do, watch out. Don't dismiss, but challenge every assumption. Always have a look at things the other way around, Kate; be very suspicious of group think. Inside out, upside down, Kate. Never blindly accept what seems to be obvious."

And Leo does have considerable justification for his arrogance—at the very base of his fortune is a simple reversal. While everyone knew how to change the shape of metal and reduce its size by various means, he saw the economic advantage of doing the reverse and increase the thickness of sheet metal for a specific purpose in a local area. "Upside down, Kate."

And there you have it. Everyone thinks John Martins is a bad person—ergo!

Just for now she will keep these logical conclusions to herself. When the time comes, Serafina might need to be persuaded. Leopold? She's got him cold.

"If it's alright," Serafina asks with some hesitation, alternating her inquisitive look between the two of them, "I'm going to make a call. I have some days coming at the office and I'd like to stay around here."

Would it be alright? Just like a family. "Great!" Kate is beaming.

Leo seems just a little surprised but pleased. "In that case you're going to have to earn your keep around here too, you know."

"Doing...?"

"Working in the stables with Kate, what did you think?"

"Oh."

Leo nods eagerly. "I can probably come up with many other tasks and so no doubt can Manuel. This is going to be great and low-cost to boot... you'll work for food. Horses for now, that's a good beginning. We spend many of our mornings in the barn anyway. Something satisfying about looking after horses, you'll see."

Kate is tidying up as he explains that there aren't going to be any fast training miles today. They'll be jogging horses, but that's it; part of the track is frozen.

"I'll try to come over," he says, "after I deal with this situation in England."

"What's the problem? Does it have to be today?" Kate asks. "I really have in mind taking another look at the fence-line at the back."

"I'll tell you about England. But let's do that, Kate, around lunchtime the three of us could go over to your spot, where you found that rock."

"Sounds good," Serafina says, "but won't it be four of us, with Blue?"

"Okay," Leo attempts a joke, "you can come too."

"What about England then? It's Ian Braithway again, I'll bet, right?" Kate is carefully pulling some burrs out of Blue's hair.

Nodding, Leo keeps leafing through stacks of documents now on the kitchen table. There seem to have been streams of them coming over the fax this morning. She has a pretty good idea what it's all about. Leo owns an assembly plant in England and this is not the first time that there are issues with Ian. Luckily she'd stayed out of it when Leo had tried to involve her before. Send her all the way to England, he was going to. Braithway, the head of procurement and resources over there—so named by Ian himself—has been frustrating management and Leo for some time now. The function is an important part of the business, but Ian Braithway has a way of making it seem critical, himself indispensable, and apparently has done it again.

"Is he...?"

"Is he what?"

"The shopaholic, is he trying to take advantage again?"

"I didn't call him that, Kate."

"I know, I did."

"Right," Leo says, making a note on the yellow pad. "It's beginning to feel like blackmail. I hate getting pushed into this position. He's over in Sweden with his assistant at one of our suppliers and he's talking about other opportunities they both have and will seriously consider if we don't work with him on his revised budget for the department. I hate this." Leo seems almost angry. Not something she sees often with him.

She feels just a bit sorry for her father. "So what will you do?" Perhaps she can strengthen her own case while sympathizing with him. "Is this a case for upside down thinking?"

"Not exactly; to me this goes more to fundamentals."

"Well then, what are you going to do?" says Serafina, seemingly also concerned about this additional pressure he surely doesn't need today. "It has to be now?"

Leo stops shuffling his papers to look up. "I'm about half done. I need a few more hours before I know who exactly is buying what and why. We'll finish this one way or another today."

Barely daybreak when they get there, but the barn is already alive with activity. There are two other grooms besides Lisa. Robert, the assistant trainer, is out on the track jogging one of the horses and Bill is hooking yet another one to a jogging cart in the arena.

"You look so cute." Kate hands Serafina a pitchfork. She kind of means it; just so fortunate they are both full-bodied. She has given her some of her own stable clothing while she is in a driving suit. She's planning to jog a horse or two herself.

Serafina has been to the races and the barn before, but not to muck out stalls. Lisa shows her, and after a while she pretends to be proud of her own effort. "I can do this," she proclaims, "yes I can. I just don't know about working that close to the horses."

"Be careful about that," Bill cautions her. He has just come back into the arena with the colt he has been working and the horse is steaming hot and breathing hard. "Never show them any fear," he says. "Don't walk around, brush right by; contact is best. Don't focus on them—they look at you funny, give'em a shot in the ribs."

"Yeah right. I'm gonna start a boxing match with a horse."

"He's right," the groom Joseph says. He might well know, given his advanced years, the scar at the side of his head and the kink in his forearm. "Don't show fear or too much respect; it's hard to reverse once you do." Serafina doesn't look very convinced to Kate, but she stays out of it.

It's her turn to jog one of the pacers and when she comes back, the horse is as hot as she is cold, but there's coffee and that tastes good. Manuel has been around the barn as well to talk with Serafina a couple of times; they whisper quietly in Spanish and Kate has no idea what they're going on about. Earlier he had gone out and come back with several machetes and shown them to Serafina. One of them a rusty old thing, the other one looked new—a prized possession from the old country?

Good to see Serafina catching on so quickly. Steaming horses rolling in the straw after getting a bath, snorting happily, munching on their hay. A sense of caring among everyone in the barn—no, not a bad way to spend a morning, Serafina has already agreed. Blue too is part of it; he doesn't bother the horses and they don't bother him.

They find Leo still buried in stacks of paper when they come back into his study. "How did she do?" he asks. He's smiling at Kate, but nodding in the direction of Serafina.

"Good, Dad," bubbles Kate, "she's particularly adept at—"

"Tomorrow," Serafina interrupts, "I'm gonna be jogging horses. It looks like fun."

Leo strokes his chin and Kate tries to hide her skepticism, managing to sound nonchalant, she's certain. "I'm going to have a shower and then we'll still head over to the lake, right? How're you making out with England anyway?"

"I'm almost finished. I'll tell you when you come down, okay? Ian wants the answer today. We're going to give him one."

Kate is first to come back down and hears Leo listen to *Aida* in his study. *Aida* is serious enough, what with people dying and all, so he must be feeling good now—relieved, at least. He too has freshened up and is wearing a dark blue track suit. All the papers are now in one neat stack on his desk.

"We'll have to keep an eye on Serafina," he says. "Jogging horses? Did she really like working around the barn?"

"I think so... Maybe it's the mother instinct in women. You know, taking care of animals."

"Always thought animals are more comfortable with women than men anyway—here she is."

"I'm gonna have to get myself some clothing," Serafina says, "I can't keep on wearing all your stuff."

"Oh, I don't mind. It's not as if I don't have enough." Kate wags a finger. "Just as long as you don't put rhinestones on everything."

"Meow," Serafina whispers. She has a hand on Leo's head and is looking at him.

"You better not be talking to me, Gomez." He gets up to turn off the music. "I've got my second wind. I'm alright. "I will call Ian now—you can stay."

Kate knows why he wants them to stay. Pragmatic as ever, Leopold Walter is likely not going to live forever and has not yet fully accepted that she will never run a business.

"Hello, Ian... I'm fine... That's good to hear..." Leo is looking at the top sheet of his paper stack while he's listening. "No," he says, "not anymore, but I will get back to it one day.... Listen, Ian, I have good news for you—about that other opportunity you have, you and your assistant—take it." Leo moves the phone away a couple of inches from his ear and squints his eyes while he listens. Kate can't make out what's being said, but she can hear some muffled sounds. "...No, Ian, management and I are in agreement on this. You don't need to worry about the department anymore..."

Leo moves the phone away again. "No, Ian, you misunderstand, you don't have to worry about it—ever again. There no longer is a resource department and we don't have a job for you anymore. Ian,

Ian, hold on ... it's not clear to me whether you and your assistant actually quit or whether you're being fired; either way, don't worry about it, you will be compensated in the appropriate way—I do wish you good luck, Ian, ... I do."

Leo hangs up and Kate is quick to ask, "I don't know, Dad, are you sure this goes to fundamentals? Isn't this more like inside out thinking?"

"Hmm ..." She sees him pondering what she said. "I looked carefully at what we're buying. Some items are in the pipeline and under control, others I'm not so sure we even need. There has been too much waste. But all the other departments are going to look after their own needs from now on. The biggest problem will be the production department components. That's a big job. But, as it turns out, they will in fact be more comfortable controlling their own supplies and we can accommodate all the other people from the department within the organization. Inside out? Well, yes, maybe."

She was right. She does have him down cold.

– 18 –

There aren't many traditional general stores left in these parts, but Tim Hanson's is a good one. Here they will find what Serafina doesn't want. Kate is certain of it.

Earlier in the morning, when they had been in Leo's study while he was dealing with the situation in England, he had taken a moment to carefully study Serafina and, barely able to disguise a smile, finally rested his eyes on her shoes. "If Serafina is going to be your stable hand and wants to come along into the woods with us, we'd better get her some sensible footwear. Why don't you take her into the village? I'm sure you will find something suitable at Hanson's."

Sensible shoes! It hadn't been difficult to see how she felt about that idea.

You name it, Hanson's has it. You need baby formula or a shotgun—no problem—canned goods, sewing kits, Coleman stoves, coats and sweaters, pots and pans, hardware, milk and bread. Candy if you want it. Hunting knives, feminine products, fishing rods, and yes, shoes and boots.

Kate sees Serafina eyeing a pair of Rocket hiking boots with suspicion. "You remember that little necklace Leo gave you for your birthday, the one with the gold shoes and diamonds?" she asks.

"I still wear it sometimes."

"The little poem he made up with it, remember that?"

Holding a seemingly offensive boot at a distance and looking at the price tag, Serafina frowns to say:

> "Shoes are good
> More shoes so fine
> When shoes are freaky
> Shoesie's are mine."

Kate laughs. "That's it. I would look at the taller boots, the ones with the fur at the top. They don't look bad."

With that, Serafina's fate is sealed. But now she wants a hunting knife.

"And you must have a knife...?"

"When we go into the bushes, shouldn't we have something to work with? What if we have to cut a branch or a rope or whatever?" Gee, she had forgotten all about that. The woods are often full of dangling ropes. So, it's a pair of sensible boots, a hunting knife and some tea biscuits for Kate.

When they step outside, Serafina wraps an arm around her. "See the limo over there at the gas station? That's the car from last night with those people." Kate sees two men getting out.

"Let's go over and say hello," Serafina says. Kate's not eager—neither of the men is John Martins and no one else is coming out of the limo.

"Come on"—Serafina is almost dragging her—"best to know your enemy." Kate sees the smaller of the two men take a canister out of the trunk and hand it to the big guy in the long coat. When the tall man spots them, he puts it back in the trunk and comes walking towards them, grinning.

"What are you doing here?" Serafina asks, looking at the smaller man who is staring at her but doesn't reply. The tall man answers. "Just getting supplies. You?"

He reaches out his hand and Serafina takes it. "My name is Ely and this," he grins at the small man, "yes, this is Aholl."

"I'm Serafina and this is Kate. Aholl? That's some kind of Eastern European name, isn't it? Or Turkish?"

Ely is laughing out loud. "No, not Eastern European or Turkish. It's more of an international name. Look at him." He towers over the small man and keeps laughing. "Asshole, I call him, don't you think it fits?" There's no visible reaction from the asshole and Kate cringes. Why must Serafina hang around these people? The big man stares directly at her now and then shifts back to Serafina. "You girls wanna have a beer sometime or something?"

To Kate's dismay, Serafina doesn't say no and instead asks, "You guys work over there for that D.R.T. outfit, right?"

Ely nods. "Yeah, so we'll see you sometime for a beer?"

"Ah... I meant that Mr. Martins," Serafina says, "is he the main man over there? You guys answer to him? And where do you hang out when you're not here?"

"That dance club, Bunny's north of here... we can take you girls there if you want. That's a really nice place." Ely smacks his lips and Aholl nods.

"Martins," Serafina reminds Ely, "is he the man? And I meant—where is your home base in the States?"

"Him...? John? Na... It's Curtis. And we hang in Seattle—if you girls ever want to come down, we'll show you around. So what about the beer?"

At least she's evasive now. "Can't be today. We've got to go for now, but maybe... yeah, maybe we will see you guys around; we'll probably have to be back here tomorrow for something about the same time, okay?"

"Don't forget, we'll know how to find you."

The two keep staring at them until their car turns the corner and they're out of sight. "Wonderful. What are you doing?" Kate is shaking her head. "How is this going to help us to solve a mystery? You're going to get us into a spot. If we're not careful, we are going to wind up double-dating at the bunny hop."

"Hell no! I told you it's best to know what you're up against." Serafina hesitates. "Unless you really, really want to."

While Serafina is driving, Kate is carefully reconstructing her logical jigsaw puzzle another time. She also tries to be fair and true to her own belief that there is some good in everyone. Ely and... Aholl. Just this very moment, she can't come up with anything.

– 19 –

Back at the farm, Serafina is walking around outside trying to break in her new boots while waiting for the others to get ready and join her.

"You're sure, Leo?" Serafina is still trying when he comes out. "If we take Manuel, he can bring his machete. And why not bring along the shotgun?"

He gives her a long look. "Gee, woman, this is not the jungle and we're not planning on starting a war. We're just going to have a look at that location. Nice boots, by the way."

"Yeah, yeah." She smirks at him while she feels at the back of her pants for the knife she has hidden. "Let's go then."

Blue is in the lead, Kate right behind with her and Leo following. She has flashbacks of walking alongside Manuel in the mountains in rough, dirty boots and she tries to make herself not think about it without success.

"Are we there yet?" she says. "Are we—?"

"I wouldn't be so impatient if I were you." Kate looks back. "Just because you're allowed to come along doesn't mean you'll get half the treasure, you know."

"I know that, it's gonna be four ways—me, Blue, Leo and you."

"Well, okay then. But not in that order."

"You definitely will stay with the title?" she hears Leo ask Kate.

"Yes, it works, I think. You don't? Though I've been warned that if used in that way, 'of' is a nothing word."

"Well..., be that as it may. You've got time, if you change your mind about what to use it for."

"What title is that?" Serafina asks, tapping Kate on the shoulder.

"*Of Flying Children.*"

"That's a different approach. You have a title but not a story. What made you think of that?"

"I didn't exactly. It sort of came from Leo."

How very surprising. Here she goes again.

"You explain it to her, Dad."

"No, you do it."

"I don't know if I remember all of the elements."

"It's not that complex, Kate, you can tell her."

"Jesus!" Serafina stops and sits on one of the many fallen tree trunks. "I don't care who tells me as long as somebody tells me! Today sometime, if possible!"

ENIGMA IN BLUE

"That's how Leo thinks of people, right Dad?" He doesn't answer as Kate tries to motion Blue to come back. "He thinks of humans as children, meandering about aimlessly, inventing gods and religions; countries, philosophies and boundaries; laws and kings. I am forgetting something. Appointing prophets ... raising the process of gathering nuts and profitably manufacturing nails into something approaching the merciless conduct of a worldwide holy war—if it's overly organized on a grand scale, right?"

"You have it about covered."

"Well then, does it include you?" Serafina is asking Leo but at the same time gives Kate, who is shouting for Blue, a quick look.

"In a way"—he hesitates far too long before not completing an answer—"In a way..."

Good God, Serafina shakes her head. These woods are likely crawling with Ely's and assholes and those two are going on and on about flying children. Boy, which one of them to pity the most? Leo at times confuses you—can he even always cope? Fair enough, he's had to come a long way from literally an outhouse and his early—he has called them formative—years at the end of the Second World War as a refugee from East-Prussia. But that, by his own account, was at the hands of two caring women who, by example, demonstrated to him the virtues of silence, uncompromising self-reliance and intellectual simplicity, while at the same time growing their own vegetables and cooking the most delicious potato dumpling soup ever. Mother Enna along with her sister themselves—according to Leo's version of family history—the offspring's of East-Prussian small-town merchants of flowers and vegetables which they grew on their small farm just outside of town and transported to their modest store via horse and buggy. Excellent training, Leo had proclaimed, and a wonderful foundation for all the hardships and so many of the disappointments that awaited the two during the rest of their lives. But all of this should not really be sufficient reason for Leo to now be afraid of bottled water, hand-held electronic communication devices and sushi.

And how can Kate be expected to act the more sensible of the two? She's never known a mother. Unlike Leo, she's not had the opportunity to mature as a result of exposure to the horrors of a World War, and most of her time is taken up with her flying things, of which Leo is surely one. Thank goodness, at least he seems to have some awareness of that. These people need help and she's going to involve Manuel whether they like it or not.

She still hasn't seen Blue in the last few minutes and is about to ask when Kate points ahead. "We're almost there. See those pines over there by the water? It's right behind them."

"If it is," Leo says, "it's real close to the line. There used to be that old cedar fence back there. I haven't been here in ages, but even then it was all broken up and rotting away."

"Yes, I couldn't see it either when I was here," Kate agrees. "Look," she's indicating something on the ground, "somebody's been here."

Serafina can see it now, a small brown bottle. A beer bottle?

"It wasn't here before," Kate seems certain.

"You could have missed it," Leo says. "Maybe it's been here for ages. Can you tell, is it an alien or earthly brand?"

"Christ. I came exactly this way. I didn't miss it and it's not been here for ages. It's clean."

She herself sees a yellow candy wrapper and she makes out the word coffee on it. She shows it to Kate who nods. "Definitely. Somebody has been around here. The spot itself doesn't appear any different."

Just as they are trying to get a closer look at it, they are startled by a yelping noise coming from the woods at a distance.

"Blue!" Kate screams.

ENIGMA IN BLUE

They're shouting Blue's name as they stumble towards the thick woods on the right. There's no other sound nor any sign of him. They have fanned out, but she can still hear Kate hollering, "Blue doesn't whine, he must be hurt!"

"Stay close," Serafina shouts back. And then she sees him first. "There!" she screams.

Blue is half sitting, struggling to get up. Maybe he twisted or broke his leg. When they get close to him, it's no mystery—there's an arrow sticking in his upper left thigh. A short arrow.

"From a crossbow," Serafina is pretty sure.

"Damn careless hunters," she hears Leo speculate in anger.

Hunters my ass, she decides, and helps Kate hold down Blue's head to keep him from moving. "Leo, go get Manuel and bring that four-wheeler as close as you can."

Leo doesn't second-guess. As he scurries off, she keeps holding Blue with one hand and feels for her knife with the other as she keeps looking around.

"I think he'll be alright," Kate says, swallowing hard, "it's not near any vital organ."

"Yeah, but he'll be laid up for a while."

"Damn hunters," Kate repeats.

Serafina knows differently.

– 20 –

Ely closes the side door to the great room behind them with that exaggerated authority John is too familiar with by now, and the two guys just stand there as he turns over a notepad and steps away from the writing desk. He is tempted to ask the small man about the ball-peen hammer in his hand, but thinks better of it.

"You've looked around over there?" John asks, walking towards the men.

"Yeah." Ely is shaking his head. "There's nothing there."

"You're sure?"

"Somebody's been digging there, that's all."

"On our land?"

"Can't tell for sure, but I think so. It's right where the trees start by the water, where you said."

"You didn't go across, did you?"

"Hard to tell, there's no fence."

"And you didn't see anybody there?"

"Nope."

"So that's it?" John can feel himself getting impatient. The Balkan has something else to tell him.

"Nope."

"Well...?"

"Tapes." Ely reaches into his coat pocket and brings out a plastic bag.

John sees the first sign of life in Aholl when he looks up and gives Ely an admiring grin when repeating. "Tapes."

John wishes that they had not succeeded. He shouldn't have agreed. "Leave them here," he says, "I'll check them out later."

"They don't talk much on the phone," Ely volunteers.

John has the tapes in his hand now. He doesn't really want an analysis of them from Ely and walks back towards the desk, shrugging his shoulders.

"No, they don't." Ely persists and goes on when John doesn't answer. "They gave the boot to somebody in Europe." He hears him chuckle. "And they're gonna have a helicopter fly around here too."

John is startled. He hasn't told anybody. How would Ely know that he has arranged for a plane to fly over the properties? He heard him say "too."

"What do you mean 'too'?" He turns around and walks back over to the man by the door.

The Balkan looks at his sidekick. "Too? I didn't say that. I just said they're gonna have a plane fly over."

"I thought I heard you say it," John says without urgency now, having decided to soft-pedal for the time being, knowing full well that the guy is lying.

Ely is buttoning up his coat and exchanges glances with Aholl who appears to be in total agreement today—with everything. "We'll get a lot more information anyway. If there's anything in particular you wanna know..."

"How you gonna do that?" John asks with real apprehension.

"You'll see from the tape. The one girl over there—she kinda likes me. She's breaking up with some Frank guy, anyway."

"Who're you talking about?"

"You know—the fat little half-breed over there. Aholl and me, we saw her at the store. The other one too."

John has turned around towards the desk. He doesn't want them to see his face.

"They said they might have a beer with us, or something," he hears Ely say.

He needs to think. "I'll talk to you guys later," he says without turning back. "I've got to call Mr. Curtis, anyway."

"Well, tell him everything is under control." Ely's voice is brimming with confidence. When he hears the door close, John slumps down on the chair in front of the desk.

* * * *

It's windy on the lake. He could have taken the cabin cruiser, but has chosen the dinghy instead. It has back-up oars.

It's a small lake of about thirty acres and the view in any direction is normally calming and pleasant. The only structures visible are three docks and a boathouse. With the adjoining conservation area, you see mostly fir trees of varying kinds, intermingled with some thick brush and maple trees. The white trunks of a few birches are a stark contrast to the dark evergreens.

John isn't going anywhere in particular. Near the middle of the lake he closes his eyes and listens to the sound of the oars splashing in the water. He doesn't get the feeling he's hoped for and thinks instead of the tapes and the recorder in his pocket.

He steers the boat to look in the general direction of where Kate Walter lives. That damn Balkan, he couldn't have meant her. She does seem to be of mixed blood and is pleasingly, well almost, plump, but not... was he talking about the other woman? Serafina, that was her name. No, he had talked about both of them.

He takes the tapes out of his pocket and then hesitates. Ely and Aholl—and Kate and Serafina. He puts the tapes back and takes out his cellphone instead. He has not been able to reach Marshal so far and his message has not been returned. This time he connects.

"Curtis."

"Marshal, John..."

"How's everything at the camp?"

"That's why I'm calling. Are you sure it's worth going after—?"

"John, listen. First of all, that political thing. Forget all about it for the time being. I think I owe you an apology. It certainly wasn't your doing. I must be sure we understand each other. It's a non-issue."

"Good. My heart wasn't in it anyway, I think you know. I actually got to like—"

"Forget all about it," Marshal says. "It's of no consequence, you—"

"Right." This time John interrupts. "As I said, this situation here. Are you sure it's worth my time? Ruth or any of your assistants could handle this, if you still want to stay on top of it."

"John, I think you're underestimating the importance of this. In the first place, there's every reason to believe that people are stealing from me with the location being what it is. And secondly, I've had additional indications that this may not be the joke we initially thought it was. No, John, you know how much I rely on you. I need you to stay with this. And we don't want to be betting zero for two, do we."

"Marshal, these neighbors of yours, they're—"

"John, John, you know I have neither the time nor the inclination for details. That's where you come in. I have total confidence in you."

"That brings me to the real problem." He pauses to give Marshal an opportunity to say something he would like to hear; without success. "Ely and his sidekick, what exactly—?"

"John, you're in charge, but have some sympathy for me. The way you're going, one day you'll probably find out for yourself. I have pressures and threats coming at me from all directions. I need competent protection. No matter what you think of Ely personally, he's very good at what he does."

"But he's not there with you, he's here with me. I don't need protection."

"He's there for the moment because that's where my front line is right now. I told you this thing may be more important than you think. And, by the way, having a close and discreet aerial look at the property line for the time being is a good idea. It may cost a fortune and take forever, but there may be a way to deal with this legally."

John wonders how Marshal too knows about the aerial review of the property line, but decides to talk about the legal aspect only at this time. "This is Canada, Marshal. Even I know it's not as easy as in the States to sue anybody for anything with a shot at success, just because you have the money. Besides, it doesn't look like that rock is from your property. But then, I think you already know that."

"It doesn't hurt to attack a problem from all angles," Marshal says. "Keep working with Ely."

It definitely isn't what John wants to hear. "What's wrong with you, Marshal? This is gonna get messy. Since when do we work like this?" He tries to be even more direct. "Ely and this Aholl guy have been—"

"John, John, I've got to go. After all these years, you should know me. Why would I want to waste your time with something that's not worthwhile?"

The line goes dead and John realizes that he didn't get to resolve anything. He had pulled the same stunt himself when he was a kid. Most kids probably had. When somebody was going to tell you something you didn't want to know and didn't want to hear, you would stick your fingers in your ears and keep blabbing—la, la, la, la, la. That's what Marshal Curtis has just done to him, isn't it?

There's a well-equipped tech-room at the retreat, but John decides to go to his suite and locks the door.

He puts one of the tapes into the recorder and thinks for a moment...

Click.

"I know, I know, Joe." He recognises Leopold Walter's voice. "I always thought it was a clever concept you had. Don't get discouraged over this."

He hears another voice say. "There's no chance?"

"No, Joe. Absolutely not. Let's learn from this. The truth is that the very clever element at the core of this is also its Achilles heel." Click.

This doesn't relate to anything of interest to him. He searches through the tapes. Click... Click. "... can do that"—a woman's voice that John doesn't recognize—"we probably have an overview in our library, but it wouldn't be that focused or close up."

"I can fax you a copy of the site plan," he hears Leopold Walter say. "I'll mark with an asterisk the particular area that I'm interested in. I'll send it to you now while we're talking."

He's paying attention now as he hears some paper rustling. "I shouldn't be saying this," the woman voices, "but why wouldn't you use a surveyor to get it exactly right?"

"No. At this point it's not what we want to do. That may come later."

"I got your fax now." The woman's voice continues. "That's strange."

"What is?"

"You have somebody else making the same request?"

"No."

"Well, then, we've been commissioned by somebody else to fly over and survey the same area." John hears the woman laugh. "This may not be good for business. We can probably kill two birds with one stone."

Click.

It's not a mystery to him. But how did Ely and Marshal know that he has made arrangements for the fly-over survey? I'm not going to use a hard line or the tech room again, he decides.

Click.

"No, Frank." He knows this voice. "There's something going on anyway and—"

Click.

John doesn't feel good. He gathers the tapes, folds them into a hand towel and sticks them into his overnight bag. He's going to go for a drive in the country and sit under a tree. Heading for the garage, he has to pass by Ely and Aholl who are polishing the limo. Ely winks at him. "We're gonna go and find the girls now."

"La, la, la, la, la...."

– 21 –

Kate just hates that moment of walking away and leaving Blue behind on his own at the Orangeville animal clinic. Every time. She knows it to not be so, but there is that feeling of abandoning him to his own devices...

He hadn't gone into shock. The arrow had almost pierced through his thigh. They had cut it and extracted the pointed end from the other side. No major arteries had been severed and none of the tendons were seriously damaged and he was to stay at the clinic for another couple of days. Partially sedated, Blue would be monitored for possible infections.

All their farm chores done for the day—according to them—Serafina and Leo have gone into the village for lunch at Mrs. Aubrey's. Strange feeling for Kate...walking around by herself. She hears herself take a deep breath as she becomes aware that she's heading north instead of the usual direction she would go with Blue.

In places the ground is thick and colorful with the foliage, it feels like carpet. She climbs over a small fallen tree and looks up when she hears a noise overhead. A plane. Kate turns left as the lake comes into view. Should she go there? The noise has come back and she sees that it's a helicopter, circling. Maybe someone in the area has a chopper now? She's never been aware of one around here before, she thinks when the helicopter disappears in the distance and she keeps walking.

ENIGMA IN BLUE

She hadn't felt good about calling Frank, but he seemed to have understood and they've left it for another time—perhaps.

Kate is approaching the trees and the site when she decides to veer off to the right and not go there. It is then she spots the man coming her way. She halts and sees him slow as well and she's about to turn around when she realizes who it is. John Martins too seems to have recognised her and waves from a distance.

How to handle this, she wonders. He has taken his other hand out of his pocket and comes walking her way.

"Are you alright?" he asks. "Out for a walk, Miss Walter?" He starts to move his hand forward haltingly and then stops. He seems uncertain whether she would take it.

"Mr. Martins. Hello." Clever that: Mr. Martins, hello.

"You couldn't call me John?"

Kate lifts her eyes slowly. The round face and the equally round spectacles; villainous people don't look like this, she doesn't think. She has seen younger versions of the same face on nationally televised spelling bees, but that doesn't mean she's going to make it easy for him.

"I'll admit this. I am not at all sure about you. You'd like me to call you John," she says, "after you threaten to force us from our home? Sue us? This is your way of trying to be funny?"

"Kate," he takes a deep breath, "this is all such an awful mess. It's true that Curtis still wants to buy your property and he would certainly pay top dollar for it, but Grimsby was totally out of line."

Presumably, Grimsby was the lawyer's name. Had she not been suspicious of him all along?

"I don't know." She is drawing out the k-n-o-w. "You seem to be in charge and now you're blaming a lawyer."

"That man will never do legal work for D.R.T. United again," he says. "He was acting on his own. He must have thought we discovered a gold mine or a large oilfield." He's laughing, but Kate heard him say "we."

"That was not my impression," she says, giving him what she thinks is a stern look. "I don't believe he was acting totally on his own."

"Kate, please believe this, he was and you won't see him again. You will see me again, though." He's been looking directly at her. "And we will definitely still be trying to buy your land."

"You're off to a real fine start with that... you are. Wake up. You cannot be so naïve... to think that this is about land or money. I'm sure you know by now that you're not just up against my father. A total waste of time is this and so unpleasant to boot."

"Peace, Kate," he says and offers his hand again, with some confidence this time. Kate hesitates and then takes it. " I do so hope we're done talking real estate deals," she says. "I mean that."

It seems to her that he isn't sure whether he is expected to walk away now. She knows what she thinks he should do, but isn't about to tell him.

"You wouldn't remember," John says, "but I saw you before I came to your house. At the doughnut shop."

She shakes her head. She doesn't remember that.

"You were in a pickup truck and you had your dog there. You bought him a doughnut. The man with you did."

She feels herself twitch when she's reminded of Blue.

"Where is your dog anyway?" John looks around. "Isn't he with you?"

"He got hurt, he's in the clinic."

"... clinic? What's wrong with him?" John asks.

"Nothing's wrong with Blue, some damn hunter... somebody shot him in the leg with a crossbow, right around here. That's what's wrong."

She's startled when she sees that much distress on his face. "We don't think they'll start shooting at us. At least we better hope they won't. He's going to be alright," she says, "he'll just be out of action for a while. I'd better go now. I was going to check with the vet again."

"I feel odd about asking," she hears him behind her and turns back. "Are you going out with our driver, the big Balkan guy?"

"Heavens, no! What made you think that?" He looks as awkward as she feels.

"Ah, somebody said something. Anyway, don't. He's not the nicest fellow you'll ever want to meet."

"No kidding. Well then, bye John."

Now she does walk away. When she looks back, he is still there, giving her a reluctant wave.

Making her way slowly through the brush and trees, she feels she did well acting cool, but knows she was anything but. Her steps become more and more hesitant. She's not ready to face anyone—best to clear her head first, think of something else. She comes to a huge maple tree with plenty of leaves on the ground and sits, leaning against the massive trunk. Could that face and that voice be conning her?

She takes out her notepad to write: "Puppy name now—Li'l Johnnie."

The tension mounts in the hall. It'll soon be Li'l Johnnie's turn.

"'I will have order in the auditorium,' the big dog barks with authority. 'I will tolerate no interruptions.'"

Kate studies the eraser end of her pencil and then writes: "Johnnie could do this."

The battle between the puppies has raged for days and now the first annual intergalactic spelling bee is coming to a close. Everything is on the line. The home team has one final opportunity: it's all up to Li'l Johnnie. Luckily, dachshunds in general, and wire-hair miniature dachshunds in particular, are known to be very apt at spelling; but the pressure is enormous. Li'l Johnnie walks slowly to the podium and carefully adjusts his round spectacles.

"Order," the big dog's voice booms once again, followed by the command, "proceed."

There's a hush and then a clear voice: "Spell—kemancha."

Immediate nervousness among the home team. Oh boy, now what?

Li'l Johnnie shows no emotion and calmly asks, "May I have that in a sentence please, Sir?"

"Kemancha—the most vivid memory of my recent travels is the lasting impression made on me by the beautiful kemancha."

The home team is ever so surprised to see Li'l Johnnie still that unperturbed. In fact, don't they see him methodically take off his glasses, rub them carefully against his sweater and then put them back on?

"Kemancha," Li'l Johnnie says so very slowly and then spells:

"K–A–T–E–––––kemancha."

The agonizing silence seems to last forever. Then that clear, pleasant voice:

"That is correct!"

As the home team rushes the stage, the whole auditorium breaks out in thunderous applause.

Li'l Johnnie has saved the day.

– 22 –

Seeing Leo paint can be stressful—watching him start a new painting, as Serafina and Kate are doing now, particularly disturbing. He paints mostly in his study and there is evidence of his rampages everywhere. It is probably a good thing that he's not skilled at mixing paint. He tends to blend too many colors and the results are muddy tones, present in his paintings and everywhere else in the room.

The subdued, sandy-colored old chesterfield, for one, is definitely better off with those muddy smudges than it might be with bright red or purple. Sections of bookshelves appear to be color-coded, but they're not. Violence has been done to his massive antique writing desk, and the splendid period wingbacks, imported from Ireland, have also been assaulted. The smell of oil paint, mixed with that of cigarette smoke, Kate had gotten used to and almost come to like. The scars left by scraping devices of varying kinds on the mantelpiece of the wonderful old fireplace are a different matter entirely.

He really is an awful painter. Kate can remember how he first started. He had gone to an art supply store in the morning and bought panels of assorted sizes, a selection of brushes and several tubes of Windsor oil paint. The fact that he had not bothered with or forgotten about an easel was probably the foundation for the destruction of his study that was to follow. For that very afternoon he had placed a panel on the mantelpiece of the fireplace and proceeded to...paint.

He painted very little and she cannot remember him ever discarding anything he started. She can remember him using hammers, files, tissue paper, nails, scissors, and his fingers and, yes, sandpaper quite frequently.

Years ago, she had laughed along with Sam Randolph. "Yes, Katie," he did say, ruffling the top of her head, "that's sort of the way he develops products." Now, that's how she would like to think of Sam—a face less red and a voice more gentle. What's the matter with him anyway? Maybe she should just ask him straight out one day: are mixed race children cute, but only up to a height of fifty-one inches and then not so much when they become mixed race teenagers with increased brain function—or what? So much of what she knew of her father's earlier life actually came from Sam who always seemed to have a genuine respect, even affection, for Leo. "For a young guy who came to this country with only a most elementary education and few dollars in his pocket, he's done well." That's what Sam had said.

"He's insecure and afraid of failure," he had also speculated. "It's primarily his constant anticipation of failure that has led us to some of these productive innovations. We would be prototyping a latest level device and see him sketching a revised component, expecting the one being tested to fail. He might personally start to work on that new part, having already designed a third version for somebody else to make."

Fear of failure and insecurity... Sam could be right. She remembers Leo being somewhat apologetic; not about pursuing success, but trying to gather too many riches and his effort to justify it to her: "If you let them, they're gonna get you." It hadn't been totally clear to her just who "they" were, but she suspected that it was everybody. "I think there are two ways to be relatively independent and secure," he had said. "One is to gather a fortune and buy what you need; the other would be to live in the ghetto, own nothing but a pair of jeans, a tee-shirt and have access to a gun." He had seemed to mean it. "I can see that as a viable way to live an independent life—as long as the man doesn't get you, that is."

Kate studies his finished painting above the fireplace and again becomes aware of all the things that are not there. There are no houses or fences, nor are there flowers or boats. There are no animals, no people and there is not a signature.

Kate hears Serafina make a clicking sound with her tongue and sees her carefully walk around Leo, still working away at the canvas; carefully presumably for good reason.

"Those United people," Kate says, "they seem pretty sure there's something of value there. Let's put a fence around it and keep an eye on it."

Serafina nods in agreement.

"Not so fast," says Leo, straightening his back but still beholding his latest masterpiece-to-be, "we don't want anybody to do anything aggressive. Besides, I now have the results on the visual survey. It's closer to the line than I thought. In fact, you could almost argue that it touches the line. We won't know exactly without a proper survey, but that's how it looks right now."

"What if they just claim it?" Kate protests.

"No." Now he puts away his brush. "You found it; you're not going to let that happen. You said yourself this Martins fellow told you they still want to buy our farm." Leo laughs. "Ja, that will happen. You still ought to be careful, walking around out there by yourself."

Serafina is shaking her head. "Yeah, you're not taking this seriously enough. Blue didn't get shot by a hunter. It's those people over there."

"Slow down, slow down," Leo says and looks from Serafina over to her. "Remember when we cruised into that bay at St. Thomas— what we talked about. The night-trip?"

She does, yes. That had been one of the more pleasant trips, gliding almost silently into the bay with the moon above and the shimmering lights from the various huts, houses and guest cottages everywhere on the steep mountainsides, almost surrounding the bay. They had fantasized about being on an old, wooden sailboat in the service of the Spanish Crown, expected to make landfall and take over the island by force from inhabitants they knew nothing of. "We'd jump overboard and swim away," they had agreed.

"Defensive action only," she hears Leo say. "We don't wanna be like them."

Kate is reluctantly considering to agree, but not so Serafina. "Sometimes, Leo, offence may be the only defense. And what is with the we, we? Aren't you mixing your I's and we's again?"

He scratches his head, picks up a brush again and says, "Hmm..."

"That'll do it every time." Serafina mocks him, carefully examining a bright yellow spot on a dark-green lamp shade. "Hmm..."

Kate feels a sudden cold draft and looks up to see Manuel standing at the open front door. "Sorry," he says, making a knocking gesture.

Without Blue there's no early warning, but they're comfortable with Manuel around and he knows that and she motions him to come all the way in and he does.

He's not to ever know it, but he sometimes makes her think of a gorilla. Bow-legged, squat and immensely strong. He's also resourceful and determined which is probably why Leo likes him so much. You give him almost any task and he will find a way. He takes great pride in presenting what is finished and functional and will not involve you in the steps it has taken to get there. Leo's kind of man. No wonder Serafina likes him too. Of his background, however, they know nothing.

"Come over here, Manuel," Leo says.

"Found it." Manuel is holding up a piece of thin wire with a wooden stick attached to one end.

After putting down his paintbrush, Leo steps towards him. "What is it?"

"Sling. Catch animals."

"You're sure?" Kate asks as Manuel nods so emphatically, it alarms her. He is ever more comfortable with sign language and has made great strides in that regard over the last few months.

"Where did you find it?"

He hesitates for a moment. "By water...where trees are."

"What made you go over there?" Leo looks at Manuel, who hesitates again and has Serafina answer in his place. "I asked him to go and check around over there."

Leo gives her a bit of a stare without saying anything. "Was it on our property?" he asks Manuel, taking the sling out of his hand.

"Yes. Not all. I see man—see him far—man in big coat."

"Did he say, do anything?" Serafina asks, getting dangerously close to wet paint again.

"No. He see me...go away. He have crossgun." He glances at Serafina. "Crossbow," she says and he nods.

There's a silence before Serafina slowly walks over to look at Leo. "So...?"

He squints his eyes and repeatedly nods to himself before he turns. "I...we don't want anyone else involved. I'm going for a walk." He reaches for his windbreaker when passing through the kitchen and walks out. Before they leave the study, Kate again takes a long look at the painting above the fireplace. The lone tree is devoid of any leaves—the light reflecting off the water is white and cold—and the sky is an ugly dark-green. What, if anything, it means she cannot say; but ugly it is.

− 23 −

Mark Reeling has barely lifted his eyes from the workstation in the last little while, so Toni Stanton sits up on the sofa and continues to meticulously blow on his fingernails, the way he usually does when he's finished painting them. The little girl, her dark eyes wide open, the long brown hair flying everywhere, is jumping up and down next to the sofa. "My turn my turn, uncle Toni, my turn."

"Wait wait, Katelyn." He interrupts blowing on his nails and sighs loudly when he looks over towards Mark still busy on the computer. "Next your Mom won't let me come to your birthday party; then what? You promised. Has your Mom ever let any babysitter paint your nails?"

"Oh yes." It's Mark answering without looking up, "go ahead. Did your Auntie...did she go along to the hospital with your Mom, Katelyn?"

"Yes, red red with poker-dots, please oh please."

"Your Auntie, Katelyn?"

"Auntie, yes. Green poker-dots, please oh please."

Painting Katelyn's less than pristine nails, Toni smiles happily. Mark Reeling occasionally babysits Katelyn for a neighboring friend who lives in his apartment building purely as a favor, Katelyn is never confused about what she wants and hasn't ever been taught to take no for an answer. This is the fortuitous arrangement Toni has stumbled into along with Mark.

"There, what do you think?"

"More poker-dots, please."

"More...?"

"Please oh please."

Toni again sighs in the direction of Mark. "Say, Reeling," he says, "what's so fascinating about a computer screen?"

Mark finally looks up. "Don't know that you'll find it so interesting, even though it actually is."

"Then tell me."

"It's all very technical. I might bore you."

"Above the ability of an entertainer to understand?" Toni teases.

"Now now, a little respect, if you please. Children are present. There are people all over the world, it seems, who think that I am a man of importance, one who knows everything." Mark pauses with a smile. "Like these people up in Canada who found this rocky substance. And so far, I have to admit, we've been unable to determine what it is. I'm certain we will in time, but for now we can't."

"But I thought you can nail down the composition, the molecules of everything, isn't that so? I'm sure I am right about that."

"That's just it," Mark says. "There's something missing that would have to be present in anything that comes from the earth. From the universe, in fact. You couldn't really manufacture it. The known physics don't add up. I'm beginning to see it coming now, it won't be the joke it is at the moment for much longer. I'm not the only one looking at this puzzle; it's going to get embarrassing. What I'm trying to say is that the academic community traditionally would not be able to just turn their backs and shrug their shoulders. We can't just say we don't know—and wouldn't want to."

"Ooh," Toni says slowly as Mark gets up to come over to the sofa, "we'd better get cracking and check with the Russians then. They probably invented it. Where else could it come from? The twilight zone?"

"I warned you...you'd find it boring. Uh, I like this combination, Katelyn. You want to come and help me do some coloring on the computer now?"

"Okay Uncle Mark."

"Say thank you to Uncle Toni then."

"Thank you, Uncle Toni."

"Could we go back to that Argentinean steakhouse later tonight?" Toni asks. "Remember those thin, salty steaks?"

"Good idea." Mark nods. "Wear the long skirt with the buttons on the side—you know the one I like, I've seen it here—I'll spring for a carafe of Argentinean wine. Would you want to include anyone else?"

"Not tonight," says Toni as he steps aside to let Mark pick up the ringing phone.

"It's for you, Katelyn, it's your Mom."

"For me? Mom?"

"I think there may be a change of plans coming," Mark whispers while Katelyn is listening on the phone.

"...okay Mom...okay Mom...Mom wants to talk to you more, Uncle Mark."

Toni is brushing aside some hair that has fallen across her face after she hands the phone back to Mark. "Katelyn Gutierrez? Katelyn is not really a Cuban name, is it?"

"Mom says I'm American girl." Katelyn at the moment is not smiling.

"Excuse me… it's a very nice name."

"Yes," says Mark when he hangs up, "we will have extra company for dinner after all. I think you know, Katelyn, your Mother won't be home till late, but you'll come and eat out with us. What do you think of that idea?"

"IHOP," says Katelyn Gutierrez.

"What's an IHOP?" is what Mark wants to know.

"IHOP," Toni says, rolling his eyes, "International House Of Pancakes."

"IHOP, please oh please."

"What a terrific idea," says Professor Reeling.

— 24 —

"Uncle Eddie?"

"Yes?"

"It's me."

"Yeah?"

"It's John."

"John. Hello my boy."

"How are you, Uncle Eddie?"

"I'm good. Why are you phoning?"

That's his Uncle. When he asks why you're phoning, it's because he wants to know why you're phoning.

ENIGMA IN BLUE

He is not entirely truthful when he says, "No particular reason, I just wanted to see how you're getting on these days."

"Oh, just fine. Your aunt has a bit of arthritis, you know. She's at the store, but we're fine. And you?"

"Good," John hears himself say. "I'm up here in Canada on some business. I'm in a nice part of the country here."

"How's the weather up there?"

"It's good. It's cool, it's fall, but it's good. I'm by a lake. I meant to ask you. I haven't been there in so long. You know that old apple tree across the pond?"

"Yeah...."

"Is it still there?"

"No ... it died a couple of years ago."

"Oh." John blinks. "The old boat, the rowboat? Is that still around?"

"No John, not for a long time. It kinda rotted away and sank, but I have a new one. It's an aluminum boat, but it's a nice one. It's made to look like wood. You really should come and visit some time."

"Yes, I should ... I will next time I'm in the area ... I will for sure. So ... say hello to Auntie May then, okay? Tell her I asked for her."

"I will, my boy, and you keep well. Do come to see us."

"Alright, Uncle ..." John hesitates. "If I did come down within the next couple of weeks, would that present a—"

"Ay John, your Auntie and I are leaving for England on the weekend. We'll only be there for eleven days, but if you want to come right away—that would be alright."

"I'll leave it for now, but I will keep it in mind. I'm not that sure I could even get away anyway. If you don't hear back from me, you have a good trip."

"Bye then, John, don't be a stranger, you hear?"

John closes the cover of his cell phone and remembers what he has forgotten to ask—had Uncle Eddie done any yachting lately?

Probably not, now that Auntie May has arthritis and he's getting on anyway. He would have mentioned it, if he was still going out to sea.

He had looked around earlier for the Balkan and his sidekick, but had not seen them. He looks again out of the window of his suite and sees the limo near the garage. They must be back. He hasn't been looking forward to this, but he knows it has to be dealt with.

Grabbing his jacket to go outside, he thinks about the mechanics of firing people he hadn't hired in the first place in a foreign country. This he really hates. The bastards. To force him into this... He's never actually fired anyone, ever. The bastards. He doesn't see the men anywhere and starts to walk in the direction of their guest cottage when he sees Ely step outside and close the door behind him in a manner that makes it clear he doesn't want him to come inside. That's just fine; he didn't want to go in anyway.

"Did you shoot the dog with your crossbow?" John asks in a deliberate, blunt tone.

"Huh?" The Balkan manages to look surprised.

"Yeah, a big dog, the neighbor's dog."

"No." For once Ely is not wearing his long coat. He's in a heavy sweater and starts to roll up the sleeves.

"Well, the dog got shot with a crossbow and I don't see other people walking around here with crossbows, do you?"

Ely shrugs his shoulders. "Don't know anything about it." The Balkan is standing right in front of him, turned at right angles, looking towards the woods.

"It's the girl's dog over there. You shot him. I want you to stop bothering the girl."

He places his hand on Ely's left shoulder to get his attention when without warning the big man wheels around and with the back of his left fist hits him hard on the side of his face. John tumbles to the ground and tries to get up on his knees. He can feel and taste the blood squirting out of his mouth. From his crouching position he lunges at the legs of the Balkan and manages to bring him to the ground and tries to wind his arm around the man's throat, but then twists his head to look when he feels something cold and sharp against the back of his own neck.

"I'll cut you," Aholl threatens, "let go, I'll cut you."

Seeing Aholl's face, John believes it. He lets go and stands up. "You two are fired," he says, wiping some of the blood from his face.

"By you?" the Balkan says, staring. "We'll see...Mr. Curtis is coming back anyway. He wants the stealing stopped."

"Then you'll be fired tomorrow," John says. "In the meantime, stay away from the women over there. I don't want to get the police involved, but I'll do what I have to."

The Balkan has stiffened and looks at him with surprise, but neither he nor Aholl says anything more when he walks away and he wonders more and more about the level of confidence in those two sons of bitches and who it is that might in fact get fired tomorrow.

John has cleaned up and inspects the damage. Nothing too serious. A couple of loose teeth, a cut inside the mouth that has stopped bleeding, a small gash on his left cheek and a slight bend in the frame of his spectacles. Damn. If he waits too long, he'll go down with this leaking wreck. He wastes no time when he gets a hold of Marshal. "We're going to settle this one way or the other now," John says. "I'm heading for Seattle tonight. I'm only calling to make sure you'll be around."

"Don't John; I know there's trouble at the camp. I was just about to call you. I'll be there by mid-day tomorrow."

"You better not be jerking me around. I'll wait till then, but we will talk. I've about had it—I don't think I want to come along to wherever it is you're going. You get me?"

"I've cautioned you before, John. Can't you think big picture any more? Pull yourself together, for Christ's sake. Hell John, we've been friends for the longest time. What is wrong with you? Tomorrow."

John suddenly feels deflated as some of the anger is leaving him. Friends for a long time? That's what he had thought.

* * * *

John is finishing a very long, very hot shower. He's having difficulty staying with any one particular thought-process to completion. He had considered and should just have done it before—get himself a room somewhere else. He'll run into the village later and get himself set up, just in case. And he had seriously contemplated getting in touch with D'Groth, but had discarded that idea when he could barely get himself to ask, much less answer, his own question without feeling some considerable level of guilt. To what end?

Maybe it's better this way, not going to Seattle right away. I can keep an eye on Ely and Aholl, John thinks as he feels for his swollen cheek and worries about what he actually could do if called upon with these types of people.

He is beginning to realize that moving about, leaving behind a big part of his life may be much harder for him than he might ever have imagined. Perhaps he really should have been less hasty over dismissing the opportunity to work more directly for D'Groth when he had the chance a long time ago. Even during the early years he had thought that Marshal was trying to become the man that Vincent D'Groth already was. That elegant manner of accepting success after success as if it were a birthright and the casual way of absorbing the occasional setback on different fronts.

John's days of being a happy business warrior suddenly seem just so far away.

He had never totally understood the core substance of Vincent's early successes the way he did Marshal's and his own, but greatly respected the candor with which D'Groth disclosed in one of his rare interviews the nature of subsequent successes and failures as he understood them. John remembers most of the words, as he has come to similar conclusions.

'I have failed…yes, badly failed at more ventures than people realize. Don't be fooled, many accomplished people have—most. Once you secure the resources that a basic foundation provides, it becomes hard to tell what is earned and what is not. Over the years we have had to give up on many investments, real disasters among them. And I have come across truly unexpected winners at times. Without the early foundation, would we even have had so many opportunities? Could be…but I think not.'

No point in going on about it, John, probably too late now. He would no doubt fit well somewhere else within the D'Groth orbit, but might wind up looking over his shoulder for the rest of his life. Nevertheless, John has to admit; he so much prefers open doors to closing them. Why else would he even be thinking about missed opportunities.

– 25 –

The Gomez woman from Colombia had been going on and on and had come close to annoying her at first. "Don't do it, Kate," she repeated again, putting down a sheet of paper on the kitchen table.

"You've said that. Don't see the big problem with it."

"You're setting yourself up. Think," she had urged her. "I can see what you're getting at. Your children and the puppies are getting greedy. Isn't that what you mean?"

"Well, yes."

"They're tunneling through your candy-ridge mountains, gorging themselves. Then the whole thing becomes so weak, it collapses?"

"Uh huh."

"It turns to...what?" Serafina, bending over the table, had pretended to be searching for a line on the sheet of paper. "Fudge! The result is a sweet odor."

"And what's so wrong with that?" Kate had asked. She had asked at that point only to have some fun stringing Serafina along. It had become clear to her that there was a problem with her choice of words.

Serafina had put her hands on her hips. "What's wrong with that, Kate?"

"Well, okay." She had tried to act just a little hesitant. "I could change it to mysterious."

That's when the "Gomez" had started to cackle. "Kate, never, never..." She had paused, presumably for dramatic effect. "Can't you just see it? Assume a critic already doesn't like you or your book—you've made it so easy. Roda Endsman, are we that sure about her? Imagine her getting the better of her husband and making him push one of their writers. He doesn't even have to think while he eagerly types: The author no longer needs to wonder about the nature or source of the mysterious odor. It's obvious to this writer and will become so to everyone else who may be unfortunate enough to come in contact with the subject of this article."

At that point, she well knew that Serafina was right, but still persisted. "It's a children's book. Even if critics did bother to read it, they wouldn't pounce on it, would they? It's for kids."

"That may be true if it's for very young children only, but you do have some thoughtful components in here...at least you are trying. You best think about this."

Kate, gathering her papers and frowning, had come up with the appropriate response. "Yeah, yeah." Jesus, let's hope Serafina doesn't become unbearable. A few lectures on journalism and suddenly she's an expert at everything.

"I know that Serafina went to Burlington," Leo says when he gets up from the breakfast table reaching for one last slice of orange. "What did she go for? And before daylight?"

"She was going to her condo to pick up a few things, I know that."

"Hmm....When she comes back, we should have one more discussion about the people over there. Let's make certain we're not the ones making the mistake. I'll tell you something I've already tried to make her understand, though I'm not sure she did—they're at a disadvantage. It's almost not fair." He looks at her as if he knows something no one else on this earth could possibly know. It's the expression he and Blue sometimes share. "They want something, we don't. You know what I mean?"

She thinks so, but is not sure. Besides, Blue is back home and she has a plan of her own. And Leopold had taken Serafina's side about the book. Albeit that he had tried to add what to him doubtlessly would pass for a constructive twist to his criticism. "Don't get this wrong, Kate. I'm a bad writer but a good reader. I would keep on saying things straight—in time it will serve you well. Patience... It's hard, but I would stay with it." She resolves to think about the merit of that advice someday soon.

When he moves into his study, probably to continue his crime spree, she turns her attention to Blue who manages to lift his paw and puts it in her hand. He's able to hop around occasionally with her assistance, but mostly he's resting on a big blanket with his back up against the chesterfield where she is going to sleep tonight.

Back to her plan.

She pulls the long rubber boots over her blue-jeans and takes the writing paraphernalia out of her sheepskin coat to put it into the short, black leather jacket. It has an air of aggression about it and she thinks it appropriate.

"Blue, Blue, Blue," she says when he moans as she strokes him a final time. He seems resigned to his situation and raises his head just a little to keep his eyes on her as she walks out the front door to head north.

By now Kate is very familiar with the trail leading to the site. There's a stiff wind, leaves are blowing everywhere and she realizes that she would have been better off with her sheepskin coat, but that wouldn't serve her particular purpose. Sure would be nice to have Blue alongside, though.

The plan itself is a typically straightforward, logical Walter plan. It is more than fair. Always give a little more in the end than you get. The goodwill points you earn may come in handy one day.

Kate stands the collar of the jacket up around her ears and puts her hands in the pockets. She will try and find a second fragment of the material and take it along as a potential peace offering; to be held securely and independently somehow for the time being until the very nature of the find is established. She'll go through the woods and confront those people and she will start out by demanding an end to all the hostilities. Hopefully, John will be there. Possibly others with kind intentions. Only then, after making it clear that she too would be capable of shifting tactics, will she offer to show the fragment as a sign of good faith.

She looks around carefully when she reaches the site. She doesn't see anything very different since the last time she's been here, but begins to worry and dig with her hands when she's unable to find anything remotely sparkling. Black as coal, all of it including her fingernails. She's starting to think about having to come back with a shovel, when finally she feels and lifts up a fragment. It's smaller than the one she had found previously, but it will do. It does have the tiniest spark at one end. Looking north, she decides to stay close to the shoreline, knowing that the main house is near the water and this way she can't possibly miss it. The terrain is rough and she stumbles over a boulder on the ground. Some of the branches she has to push out of the way.

ENIGMA IN BLUE

She slows down when she comes to a little clearing and looks at the lake. She knows this area from the lakeside, but not from this direction. A thought has been running through her head and she takes out her notepad to write:

> Why then do I often fear
> That things are just as they appear?

A good thing she had opened the notepad. She might otherwise have forgotten. She is to meet up tomorrow with the prematurely returning baby Peekaboo and the schnauzer.

They, she had gathered from Louise's carefully worded and thorough communiqué, had definitely not been cut out for extended space travel and should never have volunteered. The not that distant galaxy Andromeda is as far as they had gotten, all the while clinging to one another, starting with their departure from the Sea of Tranquility on the moon. Peekaboo, in particular, couldn't handle the periods of isolation and together they were jeopardizing the mission with their silly efforts to divert themselves by playing pointless games, according to Louise.

Kate had agreed that it would be best, under those circumstances, for the two to turn back. But she will have an extensive debriefing session and is looking forward to that.

Kate puts her notepad back and moves on. Still quite a way to go, she realizes, when she's startled by a noise off to the right. She looks over and sees some branches moving more than they should with the blowing wind. She stops and keeps looking in that direction, but there's nothing. A bit reluctant now, she moves forward ever more slowly while continuously glancing over to her right.

There it is again! And something dark... moving. She stops and looks behind her—nothing she can see. She's beginning to debate whether it's wise to go on. Without Blue? What if it's some big animal? She takes a few more careful steps and then...again! Only this time there's no doubt. There's a small dark figure moving through the bushes, following her along. She can feel her heart pounding. Should she go on?

Fortunately, the need for a decision is taken out of her hands. Nature has intervened and made any further deliberations academic. A confrontation wouldn't be that effective anymore—she has peed her pants.

— 26 —

There is concern and confusion on Mrs. Aubrey's face when she wipes her hands on the well-faded apron. "But you're staying at the lodge over there, eh?" she says. "What would you need a room for?"

"I'm not even absolutely sure," John tries to explain. "But for personal reasons I need to know whether I can have a room here for a few days, if I need it."

"Well sure." Mrs. Aubrey laughs as she looks around her tiny place. "It's not like we're overbooked this week. You're ready for your pie now?"

"That'll be great," John says while he reshuffles some of his papers on the table, "and I'll have another cup of coffee too. I'll have a look at the room later."

"Sure thing," she says and heads back to her kitchen, nodding thoughtfully at one of the pictures on the wall as she does.

With Ely and Aholl having gone to the airport to pick up Marshal, John has plenty of time. Too much time. He's been coming to Mrs. Aubrey's in Good Hope to have his meals for the last few days and more often than not he's the only customer here. Not really a bad thing. It allows him to sit at his favorite table, a safe distance from the many photos on the walls of that jolly-looking man with the rifle and usually at least one dead animal—the man she calls "the Mister."

As far as he can tell, Mrs. Aubrey's is little more than a bed and breakfast, although the woman can cook. Through the window he sees a man filling his car at the gas station and a couple of other vehicles are in front of Tim Hanson's. One of them a nicely dressed up, lime-green collectible Camaro—maybe a Pontiac. Except for the color, not unlike the one he keeps in Seattle. He takes another sip of his coffee and gets back to reviewing the weekly summary in front of him. As his eyes run down the columns again, he halts at the currency translation line, highlights it in red and scribbles the name Sato at the border. On a subsequent page, the SG&A section gets a yellow line and an exclamation mark.

With the exception of the seriously bleeding publishing arm, a small, newly acquired gas exploration services provider in western Canada and the habitually lagging plastic parts manufacturer in India, the numbers at D.R.T. United look good alright and a better position for him is difficult to imagine. He's very well compensated and effectively supervises a profitable, well-oiled machine from a distance. Not that he doesn't deserve it. He, himself, has done much to make the job what it is.

They have become experts at essentially doing the same thing over and over again. So well, that maintaining these successes has become the equal in importance to creating them in the first place. Every new venture has to have a defined and limited risk. No undertaking has been exposed to the fortunes of any other. Think big at the top, small at the bottom. Even the days of their overreliance on the marketing genius of Marshal are long gone; some of his approaches have been transplanted to other D'Groth holdings.

Their devotion to in-house developed proprietary strategies and technologies have paid off well in that they have made possible the cost-effective entry into foreign markets.

Without narrowly defined responsibilities or titles, he has the authority he needs to deal with specific problems and issues which either he or Marshal deems to be of potential key consequence. Over the years he has helped Marshal establish a system in which no single operating entity has been vulnerable to the ups and downs of another or the whims of any single individual. There would always be two, sometimes even three, key people. It never mattered how competent a particular manager was—United would never be in a position to depend on him or her alone. What better job? An overpaid go-fer and part-time firefighter is he.

"I'm gonna like this," he says when Mrs. Aubrey places the pie in front of him. He means it. She deliberately burns the crust a little and smothers it with maple syrup, complementing it with a scoop of vanilla ice cream that goes well with the hot apple pie.

"You enjoy it then," she says and then points outside. "There's Manuel."

Looking through the window, John sees the grey pickup in front of Hanson's now. That's the man he has seen at the doughnut shop getting out of the truck and going into the store.

"Yes, I've seen him before," he says, looking up at Mrs. Aubrey. "And the young lady with her big dog."

"You mean Miss Kate?"

"Yes."

"You know her then, eh?"

"Yes, I've met her. Very nice young lady." Aware that Mrs. Aubrey had noticed earlier the bit of damage at the side of his face, he had appreciated not having had to explain it—so far.

She suddenly seems alarmed. "Miss Kate?" she asks, looking earnestly at him. "This isn't that kind of hotel, you know!"

"No, no, no." John is shaking his head energetically. "I don't know her that well. It's not what you think."

She looks directly into his eyes and pulls back the coffee-pot she was about to use to top up his cup. "Well, just as long—"

"No, absolutely not. But I will rent a room. Can I go up and have a look?" Not much of a chance for him to chat with her about Kate Walter now.

Not exactly what John is used to, but it is a clean, very small bedroom with its own bathroom. There's a radio, but no television or phone. The furniture is all pine reproductions. There's a little desk by the wall and the drapes are floral and friendly.

John thinks of fallen apple trees when he takes the hand towel out of his pocket, unwraps the three mini-cassette tapes and looks around. He carefully examines the bathroom, opens all the doors of the closets and finally decides to place the tapes flat under the bible he finds in the drawer of the night-table.

– 27 –

"Thanks for holding the fort," says Marshal.

There. Direct eye contact and that smile. Marshal is clasping his arm around John's shoulder with a firm hug; he seems not to notice his black eye and the cut on his cheek.

John is not all that surprised when he sees Sharon Epstein get out of the limo. That changes when she is followed by Matthew Surtees and a blonde woman, rather familiar to him, but whom he can't place immediately.

"My right hand, John Martins," Marshal says, "Mrs. Sinclair, Ruby Sinclair. You two should remember one another."

Ruby Sinclair searches his face while they shake hands and he remembers. "Oh yeah, you were at Marshal's birthday party... Press... right, Mrs. Sinclair?"

"So formal. Ruby, please. I do occasional columns, yes. What happened to you?" she asks, lifting a finger in the direction of his head.

"Would you believe an accident?"

"You ought to be more careful then," she winks, rearranging her scarf.

Matthew Surtees, whom he has worked with twice in the last three years, he knows well. Shaking his hand, he sees Ely and Aholl unload additional luggage from an airport limo that was seemingly necessary and had followed the company limousine; it looks as though the party has arrived here prepared for an extended stay. Marshal is already a couple of steps ahead of John. But as they make their way to the door of the retreat, Marshal turns to steer him off to the side and says quietly, "Let's get settled in first, maybe have a chat with Sharon if you get a chance. Then we'll talk as soon as we have the opportunity, alright?" John would rather not wait, but Curtis is already striding away to catch up with Ruby.

Ely and Aholl have been carefully avoiding him while carrying in the luggage with the help of the housekeeper and one of the maids. Inside, Marshal looks at his watch. "How about we all meet in the great room in about an hour? Give everybody a chance to freshen up. Maybe then John will give us some good news about our discovery."

Of everyone there, Sharon seems the least at ease. He has caught her giving him long, searching looks more than once. She starts to follow the maid upstairs, but turns back to come over and grab the sleeve of his jacket. "Marshal seems quite worried about something. Does he have reason to be?"

"Don't know. What's he worried about?"

ENIGMA IN BLUE

"You're playing possum with me?" she asks. "Think, John, think. Even I'm not convinced that Marshal necessarily believes there really is something to that blue rock. I don't think—and I'll bet you he doesn't—that it really matters any longer. It has just gotten too big to let go. Think, John, think." Now he watches her go upstairs. That possum remark? It hadn't sounded like a question at all.

When John hears faint voices again downstairs, he takes a last look around the suite. His overnight bag is by the door and next to it the nearly empty briefcase. On the writing table he has prominently displayed the laptop and a stack of documents relating to D.R.T. Business activities together with an envelope, addressed to D.R.T. United, containing his resignation and seventy five dollars. The money being the fair value he had placed on the dagger-like letter opener he had taken and slipped into the breast pocket of his leather jacket.

"Time's up and fuck you all very much," says he.

Oddly, Dr. Matthew Surtees commands attention in spite of his physical appearance. John himself is all too familiar with the doctor's reputation for his occasional issues with anger management, having once been threatened with retribution from above over his failure to enthusiastically agree with an assertion made, the substance of which he could no longer remember. Marshal never fails to refer to him as a dear friend and spiritual advisor. He is tiny and frail, he nearly disappears in the corner of the large chesterfield by the fire. What little hair he has left is grey and John wonders about his recent health issues and whether he should be drinking sherry, as he's doing now. But then, at his age and in his condition...

"Were you aware, dear lady?"—Matthew Surtees leans to direct his question at Ruby Sinclair—"it is the position of the mother church... questioning what came before the so-called Big Bang is not encouraged."

She wasn't, John is certain. Not everyone is into church doctrines that much. To her credit she is taking time to think out her answer.

"But if it does turn out to be unavoidable, re-examining this position," she says, shifting her attention back to Marshal, "who better, under the circumstances, than Marshal Curtis."

Dr. Surtees seems to agree grudgingly with a narrow part of that and smiles alternately at Mrs. Sinclair and Marshal, who eagerly protests. "I don't claim that, but it is what it is. You couldn't make it up. We're explaining the nature of the universe in our articles and possible evidence, disputing what we're saying, is found on my property. Can you imagine?"

It's now on his property. Not maybe, not close to, not on the line. And he isn't finished. He has started to pace around in a circle with his arms clasped behind his back.

"Think of it." He is talking rapidly, no longer able to hide his frustration. "From a possible speck of matter, fifteen billion years ago to today's modern man." He has stopped pacing by a window at a point furthest away from everyone else and it has John wondering whether he is able to see his own reflection in the glass.

"I'm but a step away…" He pauses to put one hand against the window and then turns slowly with a deep sigh. He may have forgotten that he's not alone.

"That's where Ruby comes in," Sharon ends the momentary silence to explain. "A small scientific publication in New York has gotten wind of this. I'm told they can be aggressive and careless. We've definitely decided to take the lead, no matter where this goes. I've had another meeting with Hugo as well; he's on top of it." She goes over to the table of refreshments to pour herself a cup of tea as Marshal moves over to the sofa, sits next to Dr. Surtees and puts his arm around his shoulder. "What you could do, Matthew, is check out how we can be most helpful around here through our Foundation. Make contact with some local leaders and see what the primary needs are in these parts."

"That's so very generous of you, Marshal," says Matthew. "I'd be happy to do that...maybe Mrs. Sinclair could help," he adds, looking over at her, but getting no response.

Ruby has been more focused on John, studying him openly when she asks Sharon. "He's an awfully quiet fellow. Is he always like that?" She's noticed, probably not so difficult.

"No, not usually," Sharon says and adds. "Something the matter, John?"

He doesn't respond but shakes his head when she indicates a direction. "Grimsby told us that the man over there acts a bit strange, maybe senile."

Sharon had pointed the wrong way, but he knows who she means.

"Don't think so. D e m e n t i a, you mean?" He had drawn out the word.

"You know...?" She stops, giving him another one of her inquisitive looks. "There's a woman over there talking to people from Central America about doing security work around here."

No, he wasn't aware of that. And how could she be? She too must be in on whatever it is that he doesn't want to be in on.

He turns to Marshal who is unaware as he is scrolling his Blackberry. "Marshal," John says and finds himself having to repeat. "Marshal."

"I really, really mean well," Marshal says when he finally does look up. "I just want to buy the property or settle this matter financially in a fair way. Grimsby mentioned that you get along really well with the daughter over there. That's so?"

John stands up. "Too late for that, damn it. I want to have a word in private—now." He says it loud and clear and isn't worried about alarming anyone.

Marshal doesn't look particularly perturbed to him either when he too gets up. "So be it. We need to know whether you're with us in this or not anyway. My office."

"Marshal...?" Sharon asks. She also is standing.

He shakes his head.

Curtis closes the door behind them and the thought of a supposedly unethical enabler crosses John's mind. What had she said?

He hadn't intended to sit down and neither does Marshal. Right.

"Sorry... after all the years." He gets it out quickly so Marshal can't beat him to it. "You're gonna get yourself and me in trouble. I'm out."

There's no reaction on Marshal's face.

John steps towards the door when Marshal comes around and partly blocks it.

"Aren't you forgetting something?"

"No. You'll find my laptop and all the papers relating to United in my room."

"The tapes," Marshal says quietly.

"You'll find them at the bottom of the lake, if you want them so badly."

Marshal looks skeptical and is slow to clear the doorway. "Be smart, John," he says, "and take care. Think hard before you wind up making a real big mistake. God, man..., I don't get it. We were a team."

John doesn't answer and firmly closes the door behind him on his way out.

When he comes back down after gathering his overnight bag and briefcase, the only person around is Sharon Epstein.

"You sure you know what you're doing?" she asks. Her voice is steady.

"I'm sure."

"Marshal says for me or somebody to drive you anywhere you want to go. You want me to or the housekeeper—?"

"You've been surprising me enough, Sharon, I don't think I want you to do anything more for me. You'll no doubt go far, especially with all the new openings at United. I'll just walk."

And that's what he does. He has his cell phone and could try to call a taxi once he gets to the road. He starts out down the middle of the driveway, but finds himself looking back a couple of times. There's a narrow walkway, running parallel with the driveway on his right. It's sheltered by trees on both sides.

That's where John walks until he comes to the main road.

— 28 —

Serafina feels a tad guilty about not having told Kate or Leo that among the things she had gone to pick up in town were two tough friends of Manuel's from back home, men she also knows. She has the opportunity to correct the situation when she sees the two of them near the barn, but doesn't take it. Leo has just asked her. "Who are these guys?"

"Manuel didn't tell you?"

"Tell me?"

"He said he talked to you about it," Serafina says.

"I still don't know what you're talking about."

"Manuel told me you had agreed. Some of the old trees near the run-in shed on the east side need to be cut down and there's some fence-mending to be done."

"I thought that was done weeks ago," says Leo. He looks befuddled and she decides to try. "Maybe you forgot? Or the job didn't get finished?"

He scratches his head and says, "Hmm...."

Might as well go with it. "They're sort of free-lancers. They're gonna bunk with Manuel for a few days. He says there's quite a bit of work to do and those guys are good."

Lucky she was right about her perception over his level of trust in Manuel and is relieved when he strokes his hair again and repeats his "hmm…" in a softer, more accepting tone.

They're walking back to the house from the training track where they had been watching Bill line-drive one of the yearlings, Bill behind the horse and a groom on either side, steadying the colt with long extension lines.

A spirited horse, Serafina had thought, maybe even crazy. She admittedly isn't an expert on horses, but it hadn't been difficult to tell who got most of the workout. Not the colt.

"Can we be sure, I'm trying to say, can we know if the horses like being trained? You know what I'm saying?"

"Well ja, I sometime wonder that myself," says Leo, "this one just now liked sticking it to Bill. I think he started out nervous, but wound up toying with his masters. We do take care of them in many ways. So far I've been able to convince myself that it's a fair trade-off. So far."

"I know something must have upset Kate earlier" she says as Leo has stopped walking to look at the window of the upper level of the house.

"Yes, I know. She just rushed in and wouldn't talk. I know she's upstairs, hopefully just busy with her notes."

"I'm not saying I would do it, but I'm curious. Why wouldn't you and Kate just sell those people an acre and be done with this thing? What does it really matter who found the rock?"

"It's Kate who found it and she should really make that decision. And I think she does care… more now. I'm satisfied that it's from our property and now it's becoming a matter of… you can't let people push you around and threaten you."

She has a nagging suspicion that Leo is not at all certain the find comes from their land. He could have had a surveyor here by now.

He's afraid he might find out it's not. And that could disappoint Kate. "I'm with you, but you do have an ego, don't you?"

Leo looks a bit embarrassed. "Well, never claimed I didn't."

"Is that what you're getting at when you say we have the advantage?"

"I don't get it. You're not making sense."

"Well, with you it's all about what you know and what you think in spite of what you say about Kate, isn't it? You think that with them it's all about what the whole world knows and thinks of them, right?"

"You do have a way of making a point—and you're not so wrong. When I was younger, wanting things or asking for favors used to make me sick to my stomach. I'm lucky, because there's really so little I want now. I think it would still make me sick, even today. Having a need weakens you and I'm guessing that's the position they're in."

"You still don't want to involve the authorities?" It is Serafina's last question on the subject and she is not surprised to find herself relieved when he answers with a decisive "No."

As they continue their walk, she commends herself on her decision and her insight into how he thinks. He's happy only when he's miserable. Maybe that's an overstatement, but he likes stress. He needs it. He seems to have worked hard most of his life to make things easy, but can't handle it when they are. She wraps her arm tightly around his and thinks: no wonder that he doesn't want Kate to be like him.

— 29 —

Kate had seen Serafina and Leo walk over to the barn from her bedroom window, but hadn't felt like joining them. Not today. Dear, dear.

Blue is showing some signs of recovery. She had sat with him downstairs for a while until he had gone to sleep. Just so unfortunate that he is laid up right now. A sensible, wise and mature type with plenty of experience like Blue is probably exactly what is missing among some of those unduly ambitious intergalactic space adventurers up there. Her first indication that there was good reason to worry had actually come when she debriefed immediately after their return the schnauzer and Peekaboo. It looks now as if she should have taken more seriously what she at the time thought to have been idle gossip.

COMMERCE in space. Goodness me. Not small, hands on start-ups to fill local needs. No, big business via acquisition mostly to concentrate the most economic power possible into the fewest paws as can be arranged for some still to be defined purpose. Goros paws, it would appear, and she had clearly underestimated him—and his appetite.

His request for authorization and seed resources had been backed up with logic of a kind. Timing would never be more opportune—there's virtually no competition. Not many of the potential partners and sellers seem to have a real good sense of the value of their commodities. He knows of one place where the inhabitants are willing to exchange, on a pound for pound basis, their gold for sweet potatoes. A huge lake of very excellent molasses is available elsewhere for the asking and a commitment to improve a portion of the dam required to keep it from overflowing. Intellectual property too is readily accessible. The plans for duplicating the Fornaxiens' method of growing bacon strips in orchards could be secured for no more than a promise of a small share of future profits. And better still, they would agree to a non-competition clause covering all of the remainder of the universe. Undoubtedly Miss Kate will appreciate the possibilities presented by virtue of the fact that too many amateurish entrepreneurs are mucking about in the galaxies and that these serious opportunities deserve the attention of a serious player. He, Goro, would be prepared to tackle this challenge.

Kate is looking carefully at the point of the pencil. She is unsure. What would be most appropriate? Dear Goro… …Dear Mr. Goro?

'My dear Goro, I am in receipt of your space fax and thank you so very much for the detailed, thorough analysis of the economic potential you and your associates have uncovered in outer space. Truly spectacular concepts, to say the least. I so wish I could follow our usual practice and consult with everyone before formulating this response. In this case that is just not possible with so many of you so far away and the remainder of the home team still upset over Benji's accident. Don't you start worrying about that up there now, he's going to be alright. When all of you left for space, we wound up a little short for our ongoing circus play and Benji volunteered for a second role on the trapeze. He fell into a vat of marshmallows.

Also, dear Goro, I don't mean to shirk my responsibility in this. I am admittedly afraid of and don't really believe in bigness for its own sake. I do try to be fair and appreciate the benefits of productive efficiency, but the unintended consequences of excessive consolidation and domination can be, to my way of thinking, destructive—and even a bit sad. You might remember the time we all went to Barrie to that puppy fair, those two nice ladies promoting their Company's new line of treats? I just saw one of them, Rose, at the bookstore. She told me that they were unable to gather up enough money to exercise their option to buy for themselves the little business when their boss received an offer from GIGANTUS INC. She says she is fine with it now, selling books, but I'm not convinced. The other lady is working at the unemployment office these days.

Goro, I promise that soon after your return we will arrange for a major meeting and fairly reconsider your ideas. Perhaps we can find some common ground. I am thinking, for example, of helping aliens make what they need and don't know how to construct themselves. In partnership, as per your concept? I expect there will be many opportunities for cooperation.

Well then, for now with greetings from Blue and my very best wishes for all of you, I remain as always your friend,

Kate Walters.'

Kate is not going to send the letter immediately. She is going to check first on Blue and leave an opportunity to make changes—just in case.

– 30 –

Leo thought it a really good idea. Serafina had suggested she'd try and talk Kate into going out for the evening. Dinner, or maybe a movie, just the two of them. Get Kate's mind off things. He had done all he could to encourage them. "You should go. Blue and I will hold the fort. You know I don't mind."

Kate had seemed reluctant, so he resorted to a bit of trickery. "You could help me out at the same time. You could stop by a bookstore. There's a book about physics that I'm after for some research and you might find it for me."

When he saw Kate begin to weaken, he came up with an additional appeal to her kindness. "I'd get it myself, but I don't think I'll have time. I'm gonna try to take a quick run over to the harness track. Remember that horse we're interested in; can you remember his name, the Bradwood Farms horse? I heard they're putting a price on him and he's racing tonight. I want to take another look."

That had done it, but he hadn't been sure whether they were finally planning on going into Orangeville or all the way to Pleasantville.

Leo has already slipped the Arctic down jacket over his tracksuit and exchanged his moccasins for boots. As he feels for the cigarettes and the lighter in his pocket, he catches Blue looking at him and goes back to slide down on the floor next to him and lean against the chesterfield. "I know, wish I could take you, boy. But your job for now is to get better. You're just gonna have to hang tough for a while. You watch the house while I play surveyor, okay? I shall return." Blue groans when Leo rubs his head.

He isn't going to the racetrack. He's about to have a good look at the fence line near the site. Only he will start out at the extreme east end of the property and work his way towards the lake. He knows the property line to be fairly straight and has remembered that the fence, starting at the very east end, seemed pretty well intact the last time he had seen it. So, if he were to follow the line, he might be able to tell where the fence should be near the water, in spite of the fact that it isn't there anymore.

He's walked all the way to the side road and has found the edge of the property line. Here he climbs over the fence by the road and begins to make his way through the brush. Even starting out from here, what remains of the cedar lumber now is often barely visible. In places, non-existent. The terrain is not exactly level and there are a number of fallen trees to climb over.

His conversation with Serafina earlier had made him think again. Was he being fair? Kate, for as long as he can remember, has always shown strong tribal tendencies. She will have to live with these neighbors for a lot longer than he will. Unless, that is, there really is more merit to one of his theories than generally accepted— namely that death on its face makes so little sense and is in fact a matter of individual choice for those who will it to be so. But just in case that turns out to not be so, burdening his daughter with a long-term family feud might not be a good thing, though Serafina would probably help and enjoy it. Never mind what he thought, was he right with his impression that Kate did care more and more about the final outcome? She must definitely be the one to decide. Just because they've found something mysterious and intriguing on their property doesn't mean that they have to cling to it necessarily, but that will be her call.

Yes, he would...

His left leg is caught on something and he begins to twist and fall; as he does, he tries to brace himself against the shattered tree in front of him. Too late!

It's the last thing he sees.

– 31 –

They had been in Pleasantville earlier, going through some of the shops and searching two small stores for the book that Kate somehow knew they weren't going to find there and Serafina suspected didn't exist in the first place. They had made the short drive over to the Chapters on Dundas Street and there they had found it.

Kate is comfortable with the atmosphere of bookstores, especially this one with the coffee shop attached in the corner. She would have been more comfortable had it not been for the man sitting at "her" favorite table in "her" favorite corner. They had sat nearby talking and enjoying their coffee until Kate became increasingly aware that the middle-aged man at "her" favorite table would frequently look up from his book and glance at them. They hadn't been loud. Still, Kate had gotten the feeling that Serafina and she were invading this man's space—at least in his mind; not that easy to tell in the prevailing light where his space ended and theirs began—and clearly he had no idea whose space he was in fact occupying in the first place.

He had several coffee cups in front of him and his jacket hung over the back of his chair. He had the air of someone who lived there. Not an entirely unfamiliar sight to Kate. Normally, this kind of demeanor adds to the relaxed atmosphere of a bookstore; when it doesn't involve "her" favorite table. Oh well, maybe he just liked one of them? At one point he had managed a little smile. Yes, Kate had decided, he was the typical, shy loner. Serafina's vote had been for "disturbed pervert" or war criminal, doing research for future evil acts. She did relax her "war criminal" judgment just a little after they observed another lady customer stop at his table momentarily to exchange a few words in a way that made it seem she knew him.

They're back in downtown Oakville now and are finishing their dinner at the Black Orchid.

"I can't really blame the saleslady," says Serafina with just a tiny smirk, able to maintain a fairly straight face for the moment. "I sure hope she didn't think that was my taste in reading."

She has to watch Serafina take the two objects of her amusement out of the bag and place them on the table in front of her. "*Gods and Physics*," says she, beholding the thick, dark volume to her right and then redirect herself to the thin, greenish one on the left: *Petula's Excellent Road Trip*. Now she cackles and touches the two books in front of her. "The taste of a woman who frequently pees her pants."

Kate takes exception. "Once," she says, "I suppose that's never happened to you?"

"Actually"—Serafina gets sort of serious for a moment—"I wish I could say that."

Kate places a hand over her own glass when the waiter comes back to top up Serafina's wine. "John Martins, did you form an opinion of him?" she asks.

It concerns Kate when Serafina doesn't laugh, giggle, smirk or cackle as she puts the books back into the bag. "Aye, yi, yi," is what she says.

"Aye, aye what?"

"That's the guy you like? Are we sure?" she asks.

"We, we? You already know I do."

"Aye, yi!" The smirk is back when she says yet another time, "Aye, yi!"

"We really don't know much about him," Kate says. "He didn't threaten us. Isn't it possible he just works for the wrong people?"

"Isn't it possible, isn't it possible? Anything's possible. But he didn't look like a lightweight to me. A little surprised and confused at one point, yes. But definitely not a flunky. And to hang out with people like Ely and that other... Aholl?"

"Be reasonable. I told you, he warned me about them."

"Yeah. How do you know it's not all part of it? A set-up. Good cop—bad cop, you see? Sometimes, Kate, it can be liberating to assume the worst. Stop being so trusting."

"Huh...? At least keep an open mind. Things are not always what they seem, you know."

"That's what I just said. Only you're saying it the other way around."

"Well, yes, exactly," Kate says and decides to stop right here before she gets totally confused.

Serafina suddenly relaxes. "Your father will be so pleased. He may lose his daughter, but he'll gain an outlaw for a son-in-law." Not a line to be proud of, but she keeps right on cackling anyway when she gets up. "Let's go. You're driving. I'll point out some of the scenery to Petula."

* * * *

The pain has become worse. He has tried to raise himself up, but hasn't been able to. He's half hanging, face up over the fallen tree

ENIGMA IN BLUE

with his left leg boot trapped and his right leg up on top of the tree. It too is pinned by a sharp branch that has gone right through his calf muscle and there's blood, a lot of it. He tries again to no avail. His upper torso is hanging down with his head touching the ground and he just doesn't have the strength to raise himself up. He can move his left leg a little and could probably pull the boot out from under the tree, but he hasn't figured out a way to reach and undo the wire sling around his leg. Relax and conserve energy, he tells himself. Even with what he can see from his angle, he's pretty sure his right knee is shattered.

He again shouts as loud as he can, "Hello, hello!" and as before there's no answer.

They will find him in time, he is certain, but the blood loss scares him. He can't think of anything he can use to tie around his leg. His tracksuit doesn't have a belt. Calm down, he tells himself again. A cigarette would help and he feels for them. They're there, but not the lighter—it must have fallen out. He looks around and he can see it, but it's just too far away. A horse, a horse, my kingdom for a...

Kate and Serafina won't be back till late. Who's going to feed Blue?

"Hello, hello!"

Maybe he shouldn't have made up that story about going to the racetrack. If no one else finds him soon, they will wind up worrying all right. But that will not be for a long time. Maybe he should have listened to Kate. She had urged him to get a cell phone, but he had never wanted to.

In the years gone by, for him to be out all night would not have caused undue alarm. He can feel himself manage a little smile as he thinks of olive-skinned, bi-sexual girls, frolicking in the hot pool—champagne flowing and chicken bones flying everywhere.

"Hello, hello!"

Maybe something good will come of all this. The steel rod in his left leg has given him the limp and now it's his right leg; there's just a chance...

Strange. When he had broken his upper femur in the race car, he had felt virtually no pain. He had worried about other injuries that maybe he couldn't feel at that time, but the leg had not hurt bad. He had even managed to ask for—albeit unsuccessfully—a smoke while the rescue team was debating how best to extract him from the wreck.

"Hello, hello!"

Kate and Serafina—they will come to look, but they'll no doubt head in the direction of that damn site. Why would they think that he had come this way?

He gets a hold of a branch and starts to pull hard. He can feel his head and back start to lift and then the branch snaps and all goes dark.

– 32 –

"Oh no, that doesn't look right." Kate slows when she turns onto the driveway.

"All the lights in the arena and the barn?" Serafina wonders.

"Well, it's nearly eleven. That shouldn't be. We'll have a look." Kate takes the shortcut to drive straight into the arena where it becomes immediately clear what the problem is.

The colt they all call McArthur is the get of No No Never out of the outstanding pacing mare, Elvira Childers—a truly brilliantly bred horse. Right at the moment, however, he's a pitiful sight.

"Colic," a profusely sweating Bill says, dragging the horse to keep him moving.

The two new men, whom Kate now knows to be friends of Manuel, are sitting on a bench at the far end of the shed row. They have the calm demeanor of people who seem to know—there's nothing they can do. For now. Manuel is checking the horse trailer at the entrance to the arena and Bill, without stopping, turns the shank over to Lisa who continues to drag the staggering horse up and down the shed row.

Kate has seen this before and it's hard to watch. The horse will either make it or not. "We've called Guelph University," Bill explains. "They're gonna take him if we have to go, but we'll give him some more time." He lunges forward, as fast as his bulk will permit, to help Lisa support the horse who, at the moment, is particularly desperate to go down.

"He keeps rolling too close to the wall," Bill wheezes, "we found him cast on his back. Not the first time. The vet's been here. We think McArthur is actually getting better."

"This is better," she hears Serafina saying to herself and then ask, "What's that smell? Smoke?"

"Lucky," says Bill, "that's what alerted Manuel at first. The alarm woke him up. Otherwise—I don't know. There was a small fire in the corner over there. We'll check that out later. There was a smell of gasoline."

"Does Leo know?" Kate asks.

"No, we didn't bother him yet. But if he winds up at the clinic, you know, with the insurance stuff, they'll need to have authorization in case they have to, you know."

"I'll take a shift in walking him if you want," Kate offers, "but dad should know. One of us..."

"We're okay for now, just go."

She too rushes and helps to support McArthur when he makes it down to his knees in his latest attempt to throw himself. Bill pushes up from under his neck and Lisa keeps jerking and pulling hard on the lead shank. "Went down once before," she says, looking back over her shoulder at Kate, giggling. "Luckily we have experience at this, eh Kate?" Well yes, but this is experience she would rather not have.

"You know if Dad's even back from the racetrack?" she asks Manuel, who has just come back in from the arena.

He shakes his head.

"Let's take a run over to the house and check if he's even there," she says, looking at Serafina. "We'll come back."

Serafina glances at the two men sitting on the bench and shakes her head. "I'll stay."

"Okay, be right back."

Something's not right. Blue looks distraught and his water bowl is empty. That's not like Leo.

It's the first thing—fill the bowl. Blue eagerly drinks without getting up and she wonders now: has he been fed?

"Dad!" she yells.

No answer.

"Dad! I'm home!"

Nothing.

"Can't you guys handle things without me, Blue?" She pets him for a moment and decides to look in all the rooms. Leo's not anywhere downstairs and she checks upstairs. She's told him often enough to carry a phone. Blue probably hasn't been fed then and she'd better take care of that. Sure enough, she was right.

"Leopold!"

He's forgetful, but not looking after Blue? Has he left a note? He would sometimes do that and she looks on the kitchen counter. In his study... no. Some new lines in process, yes.

She looks at the composition. Wouldn't be that unlike Dad to place a message inside somewhere.

ENIGMA IN BLUE

Like a leaf in the fall, lost and cold,
Out of place on the concrete grey.
The little dead bird fading, almost not there, ?
Perhaps like a leaf so as not to offend
Once a creature of grace,
At heights not surpassed.
Frightened as all in a storm, ??
Will it not leave a trace?
Leave not a trace,
This delicate leaf bird of grace.

And as I stepped closer with envy I saw
A little dead leaf bird so small
Being carried off by the breath of fall,
Has it ever been here at all?
Having never been here at all?

A bit morose, but there's no message buried in here...is there?

She doesn't really want to leave Blue, but she has checked and Leo's car is not in the garage. Did he go to the track and get into some kind of trouble? Damn Leopold, damn poem. Now she must add suicidal tendencies and advanced senility to her list of concerns.

She's back in the barn where McArthur is groaning and breathing hard. "He's not doing well at all, is he," a stressed looking Serafina says, swallowing a couple of inaudible add-ons.

Lisa takes a drink of water on the go. "I don't know...I wouldn't be so sure. He's not getting worse the way I see it, eh Kate."

"I hope you're right, Lisa, you might just be."

"What about Leo," Serafina asks.

"He must still be at the track. His car is not in the garage."

Manuel looks up and shakes his head. "No car," he says.

"That's what I said. The car's not there."

He shakes his ahead again. "No car." He glances at Serafina, looking for help. "No car. Car in garage."

"No, I was in the garage. I told you," Kate insists; he doesn't understand me.

"Car fix... in body place."

"You mean at the dealership?"

"Yes... fix."

She feels her shoulders sag and looks at Serafina, who says something in Spanish to Manuel. He gestures at the men sitting on the bench and they get up.

Serafina's demeanor has changed. "I've been trying to tell you guys," she says, "you just won't listen. We'd better go look for him."

Kate no longer needs to be persuaded. She herself had wandered into the bushes, hadn't she? "Oh boy." She turns to Manuel. "There's still a chance he had somebody pick him up. Maybe you could take a run over to the track and have a look... stop by Mrs. Aubrey's on the way, Manuel, Dad sometimes—hurry, okay?" Kate is not very successful at controlling the pitch of her voice. "We'd better change our clothes. Round up some flashlights and start looking—around the barn and house for now, okay Bill?"

Serafina is biting her lips.

— 33 —

"Me, you don't have to worry about, eh," Mrs. Aubrey says as she tidies up the table behind the only other guest who just left. Barely a guest, the talkative widower Harper John knows to be a local farmhand and not a big spender. "I'm a night owl. When do you think

I bake my pies?" As if John doesn't know that by now. The scent of baking is everywhere. Upstairs, in his bedroom too. It's probably Mrs. Aubrey's primary source of income. He's figured out by now that she sells pies to the locals, cash only, no receipt.

John leafs through his book again: *The Care and Training of the Pacer Trotter.* He doesn't know anything about horses, but has somehow come to think that maybe he should.

Try as he might, he can't get focused right now. He's checked airline schedules to New York, Seattle and Georgia. Seattle he has already ruled out. New York? He doesn't absolutely have to go there; he could get friends to shut things down for him. Visit Uncle Eddie's place in Georgia—that might be the best idea after all while he takes the time to get things straightened out. He has substantial resources and there's no pressure on him to do anything immediately. In truth though, to leave here right now is not really what he wants to do.

He considers and would love to talk with Mrs. Aubrey about Kate Walter, but changes his mind. She had seemed so perturbed the last time her name had been mentioned. He looks up from his book when he hears the engine of a car outside. Late hour or not, someone in the Good Hope area is probably in need of a pie. Sounds more like a truck—motor running—when the door opens.

"Hello Manuel," Mrs. Aubrey says.

He seems in a hurry and doesn't close the door behind him. "Not here, Mr. Leo?"

"Leopold Walter? No, he isn't here." She says it slowly.

"Been before... here?" He seems to be trying hard not to miss anything.

"No, haven't seen him all day. Something wrong?"

"Not find him. Missing."

John gets up immediately, but the man is in a real rush. "You see, call," he says and is out the door.

"Geez," Mrs. Aubrey says, "he looks rattled, eh? That's not like Manuel; he's such a calm sort. Wonder what's going on."

John starts to worry that he might know what's going on. With so many people interested in the eventual outcome of this thing, it's only a matter of time until something else goes wrong. He had already seen Kate Walter wandering around in the bushes by herself. He doesn't think about it long. He's going to try. He has the Walter phone number and he connects.

"Walter residence. Is that you, Leo?"

"Can I speak to Kate Walter?"

"Who's this?"

"John Martins."

There's a pause. "No, she's busy... with stuff."

"Jesus, it's important, please. This is Miss Gomez, right? Serafina?"

"Yes. This is not a good time."

"I know it's not, that's why I'm calling. Can I please talk to her? I don't work for—"

"No. I don't think that's a good idea at all. You people better not bother her anymore." The phone goes dead.

John isn't about to give up just like that. He's going to get in his rental and drive over there and he suddenly realizes what a silly notion and total waste of time his flight schedule research had been.

Once John gets to the Walter farm, things just get worse. There are two men standing in the driveway. They won't say anything and motion him to go back. He tries to get out of the car, but they start coming towards him and he backs away when he gets a better look at them and their machetes, their scars and their eyes.

The very presence of the men blocking the driveway is confirmation to him that there really is a problem. The woods are probably the right place to look, but he no longer works for United and he isn't allowed on the Walter property. Damn it. If he could find the fence line that splits the two properties—he knows approximately where that should be. Maybe that would be a way to approach the site because that's where he thinks Leo Walter is most likely to be found.

He turns left and heads in the general direction of the area he thinks his search should start. This also happens to be the direction he would take if he was going to the retreat, but that's not where he's heading. The phrase "straddling the fence" comes to his mind and he wonders how tough Kate Walter is. Not tough enough, he worries.

– 34 –

There's a break in the clouds and the moon illuminates Leo's new surroundings. Has the bleeding stopped? Not too sure about that. Hypothermia? He tries to recall what he knows about it. He'd made that mistake earlier. He's managed to lift his upper body some and thrown himself backwards as hard as he could in the hope of breaking the branch that his leg was impaled on. He has only partially succeeded, blacked out for a time, and the pain has become severe.

"Hello! Hello!"

Why would anyone think of looking here?

"Help!"

His voice is no longer as strong as it had been, he knows. Serafina is pretty tough, though. Based on what Manuel had said, they both know something about surviving in the wilderness. Hell, all they have to do is put two and three together and come up with six.

"Help!"

He closes his eyes and his mind drifts off to the very first time Kate had smiled at him, the moment her little hand had reached out to touch his cheek. 'We are all born sinners!' Whoever came up with that gratuitous, burdensome bullshit?

"Help!"

So much time to think and without a smoke, not much fun. What a trip it has been though, hopefully not yet at an end. There is so much more to tell Serafina and share with Kate—whether they want to or not.

Awkward and shy when young, it had stayed with him for so so long. Is he even that different now? For all too many years he had been convinced that there was something wrong with him. Obviously, in his mind at one time, the world around him was functioning as intended and he would just have to pull himself together, understand it as everyone else seems to and then he would blend right in as he should. If he gave up his purely entertaining books and concentrated on the collective, recorded knowledge of the world, he reasoned, a definitive truth would have to emerge. How could it not.

He set about to read feverishly and kept it up for nearly two decades. What an exciting journey that turned out to be. He studied history and psychology and made himself review political systems and ethics. He gleaned an insight into the minds of great thinkers and brilliant leaders, made strides in understanding the difference between marvelous accomplishments and the nature of those who accomplished them. He was to learn that, like many before he was certain, he often felt as if he walked with giants or crawled through the dirt with midgets and at times found it hard to distinguish between the two. And he concluded that he was not alone in harboring occasional bombastic thoughts, except that he did well at hiding his, he was convinced.

Reading Dylan Thomas brought him to tears. So did a book he vaguely remembers as being about someone's Complaint, a bestselling must read of its day, where the author, in collaboration with some of his characters, had tried to drag him into their mind processes and their bathrooms when he didn't want to go. There, the tears had been for a different reason. He remembers throwing the book against a wall.

He also gained a basic understanding of the great religions of the world and paid particular attention to all the major philosophers and their views. The many contradictions, when he found them, more than anything became a cornerstone for the increase in his self-confidence.

And the day did come when it became clear to him he had done the right thing to search. There was an ultimate reality. The truth for him was that he had not been so wrong. He was on his own and there was no help over the horizon. He began to accept that he might always feel like an outsider looking in and—for him—it became a source of strengths rather than a bother.

If I don't get out of this one, he thinks, I still have the concept of the seamless whole to lean on. Not really a concept...a self-evident fact. I'm not reaching. The very debris of ancient massive exploding stars can morph into new, potentially life-giving suns. Nothing ever goes away, ever. It only changes. Our own best thoughts and inventions are just the continuation of all that has come before us. Kate too has it right. The tiny mass of a speck of dust somewhere in the cosmos affects everything else, as did the labor of a slave building a pyramid.

Still. Given a choice between rubbing shoulders with Bach, Da Vinci, Newton, Franz Schubert or even Jesus Christ, he would really rather be at the kitchen table with Kate, sharing potato pancakes.

"Hallow...!"

He opens his eyes to look up. Another break in the clouds as he twists his head to the left where he can see the reflection of the moonlight on the metal tip of the lighter. It hasn't come any closer.

He turns his head slowly towards the trees to the right at the top of the steep slope and is startled when he sees a figure between two trees. A man? The figure is wearing a long coat and a hat with the rim turned down and it doesn't move.

"Help!"

No reaction.

Leo blinks. Is it real?

"Help!"

My turn? Already? Is that a God? If it is, he must be awfully angry with me. Have I done this badly? In his left hand he is carrying a cross upside down and he is walking away.

– 35 –

Obsessive sometimes? Kate knows him to be that.

"Dad!" she screams at the top of her lungs.

Obsessive and then sad when it's done—he had said it himself. He didn't pity, rather admired and envied people who were single-minded in the pursuit of anything worthwhile; or maybe even not so worthwhile. It would certainly keep you from being bored, he had said. But obsessive about what this time? His self-imposed role as one who is responsible for everything? Some of those people over there?

Perhaps it didn't really matter what it was. It had happened so many times before. Once Leo isolated the core substance of anything, he tended to turn into an unreasonable pit bull; and then always followed by that letdown. Guess he couldn't help it. For him, it really did seem to be all about the pursuit.

Are we looking in the right place? Manuel had not been able to learn anything; Leo hadn't been seen at the track by anyone, so he probably never went and there's just nothing else she knows of that, at the moment, is preoccupying him.

They must be looking in the right place.

"Dad!"

One of the men from Colombia had stayed back and she makes out Manuel and the other man just ahead, each carrying a machete. Serafina is just to her left and she, no wonder, she's got a shotgun. It isn't intended to kill anyone, Kate doesn't think. They had grabbed Leo's old gun and some ammunition on the way out, intending to use it for signaling, Kate had been assured. But if things keep on going the way they are now, Kate is beginning to think, arming everyone may not be such a bad idea.

Serafina says something in Spanish to the man at the front and then shouts at Kate. "You too, remember those wire slings!"

Kate's aware of that and she's been careful. "We'll just keep right on going," she says. "Maybe he went all the way to the damn place over there."

"Leo!" hollers Serafina.

They have passed the site and are on the neighbor's property now. Kate keeps moving her flashlight in all directions. She's stumbled and has been down on the ground several times and she sure doesn't want to lose sight of the others and boy would she ever like to have Blue along.

Manuel stops and looks back. "Pssstt." He has a finger across his lips.

"What?"

Serafina raises her hand. "Quiet."

Now Kate can hear it too. Somebody's shouting behind them and out of the bushes comes the younger man from Colombia, the one with the short ponytail, screaming words Kate can't make out.

"They've found him!" she hears Serafina shout. "We have to go back the other way to get to him. He's hurt!"

* * * *

Stumbling back through the brush, Kate already knows who found him—from what the Colombian man told Serafina and what she had said about the phone call and the offer to help. At the entrance to the barn she sees Robert standing in front of John Martins, blocking him.

"I've already called for an ambulance," John says, "I'll show you." He runs towards his car, shouting, "It's not far!" As they pile into the pickup to follow, she can just barely make out Bill give a sign—an okay sign. He must mean McArthur.

In the woods, the men from Colombia seem to be in their element—they are deliberate and decisive. Even as they make their way through the bushes, they have started to fashion a cot of sorts. They've chopped off one tree limb and picked up another. While moving, they were hacking off small branches of those stems. One of them had taken off his jacket and started to fasten it to one of the limbs.

"Almost," says John in the lead, "over there!"

"Where? I don't...yes, there! Dad."

Leo had at first been silently grimacing while people considered how best to free him and get him out and onto the road. Kate had wet his lips and carefully wiped his head with a wet cloth. An expression of relief finally starts to come over his face, but he is barely audible when he hoarsely asks. "What took you so long?"

Serafina kneels down and cradles his head as one of the men chops away the wire sling with a single blow. Leo is biting his lips when the men now slowly lift his trapped leg. One of them pulls out a knife and cuts away at the branch, severing it. Now he's free.

It is a real struggle with the makeshift cot, but it does work well enough as they walk and sometimes crawl up the hill towards the road. Kate can hear Serafina starting to laugh; nothing unusual there. She's alongside the cot, holding Leo's hand with a firm grip.

She interrupts her laughter for a moment, looks down at him and Kate can clearly hear her hum with an unusually soft tone in her voice a tune that Kate is sure comes from the tragic opera 'Rigoletto.'

Finally the lights of the cars on the main road come into view through the trees. There is an ambulance as well as a couple of other cars and the attendants are coming towards them. It's their turn now.

The pickup has just pulled away and Serafina and Kate are inside the ambulance alongside Leo as the driver reaches for the door. "Ready, let's go," he says. Just before he closes up completely she gets a last look at John who is standing in front of his car with the headlights on. He's a mess. He has scratches and blood all over him and in a moment he'll be the only one left there.

As the ambulance drives off, Kate has one hand on Leo's arm and the other on her bottom lip.

– 36 –

What the fuck does that Epstein bitch think I am...a god damn gopher? And to tell me that Aholl has to stay behind for Curtis's protection. The asshole?

Ely hands the soldering kit he had bought at Hanson's to the smartly uniformed technician, who barely looks at it when he grunts, "That'll have to do."

Ely turns his head to mumble under his breath. "Maybe I'll just do you, fucker."

They must all think he's fucking stupid. These are not receiving dishes they're setting up, they're for transmitting signals. And the tower that's going on the roof of the log cabin has a platform for a remotely operable camera. Why has he not been kept in the loop?

Fucking ridiculous! There's just no fucking way he'll ever again be freezing his ass off bouncing disgusting, drunken perverts for little pay. And then there are the geezers. Nobody else he knows of is going to send money home to help out. Nobody ever has or ever will. He's been around a lot longer than Epstein or the asshole, and now they're always yapping. Curtis too. He's been all over the installation crew in his short sleeves. He can see him now looking at a booklet, talking to the asshole who is wearing short pants, carrying Mr. D.R.T. United's stinking laptop. Curtis actually has one arm around Aholl's shoulder when they both turn to look at him from their safe distance.

Fucking ridiculous! They'd better be careful, or they'll all need protection. He knows stuff.

– 37 –

"It's show-time!"

A happy female voice behind the green mask seems exuberant. "They tell me you've done this before."

Leo glances around. It sure looks familiar. The operating theater is large and everything seems to be pale green. It's cold and he's cold and if he remembers correctly he'll still be cold when he wakes up.

"Let the fun begin," says the green voice.

Ninety-nine, ninety-eight, ninety-seven, ninety-six, ninety-five, ninety-four, ninety-three, ninety-two, ninety... one, ninety... eighty...

The train of refugees from Prussia had made one of its infrequent stops—presumably to unload the dead people, some more dead than others Leo and his sister had come to suspect, empty the buckets of filth and get some supplies. Mother had told them to stay put while she was going to see whether she could find anything to eat for them herself. He is on his toes, blowing against the frost-covered window of the railcar that had been gutted of all seats, trying to get a better view of the outside. His sister Na-Na, two years his senior, and Harold, his four-year-old brother, are crouched on the floor, cramped with their backs against the side of the railway car. Mother will have to hurry; he can hear some of the doors being shut.

There's a whistle, a loud hissing noise and the train is moving. Leo feels a sense of panic and glances down at Na-Na, who's holding her brother's hand tightly while he is struggling to get up. He quickly looks back outside and sees Mother running alongside the train that is gaining speed. The last thing he can see is her reaching forward with her right arm and then she disappears from his view.

Leo feels a pressure against his hand and he opens his eyes. Everything is blurry, but there's no pain.

"Dad?"

He moves his head slowly to the right, blinking. "I'm cold."

"I know." Kate squeezes his hand.

"Jesus, how long have I been out?"

"For hours," Kate says, "don't know exactly."

"Are you all okay? Where is Serafina?"

"Sure, sure, don't worry about us. She's outside. I'll get her in a minute, but you best start to listen. I asked you a hundred times to get a phone. They don't explode in your hand just because you press the wrong button. You're gonna be reasonable?"

"Ja," he says, knowing that he doesn't mean it. Who always wants to be found, he wonders as the door opens and a thirty-something, dirty-blonde woman comes in part-way. "You remember me?" she asks in a cheerful voice. He sees Kate shaking her head and he too is straining.

"You don't?" the woman says. "That's alright. Nobody ever does. How're you feeling, Mr. Walter?"

He nods in her direction.

"Good. But you men are all alike, now you don't remember." She smiles and closes the door behind her.

"I'll go find Serafina," Kate says as she follows the woman out, shaking her head.

Waiting, Leo resolves not to let this become a habit. The chill is starting to go away. He knows the feeling all too well. The hurting will start in time, but at the moment he feels not that bad, even a little light-headed. Morphine will do that.

When Serafina comes back with Kate, she halts at the center of the room with her hands at her hips. "Punchinello," she says and comes over to kiss his cheek.

"Make up your mind. That's not what you called me before. I heard you humming 'Rigoletto'. There is a difference, you know. There are clowns and then there are clowns. How did you all figure out where to find me?"

"When we realized you hadn't gone to the track, we thought you might be screwing around in the wilderness." She steps aside to make room for a nurse who has come to check his vital signs and the supply of intravenous fluids. "Can you check his brain function while you're at it?" Serafina adds, "I think we have reason for concern."

"There was a woman … came in and asked if we knew her … a nice woman we don't know. Is she one of the doctors? Do you know?" Kate asks.

"Ah," the nurse shakes her head, "that old shtick. It's an inside joke. She asked you whether you remembered her, Mr. Walter, did she?"

"Aha," Leo says.

"They all pretend to be hurt, because nobody ever gets to see their face. It's an act. She's an anesthesiologist."

"Well then, Nurse," Leo asks quickly, hoping to railroad her while she's still talking, "you can tell me, what's the damage?"

"No, that's for the doctors to handle."

"I know a little bit," Kate looks at the nurse. "You will live. You'll be out of commission for a lot longer than Blue, though. The fracture in your knee is not that bad, but there's quite a bit of calf muscle damage. It's going to take time. They say you'll walk okay. I'm not so sure about that. But Jesus, Dad, this is really all getting to me. We better start thinking. I will. Hard."

He waits for the nurse to leave the room and, feeling bad, he wonders. "Really, how did you find me?"

"We didn't, Dad. John did." There is satisfaction in her face.

"John...?"

"John Martins."

"That's the guy who came over," he starts to say but she interrupts. "Yes, John Martins. He doesn't work for them anymore."

Leo looks at Serafina who is shrugging her shoulders. "That's what he claims," she says. "He had called earlier and offered to help search for you, just to be fair."

"And you believe him? I don't know, Kate!"

"I know," Kate says firmly and repeats. "He's the one who found you."

Leo, really worried now, is straining to lift his head. "Search for me to what end? Think Kate. And how could he, of all people, have known exactly where—?"

She is resolute when she stands up. "Not now, Leopold, no more. Will you please try to differentiate between John the person and that awful outfit."

Serafina also seems to be trying to tell him something when she shakes her head. "Okay," he says, "but about the spot where you found that rock—"

Kate again interrupts. "Blue and I found it. It's a little corner of land that has come to represent something else to some people, myself included. And look at yourself, Dad, you're hardly in a good position to make decisions that you could act on. Either way, I'm going to decide what's to be done. Right, Leopold?"

There are two of them standing up now, looking down at him. Leo can feel himself hesitate for a moment before he says quietly, "Alright." Inside he's beaming.

As they are about to walk out the door, he has an idea. "Try to get me transferred to a smoking room, will you?"

As long as they're taking charge anyway, maybe they can do that too.

– 38 –

Something about the arrangement Serafina has just agreed to is beginning to bother her. It no longer seems reasonable or balanced. For her very next visit to the hospital she is to cook and bring along either a hot Thai soup—her choice—or a hearty red pea soup. If she were also to endeavor to secure a pack of cigarettes and a lighter, she was to feel free to enlist the aid of either Manuel, Kate, or both. A thermos and a plain brown paper bag had been suggested for the transportation of the items, in the interest of discretion.

In exchange, he, Leopold Walter, had agreed to consider—his choice—to keep an open mind about John Martins for Kate's sake...or not.

Serafina has walked from the hospital on Avenue Road and is now strolling along Toronto's fashionable Yorkville area. The air is fresh and there aren't many people on the street.

The area is changing fast, she realizes as she looks in vain for one of her favorite haunts. A little craft store with that pleasant young couple transplanted from out west dealing in odd, mostly second-hand, but high-end items. The bronzed and gold-plated baby shoes come to mind... and mostly unsigned notes, scribbles, sketches, drawings and paintings—purportedly the handiwork of publicity-shy, but prominent Torontonians. A fun and clever concept, Serafina had always thought, owned and managed effectively by Mr. and Mrs. Prominent, little doubt. Probably replaced by something more ambitious and rewarding now; in a different legal jurisdiction, it would seem likely.

She knows Toronto's Yorkville area well. At least she did once. She used to spend a fair bit of time around here before she got involved with the country folk.

There now, at least she doesn't have to find a new coffee shop.

Her caramel amaretto generously sweetened, she sits at the only remaining available table. She's going to relax a little and then pick up a second coffee for the long drive back home. Home?

Even with all the problems over the last little while, she has really liked being at the farm and at the moment is not looking forward to going back to Burlington. Today, however, is a bit of an odd day. Leo's in hospital and Kate is going to meet with John Martins tonight. She's happy for Kate, but that's going to leave her with Blue. Probably not her worst date ever, although...

"Do you mind?" The blonde woman, balancing a cup in one hand, has been looking around helplessly.

"No, no, go ahead."

"Thanks. Busy place," says the woman as she gets herself settled in. "Must be the chill outside."

"That and people-watching," Serafina says. "And, come to think of it, to be seen."

The blonde woman takes a sip of her coffee. "Are you from around here?" she asks.

"Not really from around here, but from the Toronto area. Yeah, I used to come here a lot."

"I'm visiting from the States," the woman says, "and I heard about the Yorkville area as being charming and a good place to shop. Thought I'd check it out."

"It's been changing a lot lately; it's not what it used to be. There's so much redevelopment going on. I hope they don't turn everything into high-rises around here."

"I noticed. The building, the big one, right across the street over there."

"And to think that this was once a poverty-stricken area. Full of hippies on LSD... before my time, that." Serafina pauses. "Don't know if they're the ones who invested in the real estate around here."

The woman chuckles and reaches over. "Ruby, Ruby Sinclair." She maintains eye contact when she does.

"Hi. I'm Serafina Gomez, pleased to meet you. Ruby? Yeah, you look like a Ruby."

"Thanks, I think," Ruby says.

"Do you have family up here?"

"No no. I'm here on a job. I do some freelance writing. I used to do reporting, but doing the occasional column gives me more freedom."

"What do you know," Serafina tells her, "I work as a secretary for a small paper. Columns about anything in particular?"

"No, not really. I try to carve out what I think might become of interest to readers, look into it, write about it and try to sell it. Looking for the flavor of the month, you could say."

"What are you digging up now?" Serafina is a little intrigued. A column-writing Ruby.

"I'm not quite sure yet. I'm here with a group of people who have stumbled onto something unique, and the man leading the charge has turned out to be very interesting indeed. A many-faceted human dynamo, you might say, and charming to boot."

Serafina glances at her watch. She has time and Ruby is a pleasant person, eager to talk. "Sounds interesting," she encourages her.

"I shouldn't be telling you," Ruby grimaces. "I've come to like the man a lot on a personal level. He can be so thoughtfully generous one minute and then turn into a harsh and icy vanquisher the next. Although right now, I kind of feel sorry for him. He's really here trying to clean up a mess that's been left by some disloyal people. He means well and a man like him shouldn't have to do that. He is immensely successful in different ways. I sometimes don't understand what drives men like that. More? More of what? More of the same?" Ruby is searching her face.

Serafina's not sure she has an opinion and thinks for a moment. "It's probably a matter of ambition, pride, possibly insecurity. I just came from the hospital visiting a friend who is a bit like that himself. We could choose to flatter ourselves and think they're doing it to impress us."

"Nothing serious, I hope." Ruby looks at her.

"No, no, just an injury... it'll heal. But you haven't really told me what your column is about."

"Sorry, Serafina, I don't mean to be coy, but it's premature. Etiquette and all that, I'm sure you understand. In the end, it's really always about people."

"Hmm, I know someone who would not agree," Serafina says.

"Your ailing friend?"

"I told you. Injured, not ailing. But yes, he and his daughter... well, to a lesser extent. Their interests go more in the direction of productive vegetable beds and flying canines."

"Flying vegetables? Tell me more. I don't get it." Ruby seems to be trying not to laugh.

"Don't get this wrong. They're more to me than just friends. His priorities can be, let me say"—Serafina is looking for the word—"odd. And she, whether she'll admit it or not, at times has to struggle with that."

"There aren't any mental issues, are there?"

"Goodness no, he is quite an effective entrepreneur, still at it part-time. Just...just, you know. I'm going on here."

"Not at all." Ruby reaches over to pat her hand. "It's beginning to look to me as though our friends might well be occupying the opposite sides of the same coin. Maybe we should have them meet; they might well complement one another. My friend is truly a master communicator and an expert at networking."

Serafina is doing all she can to suppress the oncoming laughter attack. "Networking! Yes, my friend networks all the time. He networks with suppliers of fertilizer, creatures who don't speak his language and long dead poets."

"Poor daughter—poor you."

"Hmm. Not really... no, not really."

Now Ruby looks at her watch and starts to gather her belongings. "I have a long way ahead of me to get to where I'm going. I'd best be on my way. I hope your friend will be alright." She hesitates and looks at her watch again. "I have a driver here, if we can drop you anywhere?"

"No, no. I have my own car."

"Sure? I would even change my plans if you're interested in having dinner with me. We could commiserate more about our respective friends. I would enjoy that." Ruby has actually put her things back down again.

"Sounds good, but I really can't. I have a date with a dog tonight."

That draws a giggle as Ruby puts on her coat. "Poor you. Really too bad." She is looking directly at her. "Its been a pleasure meeting you. A real pleasure."

"Likewise, Ruby, likewise."

Through the window Serafina sees her wave and smile back at her as a limo pulls up.

"Merde!"

Out of the limo steps an asshole familiar to her who walks around and opens the door for Ruby Sinclair.

– 39 –

Kate is so relieved to find that Mrs. Aubrey has no customers in her little restaurant—none. There are a couple of pie-boxes on the counter, probably waiting to be picked up. Elsa...? She has to go to the kitchen to find her.

Mrs. Aubrey looks up from the pot she's presiding over when she becomes aware of her. "Heard about your troubles, eh," she says. "Mr. Leo, he's gonna be alright then?"

"Laid up for awhile, but he'll be okay. How're you, Elsa?"

"'that mean I'll not get my vegetables from him next year?"

"I think he'll be good again by then to look after his garden. We could make a deal, Elsa. If he's not, I'll try to help and you give me another lesson on making gravy. Heaven knows, I need that more than you need our vegetables."

"What was he doing there anyway? All by himself at night?" She has stopped stirring the pot and is measuring Kate carefully when washing her hands.

"That's a long story, Elsa. I'll just get mad again thinking about it. Is John Martins here?"

"Pretty sure he's upstairs. Want me to go get him?"

"If you don't mind. I have to talk with him." She did well remembering to say 'have to' rather than what she meant. "And we'll be a while, Elsa."

"Sure thing, eh. Go see if you can find an empty table." She heads upstairs.

Kate can't quite shake a sense of apprehension when she sees John coming down the stairs, followed by Mrs. Aubrey. Disheveled jeans and shirt, bruises and scratches on a face in need of a shave—she likes the look.

"Kate, how's your father?" He's come over, albeit with some hesitation.

"They operated on him the same night. Lost a lot of blood. He's going to be all good again, it would seem, as of now." She gives him a long look. "Better, I think, than whoever is responsible for all this."

He manages a grin. "That may be so, if you're able to avoid unexpected results over possibly mixing human and canine medication. You'll have your hands full, nursing two of them."

She might. "Neither Blue nor my dad especially like to be fussed over that much. I'll be all right." Kate takes a breath. "Fortunately, if there was to be a mix-up, the two of them are not so different in their basic natures."

Mrs. Aubrey doesn't look amused. "Really now, that's nothing to be making jokes about, eh." Focusing on Kate for a long moment, she relaxes. "Why don't I make a fresh pot of coffee," she says, "and if there's anything else you want?"

"Kate?" John asks.

"No thanks, but maybe later, Elsa. We'll likely have a little something."

Sitting across from her now, John waits for Mrs. Aubrey to get back to the kitchen before he turns to look at the photo above his head that prominently features a dead deer and a smiling man.

"That's Jack Aubrey," she whispers. "He passed away a few months ago."

"Ah, 'the Mister'. He did a lot of killing." John too is whispering.

"Well, let's be fair," Kate says when she looks around more carefully to take note of the two distinctly differing types of photos adorning the walls. "But yes, I have to agree, he sure did like to hunt when not busy marrying Mrs. Aubrey and getting their wedding portraits taken."

John is nodding, but doesn't seem to have anything to say for the moment except, "Yes, yes." And then he apparently has an afterthought when he adds another "yes", but in a different tone.

ENIGMA IN BLUE

Kate doesn't mind...at all. "Anyway," says she, "I sure am glad you found my father. But we're all puzzled. My father...how could you have known where to look?"

"I've seen you wandering around down by the lake, remember?"

"Well..., but that's not where you went."

"That's where I was heading." He stops to raise the palm of his hand, indicating some small level of frustration. "That's where you were looking too, weren't you?"

"Yes, and we would have been looking in the wrong place. I still don't understand. How did you wind up at the other side?"

"If you think about it..." he halts for a moment, "I tried to tell Serafina that I don't work for United anymore, but she and the others made it clear—boy did they make it clear—I wasn't welcome on your property, so in a way maybe it's lucky the way it turned out. I knew approximately where the dividing line between the properties should be and that's the way I tried to go...over towards the lake, down the middle."

Kate takes a long look at his beat-up face. There's logic in this. Even Leo would be able to see that and she can feel herself become a little less tense. "Fortunately then, the way it....I'm going to put an end to all this anyway. I've called a surveyor and we've ordered some heavy fencing. It's either ours or theirs. Then I'll decide what the next step should be. I'm pretty sure it's ours and I'm going to start thinking about ways for them to start worrying for a change and that will end it all."

"Then I'll call you Kate of Good Hope from now on." He is trying to smile, but she's sure she sees a touch of concern mixed in. "It would be awkward under the circumstances, but anything I can do to help, if you can get yourself to trust me. In the meantime, I...I want you to be careful. There are some serious people around here, I don't have to tell you. That's all we need now, for you as well..."

I want you to? He had hesitated before saying that, but she had liked it. "I will. I am wondering—I mean to ask. Have you ever been in a spelling bee?"

"A spelling bee?" John shakes his head. "No. At school, some, but not in an organized spelling bee. Whatever makes you think of that?"

"Ah, no reason. I just wondered."

"No reason? Don't think I'd be very good at it either," he says. "I'm not that great at spelling."

"I know.... don't I know," she says and adds: "Inside joke."

John reaches over and puts his hand on hers. She looks up and very slowly takes her other hand to place it on his. "Kate of Good Hope," he says again and she thinks of that corny old line: "That was the moment she knew they would grow old together." What a nice sentiment, regardless of where it comes from. Kate feels her face twitching and now that she's in so deep already, she might as well just ask. "Should I like you, John?"

– 40 –

Young Leopold, shivering in the cool evening breeze, can see it from here. The angry-looking man with the large flashlight in his left hand is blocking the entrance to the hospital and simply won't let Mother inside. He can hear him too—everyone can. "You people... you just won't understand, will you. Can't you see for yourselves what the problem is? It's always the same. You can't just come here and expect services. We're totally filled up as is and you don't have proper credentials either. I know you're not even from around here anyway."

ENIGMA IN BLUE

Mother gives him a pleading look and tries again to brush by him—to no avail. Leo feels his grip on the handle of the baby carriage tighten when he sees his brother stomping his feet in anger on the first step to the hospital entrance just in front of him. Leo again looks at his baby half-brother struggling for breath in the carriage and sees him turning dark blue, even as his sister is trying to cool his forehead with a damp cloth as mother had told her. His face had started out bright red an hour ago. He had seemed so much better then.

Mother comes staggering back. Her face is pale and gaunt and there are tears. "He won't, he just won't," she says as she too holds onto the carriage. "What am I going to do?"

A very large man walks briskly past them towards the entrance but stops, turns around and comes over to look into the carriage. "This child needs help," he says and without hesitation he resolutely pushes the bouncing stroller up the stairs and heads towards the man at the door. When he gets there, he forces him aside decisively and opens the door by pushing against it with the stroller. As he does, Leo can hear him shout. "Nurse Katie! It's Nurse Katie that's required here!"

Leo is the last one to enter the building past the mean man and when he sees the stroller again, there's a nurse leaning over it. She raises one of her arms, demanding silence. Her body relaxes and Leo can hear her say in a clear voice. "Not to worry, all will be well."

When she turns around, young Leopold can plainly see—it is Nurse Katie.

"Nurse Katie."

"No."

"Nurse Katie," again he says.

"No, it's not. You should know by now. It's Margaret."

Leo starts to open his eyes. "Nurse," he says, "Nurse Margaret."

"You are hallucinating again?"

Leo reaches up with his left hand to feel the top of his head. "Geez, that damn morphine."

"That could do it, but you wouldn't want to do without it. You'd better try to get some solid sleep. I'm coming to the end of my shift. I'll see you tomorrow." She straightens the bedcover and turns off the light before she leaves.

He's alone again and turns the night light back on. Howe long did he sleep? Ten-thirty at night. They had told him which dial to turn to increase the dosage of the painkillers. He fiddles with it and turns it down. Not much movement left in the dial. It's probably all phony anyway. Just a "feel good" kinda gimmick; hard to believe they would just let you self-administer painkillers. Just as well he woke up when he did; a chance to clear his head before Tyler calls back. Should be anytime. A true dinosaur, about to become extinct, is Tyler. Hopefully not yet. It's been years since Leo last worked with him and he had not thought that he would ever need him again. But...

"Leo," he answers when the phone rings.

"Hey, cripple, you made it through the day."

"You should talk. You're forgetting, I was there. How many screws are you up to now? You can still move, can you?"

"Yeah, yeah, fuck you too, Leopold."

"It's no fun, Tyler, and you know I hate to lean on you."

"No sweat, Leo, I still owe you. I can be there this week."

"Do it. I hate it, but I need you right now."

"Can't say I'm totally surprised; always thought you'd find a way to get into trouble again. But not about fucking space-rocks. Christ. Anyway, that Curtis is high profile alright. I got a couple of things. He does a lot of hunting... stuff happens in the bushes."

"Cut it out, Tyler." He hesitates a moment while he shifts the phone to his other hand.

"You there, Leo?"

"Money, Tyler, the I.R.S. angle. Let's keep this in proper order. You still got your connection?"

"The I.R.S? You can't be serious. Fuck. But you'll be satisfied, I'll say that much. Let's leave it till I see you, okay? But if you have to, you can let him know; he's being painted either way. Is Kate still living at home?"

"Oh yes, but I want to keep her out of our arrangement. I'll owe you, Tyler, I'll see you then."

"I need another day and I'll be there. The I.R.S...fuck."

If Tyler has mellowed with age, it is not apparent from the way he talks. With him you always run the risk of getting into as much trouble as you're trying to get out of, Leo laughs to himself; but on balance you couldn't wish for better in a spot. Kate probably wouldn't remember him from the time they had spent in the Philippines; she was only four years old then. And so much of their time had been spent on the move, not always because they wanted it to be so. Leo will not talk about Tyler's involvement, let it be low key for now—he should really keep it to himself permanently if he can, though he would love for him to meet Kate now.

He turns the light off. Still no bad pain. Kate must be sleeping near Blue and Serafina has been a rock. To the islands—that's where they'll go as soon as everything settles down. Take the yacht and go. It is hurricane season right now. But she's a good boat now. They would find a hole in the weather. Kate, Serafina and the two cripples. Just go. Look at the sunset. Play poker. Stay up all night and count the stars. Fry my own bacon and eggs with beans in my sky-lounge. Catch a fish. Rolling, rolling, softly rolling, gentle waves...barely splashing...so warm...night...

It's his turn. He goes last because he drew the shortest stick. Mother lifts the last cooking pot from the coal-fire stove and adds the hot water to the bathtub standing on the kitchen floor. She feels the water and motions him to get in—the once-a-week Saturday night ritual before dinner. He will have to hurry. Uncle Aldo isn't home yet and he doesn't really want to be parading around naked in front of him.

And dinner they certainly deserved... at least his little brother and he did. They had done well in the last couple of days. The night before, they had gotten the coal and very, very early this morning they had provided for the bread. They did what they could to help out and had become quite proficient at stealing. The coal you got by having one boy climb on top of the slow-moving freight train, throwing coal over the side, while the other would stumble along and put as much in the sack as possible and then backtrack and collect the rest he missed.

Strands of copper wire for the purpose of bartering and fresh fruit from neighborhood gardens for the purpose of eating—the unauthorized gathering thereof—he didn't know too much about. That had become somewhat of a specialty for little brother. Securing bread was a little more complicated, but they had worked it out pretty well. They had befriended the son of the local baker just around the corner, and he would occasionally let them into the bakery and the store. Most of the time they didn't really steal bread—they stole coupons. Times were hard after the war and bread, among other things, was rationed. Coupons were easy to conceal and could also be converted into cash. So yes, they were certainly contributing.

When Uncle Aldo gets home, Leo knows right away; something is up. His large, once splendid leather briefcase is really stuffed and he has a big grin on his face. He takes a couple of chorus line dance steps and opens his briefcase—wieners, full of wieners. More wieners than you've ever seen in your life. He makes a chain of some of them, puts it around his neck and adds a few more steps. It doesn't matter that Uncle Aldo smells of dead animals. There's going to be a party.

ENIGMA IN BLUE

Uncle Aldo is not really his Uncle Aldo. Uncle Aldo is with Mother and has lived with them for over two years. He's a very nice, gentle man when he's not on a drinking binge. He may be collecting dead animals now, but he's no looser. According to rumor, his hand had once been shaken by Field Marshal Montgomery, commending him on his bravery. All the more remarkable, since they had been on opposite sides during the war. He is also said to have been a reserve goalie for the German national soccer team. Oh, yeah? Just try and become a reserve goalie for the German national soccer team.

Uncle Aldo worked for the Diseased Animal Processing Center and his job was to drive to farms and haul in dead animals to be converted mostly into soap, as far as Leo knew. But every now and then luck would strike. Or rather, lightning would strike. There was some method that the farmers and Uncle Aldo had developed whereby animals that had been put out of their misery as a result of broken limbs or had obviously been struck by lightning would be diverted, even though they weren't supposed to be, and turned into delicious food that was shared among a selected few.

It happened fairly frequently and, as luck would have it, it had happened just in time to turn that evening into a perfect Saturday evening. There had been plump, fat wieners everywhere and Leo had slept solidly on that excellent night.

– 41 –

As Kate turns to drive towards the parking lot of the roadside doughnut shop, her thoughts momentarily drift to the time John had said he had first seen her there with Blue and she smiles briefly. She doesn't really expect to recognize Tyler Malone, but with only a few vehicles she can see from a distance and him having said on the phone he would stay outside and wait for her, she's not worried about finding him; perhaps just a bit about what would follow after she did.

She had first been surprised when he called. That was followed by a sense of apprehension and finally a feeling of relief and anticipation when she realized that Uncle Tyler—she has decided to call him that—shared some of her concerns about Leo, his present condition and good judgement.

Maneuvering into a parking space furthest away from the entrance of the doughnut shop, she becomes aware of the tall man near the edge of the parking lot on the other side, getting up from a bench by a picnic table to look in her direction. Stepping out of the car, she sees him motion to her with one of his two cups and, walking slowly towards him, she begins to make out some familiar features and all of it helps to diminish her level of anxiety. While clearly younger than Leo, he's not as tall as she remembers, nor is his hair as dark and tidy or are his shoulders as broad; but that element of mischief in his eyes is comforting, unmistakable even after all this time.

"My my, Kate, would you look at you." He firmly shakes her hand.

"You remember me then, Uncle Tyler?"

He hands her one of the coffees. "You mind sitting out here, Kate, it's nice enough. Do I remember you? Not like this, I don't. I'm sure one could say the same about me, only in a different way. '*La vie continue*'."

"Well, for some reason, I don't remember much at all about the Philippines. There is this one thing I often think of... it sometimes runs through my mind. A truck."

"A truck?"

"A truck." Kate twists the lid off her cup and has a sip. "Bouncing around for hours and hours on dirt roads with Dad and you. Fast sometimes, and more than once. Was there...was there a particular reason for that, Uncle Tyler?"

Tyler Malone is grinning. "Was there a reason? You could say that." He tugs on his pony-tail. "But...even now, Kate, it wouldn't be good to go on about it, trust me. However, it does relate vaguely to what you are...we are worried about. None of us are what we used to be, although in Leo's case..." He stops, nodding as if in thought.

"I need this to be between us, Uncle Tyler, but it is getting to be more difficult for me to know when Leo is drifting off out there and when it is convenient for him to just pretend. And with what's going on right now. It is not your problem and I–"

"Oh no, Kate, that's why I'm here. It's not that easy for me either to be talking with you and Leo not knowing about it. I won't claim that Leo and I are best friends—you would know, he is a hard man to get close to. But to say that we owe each other a lot, I mean everything—and I'm not speaking about riches—that would not be an exaggeration. I think you have good reason to worry about his, as I see it, increasing pacifist tendencies. He would have me...well, never mind. But know this. Once we become proactive, if that turns out to be necessary, there may not be a way to turn back. You understand that?"

Kate wraps the open jacket more tightly around her shoulders to ward off a sudden chill. "I am aware of the concept—unintended consequences. But I'm guessing that you're talking about consequences—period—intended or not. Right? All the more reason to keep everyone else out of this if possible. I'll do what I can, short of...no, short of nothing." Kate lifts her cup in an effort to hide her lips. "I will trust you, Uncle Tyler, Dad only ever said good things about you. I do wish he wasn't so dead-set against it, but maybe there is a discreet way to involve the authorities?" She carefully keeps her focus on Tyler, looking for some kind of reaction. It isn't there, at least not in any way she can discern. "I really do need something good to happen...soon."

"Let me have the day. I do believe we see eye to eye. Kate, Kate, a fortunate man is Leopold Walter."

For some inexplicable reason Uncle Tyler is laughing when they walk back to her car, trying to suppress it only momentarily when they pass by two men standing by a van. "We've been in tougher spots than this, Kate. Ask Leo. Actually, don't ask Leo. I may be laughing now, but being chased by angry old ladies dressed in black. It wasn't so funny then."

"You are not going to explain this, are you, Uncle Tyler?"

"No Kate... no."

When Kate drives off and gets another look at a smiling Tyler, an idea—a thought she's sure she would never really want an answer to—runs through her head without upsetting her. Did Leo with Tyler's help rescue or steal me from some institution?

— 42 —

What's wrong with this creepy retard anyway, Ely wonders. It had just happened a second time; different bitch, but more or less the same result. The tall, dark-haired slut, clad only in panties, had first lingered in front of the asshole on his left for a long time while he had been staring at her, then lifted his beer bottle and shaken his head. She had turned to him and put her hand on his shoulder. "Are you ready for me, honey?" She hadn't been his type at all, but he had been courteous anyway without showing too much of his sensitive side. "No."

She had barely looked at the fucker on his right and then moved on. Damn, he'd thought, he wasn't that ugly. Just because he wasn't drinking? He had kept taking swigs from his water bottle. "Fucking liver," he had said earlier when Ely had looked at him after he ordered water. That large, triangular birthmark under his left eye—is that what puts the bitches off?

The guy had been sitting at the row of tables, facing the bar. When the seat on Ely's left opened up, he had quickly moved over.

The strip-bar is crowded and you do get a much better view from here, if you turn your seat around. Occasionally, one of the strippers would climb up on the bar, but mostly they would be at the opposite side, on either the small stage or grinding away at one of the customers. It's loud in here and Aholl is moving his upper body along with the beat.

"Curtis didn't say anything to you, did he?" Ely asks and when the small man doesn't acknowledge him and keeps on bobbing to the beat, he shouts. "Did he talk to you?"

The asshole twists his head a little and gives him a dumb look.

"Did fucking Curtis say anything to you? I saw you talking with him. You? You don't even speak good fucking English."

Aholl shakes his head and turns his attention back to the dancers.

"I don't like it," Ely says as his eyes follow a full-bodied blonde girl who moves slowly nearby, looking for action. "Now...now he says security security, strictly security. And we shouldn't have listened to fucking Martins. They better not take me for a fucking idiot. I know about shit."

Aholl's face makes him think of a dead fucking fish, the way he is leering at him. He cranks his head to the right and is now looking directly at the face of the ugly man with that birthmark who seems to have focused on the fat bitch along with him. He takes another swig from his water bottle and gives him an approving grin. At least he agrees with his taste in women, but he'll be lucky to get any, the way he's going.

On his left there's no sign of consciousness, other than the bobbing and weaving. Fucking asshole. Sometimes he would be better off talking to the wall. "That Epstein bitch too. She says we fucked up—Martins and us. I don't like it."

Now he sees Aholl balance his beer bottle on the back of his right hand, but for some reason he seems to be even more preoccupied with the shoe on his left foot he has stuck out. "Are you listening to me?" Guess not, he's busy. "Maybe we should just get the hell out of here." That gets the asshole's attention. He grabs hold of the beer bottle and drops his foot while shaking his head vehemently before he turns his attention back to the dancers. Ely is getting real mad. "Not here, you idiot," he shouts, "I mean get out of this fucking country."

Aholl gives him a quick glance and then carefully looks around the room. When he's finished his review, he turns his gaze back to him and to Ely's amazement he makes a speech.

"Not me," the asshole shakes his head, "I like this smell of sweat and piss and ganja. What a country, eh?"

The man on the right seems to agree. He reaches around Ely and salutes Aholl by tapping his water bottle against the asshole's beer bottle.

– 43 –

With not everyone around the Walter homestead fully aware of the relative scarcity of Jamaican fresh farm produce in the Canadian woodlands, it had from the outset looked like it was going to be a busy day. Kate, with Serafina's help, had started out by walking Blue around outside. They had fashioned a sling from an old scarf and used it under Blue's belly to support him and it had worked surprisingly well. They'd then spent an hour in the barn, though Kate knew they hadn't been useful.

They had also made the time to go along with Manuel to look at the new fence enclosure. A metal chain-link fence with round posts, sturdy enough. It doesn't have a gate and you would have to climb over to get inside. The surveyor had confirmed; the site was on their land—just barely—but on their side of the line. One of the Colombians, the older one with the grey mustache, the one they call Alfonso, had been there. Apparently, they were taking turns keeping an eye on the area.

Serafina had been eager—as well she should have been—to get back to the kitchen and her red pea soup to be. Kate hadn't realized it at first, but it had become increasingly clear that making good red pea soup is not an easy undertaking. Serafina had studied recipes on the Internet to refresh her memory and had been able to round up all the ingredients, except the one she needed the most—country pepper. She had made several phone calls, starting last evening, followed by additional frantic ones this morning and finally located some. Manuel had, after momentarily looking at them in disbelief, good-heartedly driven a long way to get them.

And Sam had called earlier. Would she ask Leo when he should go and visit him? "And tell him it works fine. It might cheer him up."

"It does?"

"The correction process for the oval disk," Sam had said. "You know, the one where we couldn't beat the eleven percent fall-out rate? Point eight percent, Kate!"

It's not Katie, but better than Miss Walter. And she knew what he was saying about the fall-out rate. For sure, Dad would be pleased—that is a massive improvement.

She had been there when Wally, one of Sam's technicians, had come to see Leo. "We're not getting there," Wally had said. "We just can't get them to an acceptable level the way we're going now."

"Why not make them all wrong, I mean smaller, and reshape them," she, Kate, had suggested.

Wally had looked puzzled, but Dad had seemed interested and then deliberate when he said. "We're fighting thermal variations, changes in the base metal and variables in the stresses that come from the staking and changes in the tooling. I agree—we won't get it this way. We make all the grooves too small, quite a bit too small, that's what you're saying, Kate? We do have to move some metal. The automated measuring and sorting is fast, I know, but it doesn't make up for that rejection rate. Ja, Kate, we'd beef up the whole test rig and add a second wheel, strong enough to open and reshape a smaller groove, and do that consecutively with measuring it on the same rig and see what happens."

Wally had started to look interested at that point. "Not much to lose," he'd said. "I could even try that experimentally on a lathe...real simple. You want me to do that, Mr. Leo?"

"Good thinking, Wally." 'Mr. Leo' had kept moving his head in apparent total agreement with himself and after a long look at her had stated the following. "Eh, Kate, you want us to make them all wrong. I think I like it."

He should have. He had rationalized everything well with detailed words, but that didn't change the fact that the core thought was her realization that most materials were like springs to varying degrees. And that in order to manipulate them you had best pounce on them rather than fiddle in their springy range. Kind of like unruly puppies: not that she had ever actually known any.

Wally too must be proud.

"We're kind of in the same boat," she hears Serafina say from the kitchen. She strokes Blue another time and goes over to where Serafina's finishing up with the dumplings as the whole house now smells like a Jamaican kitchen; not at all bad.

"I know what you're getting at," says Kate, "running into that Sinclair lady. That would be a one in a million coincidence."

"Think of it. John Martins goes exactly to where Leo is trapped and I run into a friend of Marshal Curtis, just like that. Really too much of a coincidence." She shakes her head and stirs the pot. "If you ask me, she's either a fabulous actress or her affection and admiration for that Curtis guy is genuine. Well, could be both. Maybe we're missing something with her being an investigative reporter. Are you sure you understand that John...?"

"Oh no, not again." Kate stops helping with the cleanup. "Enough already, you guys are going to start getting to me. I've asked this before. Please try to see the difference between John the man and other bad acts. This is not easy for me, can't you see that. I trust you, so why can't—"

"Oh, calm down already. In any event"—Serafina is ladling the soup into the thermos—"if you cosmic geniuses are right, none of this will matter in time and all will blend well in the end. Just like my soup here, right Kate? Are we all set? Cigarettes and lighter? The books, Kate."

"I've done my part. Got it all. You did put the baseball bat in the trunk, didn't you?" Kate waits for Serafina to nod. "Let's get going then. Remember, if we get caught, you're the head of this gang. I think that would be self-evident anyway."

Blue's eyes follow her when they leave and she's comforted by the knowledge that he is such an intelligent dog. He no doubt knows that she is leaving only because she has to; hasn't he always had more sense than certain people she knows.

— 44 —

"Tell me when it's high enough?" Kate is carefully raising her father's hospital headboard.

"That's good. Ja." He's grinning gratefully. Like a little boy, thinks Kate, or is it more like a senile old man?

Serafina is vigilantly stationed in front of the door. "Don't you move," Kate says and puts the large cup of the red pea soup in front of him. He's already holding a spoon. "Hmm," he says and looks around her to nod at Serafina. It may be worse than she thought; a senile little boy.

"Two days at best," Serafina says. "That's what they said at the nurses' station, before you might get into a wheelchair."

It's not difficult to see—Leo is straining to analyze if that is good or bad news. "We better find a good hiding place for the cigarettes then," he says, "these nurses don't miss much."

"Who was that guy, Leo?" asks Serafina.

"What guy?"

"The older man we saw coming out of your room when we came up," Kate is probing, looking away. "I only saw him at a distance. He moves funny, as if in pain. I can't figure it, but there's something familiar about him."

"You're sure it was my room?"

"Dad!"

"I can smell it," says Serafina. "Do they use stale cigar smoke in hospitals as a cologne now? The tall guy with the pony-tail."

"Oh, now I know who you might mean. We go way back, that's an old friend. He just happens to be up here from the States. He's a good man."

Kate is quiet certain that Leo is not totally coherent at the moment, having imaginary friends now and everything. Friends, not associates. Even Tyler had not claimed to be a close friend. But that is precisely why this may be a good time to deal with her own priority.

"John says so himself, I didn't have to press. He screwed up, he made a mistake."

"That's an easy thing to say, Kate. There's no cost attached to this talk." She sees him look with concern at Serafina. "Hell, I would probably say that if I was after something. It's all everybody else's fault now, is it?"

"No." Kate is forceful. She's not the one showing symptoms of senility. "He did warn me before and now he won't talk about the others anymore. He says he messed up and he's not blaming anybody."

Leo finishes up the last of the soup by drinking it out of the cup and looks directly at her. At least what she said about John not blaming others seems to have made some positive impression on him, but almost immediately she can see his mind wandering off to something more important.

"What I wouldn't give for a cigarette now." He is grimacing with pain and Kate is about to lecture him on how little she cares when she notices Serafina struggling at the door.

"Somebody," she whispers.

Kate just manages to hide everything under a towel she has kept handy as a nurse opens the door and walks towards the bed, then stops and walks back. Reaching for the door, she looks back with a big grin. "Pepper-pot soup, is it? You'll have to share the next time, you know."

A close call and a fortunate break to have gotten this nicely unprofessional nurse, Kate realizes when she decides to give Serafina and Leo some time alone. She's going to step out for a while and bring back tea. Does Serafina want anything?

"Something cool and fresh. A beer for Leo and an extra dry martini for me," says she.

"I'll look for the alcohol dispensary."

It's a large hospital and she takes the elevator down. As she walks through the hallways, she remembers that she's thought this before—something about hospitals she likes. Everything is real. You screw up at the office, no problem. Leave your car in a no-parking zone, so what? Lose your house keys? Big deal. Mix up the oil line with the water line? Overcharge or undercharge? Send your boss to the wrong location? Blow money instead of making it? You could get fired. Here, the consequences could be death—or worse. That difference is so visible to her and there's just something about this intensity in a hospital.

Intensity. This may not be so different from what her space troopers are experiencing on the fringes of the universe. Decidedly on the fringes—beyond, in fact.

It's a crisp fall day, but Kate doesn't mind. She has taken her tea outside and is sitting on the stone edge of one of the flower beds gracing the entrance to the hospital, scouting out Leo's future smoking environment. It's like a little club. There are visitors, nurses, doctors and patients and they're smoking. Maybe they shouldn't be, as some of them look already dead if it weren't for the smoke rising from them, but they are. Leo will blend right in. The fact that they tend to be on the sociable side will just mean that he has to act completely disturbed to fend them off. Shouldn't be that difficult for him.

Kate leafs through her note pad another time. She has a couple of days before the next meeting, but she'd best get her head straight. Decisions will have to be made. The communication from the team had in many ways been reassuring, but there is one aspect that gives her reason for concern. The document had been well structured and detailed and had been signed by the three principals who had assumed leadership roles and was initialed by the still remaining twelve members of the expedition. Herman had addressed technical issues, Goro had handled supplies, and Louise had dealt extensively with moral, ethical and other interpersonal subjects.

Much of what they had anticipated turned out to be true, Herman reported. And a good thing it was, he had emphasized. Without the worm-holes and the shortcuts they could never have made it as far as they did. He was concerned that apparently, due to the speed at which they had been traveling, they had all gotten a little younger and taller by an average of three centimeters. But then, that was not totally unexpected—Jacob had predicted so correctly, except his number had been two centimeters. Kate did not totally believe either number as she had conned Leo—without disclosing her purpose—into calculating with her that very proposition and came up with less than one centimeter. They were all perfectly recognizable still, Herman had assured her, so there was no cause for alarm yet.

And yes, they had gotten to that tiny spot in the sky that had been photographed from near the earth at a distance of some thirteen billion light years and had gone well beyond there. Naturally, it all looked very different there now. And, no, they had not found a wall. Goro and Louise might want to address in greater detail what they had found and he, Herman, was prepared to continue the journey and would await further instructions.

Goro had seemed downright giddy in his section of the document. He went out of his way to compliment Herman on his clever ways of traveling efficiently while allowing plenty of opportunity for rest stops and exploration and opportunities to stock up on fresh supplies. He, Goro, had fashioned a larger pouch and was stuffing it with samples of almost everything that they had found or had been given. And he was going to bring it back with him. "You will not believe it, Miss Kate!!" He had written in quotation marks and finished it off with exclamation marks.

She is just so relieved that Goro and his handful of supporters had taken her declining of their request for start-up valuables in such good spirits and have seemingly gotten over the initial disappointment.

And yes indeed, well beyond the place where they had half expected there might be a wall, they had come across a piece of material that looked just an awful lot like the one that she had found; and that would definitely be coming back with them. So from that point alone he had written: "Mission accomplished." But Goro had refrained from offering an opinion as to whether they should continue or not on the same path.

It was here that Kate had come to the place where she had started to worry some—Louise. And it definitely wasn't that Louise hadn't been dedicated or intensely involved. On the contrary, perhaps too much so. Not that it came as a surprise, but Kate had already gotten the impression from something Herman had written that she was the one who did most of the interacting with the inhabitants they had encountered along the way.

And Louise herself had enthusiastically written about it. Not only about her own efforts to network, but also the fact that she had encouraged all members of the team to interact with one another while traveling and with the inhabitants wherever they found them.

As "fertile ground," she had at one point described the universe. No hostility to be found anywhere. All the stories about space monsters and nasty aliens: not true! Everyone, simply everyone, seemed to be very nice. And it didn't seem to matter how strange some of them looked, how big they were or how tiny. Or what language they spoke; or whether they flew or crawled or walked or skipped; they all seemed to have one thing in common. They were preoccupied with basic survival and play. "A little like old children," Louise had complained, "if you can imagine that." Oh yes, Kate could imagine that.

So, Louise, according to her own words, had taken it upon herself to educate everyone, willing to listen or not, about the benefits of introspection, self-analysis, the search for the meaning of everything and especially the joys to be derived from discovering what you are and how you are as a result of your relationships with everyone else around you. Louise had, in fact, written down with obvious pride for Kate's benefit a summary statement she had come to use at the end of every one of her little lectures, when addressing the

Flying Children, the puppies and the aliens about the wisdom of "often" putting aside practical matters for a time and doing what she deemed to be of greater importance.

And that is precisely what concerned Kate. Really, this had never been intended as a missionary effort and there must be dangers lurking out there. What if the gang started to lose focus and got themselves into trouble? She was going to have to deal with this. In consultation, naturally. But she certainly wasn't looking forward to that. It would bring up the old question again—what is more important? The single individual? The common good? Her dad had wrestled with that and so had she, but a group is composed of many "ones." That's what one of the Flying Children had said. How can you argue with that? A real dilemma.

On her way back up in the elevator, Kate's positive impressions of hospital environments are further enhanced. A well-dressed, handsome gentleman and a frail-looking, older man are riding with her, going to the same floor. To Kate, they represent the epitome of that dedicated, purposeful image appropriate for this location. Yet they both take the time to give her a friendly smile; more than one in the case of the younger man—three times in fact.

"I hope all will be well for you, young lady, and I wish you a great afternoon," he says when the elevator door opens. He hesitates for a moment with a fourth smile before he and the older man head in the opposite direction towards the nurses' station. Probably a top administrator and a rich retired doctor, who has become a benefactor.

She finds Serafina sitting on the edge of the bed, straightening Leo's hair with her hand as he tells her that he's been having dreams or been daydreaming. "It's that damn morphine, I'm sure. Sometimes it's hard to tell; it's always about things from when I was young."

Kate too is about to sit on the edge of the other side of the bed when the door opens and she sees the two men who had been in the elevator with her.

"Wrong room," says Serafina.

The younger man shakes his head and keeps guiding the small figure ahead of him. "I hope you don't mind," he says. "This is my dear friend and spiritual advisor, Dr. Matthew Surtees. You may know of him from his articles on theology." There, she wasn't so wrong, thinks Kate as the old man bows courteously while the administrator pauses before he says, "I am Marshal Curtis."

Serafina immediately gets up and rushes to the middle of the room. Kate is momentarily stunned and looks at her father who has no particular expression on his face.

"I'm going to get security," Kate says, having composed herself and now also standing. "You must be out of your—"

Curtis is just so quick to interject. "I beg you; just give us a moment of your time, please. I think you will be interested in what we have come to say."

"Dad?" she asks, but starts to feel isolated when she sees Leo nod meekly, even as the two men are coming fully into the room. Serafina is no help either at the moment. She's moved one of the chairs for Surtees and is leaning against Leo's bed. In her case it has to be that damn curiosity of hers.

"This is so very difficult for me," says a concerned looking Curtis. "There has been an awful misunderstanding. I never intended for any of this unnecessary aggression to take place and I feel so bad about your accident, Mr. Walter." Curtis comes still closer towards the bed and Leo doesn't seem to mind, although he keeps his focus on him.

"I'm as much a victim as you are." Curtis seems to feel encouraged. "I trusted some people working for me who used very bad judgment and have been disloyal. I have already taken steps—"

Kate is about to erupt, but Leo again raises his hand slightly to look at her. It's a long, somewhat pleading look and she thinks she understands—he would like them to let him take the lead in this. She'll see how that goes for the moment, but really doesn't want to.

She can sense Curtis becoming more and more comfortable with Leo. His whole demeanor tells her that he has given up on Serafina and her and that he is directing all his energy at Leo now.

"I know of course that this material was found on your property," he says, "there's never been any question about that. From my point of view, it wouldn't really matter where it was found. The profound issues raised are just too important. As you may know, we own a publication that has been dealing with the nature of the universe; and just in case this find somehow enters into the understanding of the cosmos, well, you can see... it would be most timely and convenient to connect the two."

She has to watch Leo nod his head again.

"Any prestige resulting from the find I would be more than happy to share," Curtis continues, "and absolutely compensate you in any way you wish. I pray you'll not think me presumptuous when I say that men like you and me, Mr. Walter, have no business being at odds over anything. Quite the contrary. I've come to respect you and be amazed at the numerous parallels in our respective ways of conducting worldly affairs. I, for one, would be very comfortable collaborating with you in business as well."

"Aye yi," quips Serafina, but is ignored as Leo asks. "Kind of like a team?"

"Indeed, Mr. Walter. And there's another reason for our interest in this find and its possible implications." Curtis walks over to Surtees and puts both hands on his shoulders. "You're much better qualified than I am, Matthew. Why don't you elaborate?"

The opportunity seems to really please the doctor. "My interest in all of this only deals with the position of the Mother Church.

Excessive speculation and wild rumors can only be unsettling, don't you think? The church has good reason for discouraging research into anything that might have preceded the Big Bang, wouldn't you agree?"

Oh no—that much Kate knows for sure—Leo doesn't agree. "You're trying to tell me that organized religion has something to do with that rock in the ground?" he asks, shaking his head.

Dr. Surtees seems just a little perturbed and leans forward. "Are you a godless man?" he asks, his eyes widening.

"Godless? That depends on how you look at it," Leo says. "Godless? I definitely don't... but maybe this is not the time..."

Why is he engaging the old man at all in a discussion about religion under these circumstances? She can see well enough that he actually likes the old man, but still...? He's been talking softly and quietly. Maybe he's getting tired. Is it the morphine?

Marshal Curtis seems content to just listen for now and he's smiling.

"Don't you believe in a higher power then at all?" Dr. Surtees keeps probing. There is no outward hostility in him, but there is stern curiosity. And Kate thinks she'd caught a flash of anger coming from the wrinkled face. He might well have been a tiger in his younger days.

"I don't." Leo looks tired, but Surtees won't let up and gets him to finish by leaning forward again in his intense way. "I believe that the concept of God and godliness is just that; a concept within the reach of all reasoning creatures. It is one's own sense of goodness and fairness. The responsibility for being true to that sense is within every one of us individually."

Kate is looking at Serafina who is rolling her eyes. Is this coming to an end? Not yet.

"That's the easy way, isn't it?" Dr. Surtees says with a sad demeanor.

"I don't believe that. Just the opposite. I blame no..." Leo pauses, shaking his head as though he realizes it's been going on for too long. "The burden is on me and you." He looks around. "All of us."

This is not going well. Dad had at times mildly encouraged her to find comfort in organized religion, if she so wished, in spite of his own beliefs. She knows what he is talking about. But here and now? She is looking at the person who is probably responsible for putting him and Blue in the hospital. Yet, given Leopold's logic, this room may well be filled with gods. Kate studies the face of Marshal Curtis and then sees Leo fumble for the button to raise the back of his bed a little more.

"Could you leave Mr. Curtis and me to talk alone for a few minutes? Do you mind?"

"Yes I do," Kate says without hesitation. Serafina too is reluctant, biting her lips, but taking one hesitant step.

"You stay then, Kate. If that's all right with you, Serafina?" He is using his pleading boy look and Serafina nods reluctantly.

Curtis touches Surtees's arm as he passes by him to leave the room, seemingly indicating to all observers his willingness to support the old man physically if need be.

"Well, we don't agree on everything," Curtis says, "most assuredly not on what it means to be human—but I feel that we've done much to improve our understanding of one another, Leo. I may call you Leo?" Leo nods and motions him to come and sit closer still on the chair that Surtees had just vacated.

"We are evolving into quite the inextricable team here, Marshal," Leo says. "Let's make certain that there are no further misunderstandings."

"Dad," she again protests.

He maintains his focus on Curtis. "I will admit, there are aspects to your version of reality that frighten me. Your apparent unshakeable conviction that you are a man of consequence and destiny. And just as I'm revisiting my view of mankind's possible position as the crowning jewel of evolution... here you are. Add to this the fact that you probably can't take us seriously at the moment—it worries me a lot."

Leo is glancing at his legs as Curtis gets up from the chair.

"I see you looking down at me. I seem pathetic to you, do I? Are you a father, Curtis? No... let's still try to be on the same wavelength. Get used to thinking of me and my camp as your shadow. The one you can't get rid of unless you stay far, far away or do the right thing and die." Leo is straining, trying to lift his upper body. "I'm getting old and consequences to me are not necessarily the same as they might be to you. Don't expect me to play by your rules or run to the law. No no... I'm still talking. If you ever harm or even get near any of my family again—I warn you, I'll come at you in ways you've never even thought of. You hear me?"

"I would advise you to be more careful about what you're saying before it's altogether too late." Curtis takes a step back, pressing his lips together. "You may think you know what you're dealing with. You couldn't possibly understand me or what you're up against. Others before you have tried."

"You made my daughter look over her shoulder, you son of a bitch, now it's your turn. Have a look in a mirror; that orange spot on your forehead is laser paint. You get that?"

Seeing the way Curtis again looks at Leo's legs, Kate steps up to face Curtis. "My Dad is not the only one you need to worry about, if that's what you are thinking—"

"Kate—"

"And you hurt my dog," Kate shouts over Leo's voice. "You ought to be ashamed, taking advantage of that old... and my Father... you get away from us, bad things are going to happen." Seeing Leo grimacing with his eyes wide open, she again faces the man. "We may not be as helpless as you believe! Think about that..."

"You won't be able to say I didn't try to make peace," Curtis says. "And your—shadow—metaphor is well chosen, Mr. Walter, if that's what it is. Next time you think of it, you may want to consider that others too cast a shadow." Marshal Curtis is grim-faced now, but still doesn't appear intimidated when heading for the door.

– 45 –

Serafina had not been too pleased to leave the room, but realized that Leo must have had his reason and she worried that she knew what that was. He didn't want her to be in a position to know. If she was going to blackmail or threaten someone, she wouldn't want witnesses around either. He had let Kate stay, probably in the mistaken belief that a daughter wouldn't have to testify against a father. Serafina is pretty sure that this is true only of husband and wife.

It's been awkward for Dr. Surtees and her, alone in the open visitors' lounge at the end of the hallway, alternately looking towards the door to Leo's room and one another. He had tried to start a conversation, but she had not thought it smart to respond.

Maybe that was wrong. What if he was exactly what Curtis said he was...a spiritual advisor? He looked like it, but did he have any influence? For certain, the longer this ego battle went on, the more important it would be for someone on the other side to understand the mindset of Leo. And Kate too was not likely to depart from her father's way of thinking—or her grandfather's for that matter—a man she has talked about with considerable pride. Ha! Grandpa...As immutable she had described with pride Leo's father, a man he had lost contact with since age four and rarely spoke of. Even that description using the word "Immutable" likely being an understatement to Kate's way of thinking. What can you say about a soldier so determined to try and time a hand grenade to such perfection as to pull the pin and hold on to it long enough to have it blow off his hand? Never mind Leo's cautions that there may have been a malfunction or possible issues with counting. Grandpa had apparently shown other signs of that Walter stubbornness when confronted by well-meaning and pragmatic representatives of the authorities. "Absolutely not" had been his response—as relayed by Grandma—to the suggestion that he do away with himself. He had evidently not agreed that as a cripple he could best continue to serve his country and the war effort by relieving it from the burden of looking after him.

Add to all that the possibility that Leo and Kate, with their chosen lifestyle of relative isolation in the country and their tendency to avoid human company, could easily be taken as naïve. Not a good thing, even if not altogether wrong.

If Leo were to say to Curtis, "I'm going to..." would Curtis believe that Leo was going to? She doesn't think that Leo ever would, but is quite convinced that he is capable of pulling a trigger. Never mind the little blood already spilled. But endangering Kate and trying to impose your will on Leo? A toxic mix all around, yet one she would ordinarily not be that uncomfortable with, if not for the proximity to people she cares about.

She has just checked the corridor again, looks directly at Surtees and asks. "Are you certain you understand what is really going on here?"

He appears relieved that she is talking now and has brightened right up. He seems to be carefully considering his response. "I am so cold," he answers, "you too? I think they always keep the temperature down in hospitals, Miss Gomez."

"Hmm... I meant about Marshal Curtis."

ENIGMA IN BLUE

"Oh yes, yes, yes, Miss Gomez, much good is done through the Foundation. Marshal, you must know, is an exceedingly generous man. I will soon be heading for Louisiana on a special mission for the United Foundation."

She decides to quit while she's ahead. Well... not ahead; even, maybe. "You should find the climate there more to your liking," she says and gets up to check the corridor once more as he replies, "Yes, it can get downright nasty up here."

You can say that again, thinks she. Just as well we're in a hospital. This poor little man is wasting away right in front of me and may die right here and now. The goofs down the hall are taking too long.

"Anyway," she giggles, trying to comfort and reassure the frail man, "Leopold Walter is really a kind and thoughtful man and didn't mean to offend you. Believe me."

"Not at all, dear lady. Our hearts have grown big enough over the years."

Not much room for anything else then, she thinks—and his heart she believes. "But here comes Mr. Curtis."

He walks past them briskly, seemingly unaware of her or the doctor who gives her a little wave as he struggles to catch up with Curtis.

"Anybody want to tell me what happened?" she asks when she gets back into the room. "He just stormed by me."

Leo doesn't answer and just looks at Kate. "Dad asked him not to bother us anymore and to stay away from now on," she says.

"That's it?"

"Well, Dad tried to tell him in his own way."

"Me Kate, me? What about you, Kate? Wish I could go home with you right now," Leo says. "You think we could arrange that? Whatever you do, keep away from them. The man has complex needs. Hard to predict is he. I fear this will not be the last we'll hear of him. He too uses his own rulebook, I'm sure." Leo frowns. "Still, he'll make another mistake, if he hasn't already done so. What I said still goes, Kate. We give the man a quarter of an acre for all I care and let's find a way... the old man, I feel bad for him."

"Make sure you remember what you said," Kate says. "If I decide it's the best thing all around, I might do just that. Right now, I'll say this; that is the furthest thing from my mind."

This would certainly qualify as one approach to conflict resolution, thinks Serafina. Whenever people try to kill you, give them some of your land. "I don't believe that, about him being a victim too. That Ruby lady said that as well, but I just don't believe it."

"John Martins screwed up," Kate adds, "but there's no way he would get involved in things like this, hurting people, hurting Blue. No way."

"Maybe not knowingly. We still have to be careful about that, Kate," Leo says. "But I kind of feel the same way. Maybe you want to bring him along when you come again and we can talk about this?"

She sees Kate's face light up. "Yes, Dad, that I can arrange."

Three cheers for young love, and she'll bake the cake. But just now she has noticed Leo twisting and turning and moving around on the bed quite a bit. "It's starting to hurt more, is it?"

"Nah." He's trying to smile. "You see this as a negative thing, but it may all turn out for the better."

"How could that be?" she asks, preparing for a bit of twisted logic that she's probably going to have to endure.

"After my left leg got busted, I started to limp. I think there's a good chance that, after this one heals up, I'm going to walk straight again. Balanced, do you see?"

Well, I did ask she concludes when she sees the door open and a nurse stick her head in. "There's a Mr. Coulter here, he needs to see you. Are you up to it?"

"Coulter?" Leo says. "I don't even know who that would be. I'm up to it, but not today."

ENIGMA IN BLUE

The door opens wider as a man pushes his way past the nurse. Just a bit too pragmatic at times is Leo, Serafina speculates, when she gets a good look at the man; isn't it premature for consultations with an undertaker? He's of medium height, in his forties, neatly dressed in a dark suit and carrying a coat over his arm. There's a prominent birthmark of a triangular shape under his left eye. "I'm afraid you don't really have much of a choice," he says, "Inspector Coulter, R.C.M.P. You're Mr. Walter, right?" He takes another step in Kate's direction. "Miss Walter, correct?"

"Ah...yes," she stutters.

Now he looks her way. "And you are?"

"Serafina Gomez."

"You are...?"

"A friend, a family friend."

He steps closer to the bed and talks to Leo directly. "I'm going to try and not take too much of your time today because of your condition, but we're going to need statements from all of you."

"About?" Leo asks.

Inspector Coulter seems to be trying to contain a grin. "You're joking, right? What are you people thinking? You can't just—"

"But we didn't do anything," she hears Kate cleverly protest. "Can't you see? We're the ones who have been hurt."

"I can see that," the now grinning Inspector says. "But that doesn't mean you're off the hook. How about trespassing, to begin with?"

"I didn't," Leo says. Kate doesn't respond and she isn't going to say anything either.

"How did you even know about these troubles?" Leo asks.

"You can't be admitted into a hospital, for starters, all chopped up with wire cuts on your legs, without somebody notifying the authorities. I didn't come here riding on a horse. These are not the old frontier days. Anyway, we have a pretty good idea of what's been going on and two of the people have already been arrested."

"That nasty little man," Serafina says, "right?"

"Uh huh," the inspector nods. "Dubzak."

"And the big Balkan guy," she probes after hesitating.

"No, not Ely Greguric, we're still looking for him."

"But Curtis was just here," Leo says.

"Not Marshal Curtis," the inspector says, "but he'll be questioned too. John Martins—he's in custody."

Serafina sees Kate sag and ask, "John? What did he do?"

"There are issues with hunting regulations, trespassing and wire fraud. These are not matters to be laughed at. We know about your treasure site too. You'd best all stay away from there until this situation gets sorted out. I'm going to leave now, but this will not be the end of this. Be prepared to answer more questions and stop doing whatever it is you think you are doing. This is now a police matter and your foolish game is over. Do you understand that now?" The inspector is not grinning anymore and with his hand on the door carefully measures all of them. "Anything you want to tell me about the disappearance of the Balkan man?" He waits for an answer. "Am I to take that as a no?" No answer. "I'll take it as a no for now, but I'd advise you to think hard before you answer this question again and make matters worse. Take my word. It is out of the ordinary for me to be here, I'm trying to help you, whether you can see that or not. Take advantage of your good fortune. Don't do anything else, I urge you."

When he's gone, she sees Kate hold on to a chair. "Wire fraud?" she says. "What does that mean?"

Serafina has a pretty good idea. "I think he's talking about tapping phone lines or intercepting phone conversations by some means. Or other transmitted data. That's serious stuff, alright. I think hunting regulations, that's one thing, but wire fraud? Yeah. Could be trouble." She suddenly feels a little sad. Just a little. True, this probably means the problems are over. But poor Kate, it looks an awful lot as though she's really fallen for that John. And now the man may wind up in jail. She is beginning to feel giddy and she looks over at Leo. His eyes are closed; he has fallen asleep. She gets Kate's attention by standing up and putting her finger across her lips, nodding in the direction of Leo.

Kate bends over to kiss him on the forehead. "Sleep well, Dad," she whispers.

She also rushes to gently stroke his cheek and beat the laughing attack that she knows is coming. As she lifts her head, she sees a damp spot on the pillow. When she looks at Kate, it's clear where that tear came from. Wimp.

– 46 –

"Academia too may not escape untarnished. It is expected that Professor Mercier, who has already been questioned, and Professor Mark Reeling of Florida State will be required to testify."

Toni places his index finger to mark the spot of the paper where he has stopped reading and looks with exaggerated horror at Mark. "Well... that's it then, Reeling, it's the dungeon for you; no doubt about it."

The plane has just broken through the low cloud cover on its descent into New York's La Guardia airport and is gliding almost silently above the sparkling lights of the city.

Mark reaches over, trying to indicate another place on the paper. "Why would I worry," he says, "they permit purely social visits nowadays."

"Go ahead and laugh. I doubt that is intended for people of your kind. I saw the word, here." He has moved his finger. "Right here. Blood. I'm beginning to think that inviting you to be a guest speaker at a Global Warming conference is a pretense. They want you closer to the scene of the crime. They're gonna fry your ass."

"Did you see the pictures?"

"Never mind the pictures. It says here, look, '*This reporter also regrets, having followed the story closely from the beginning, that the find–now affectionately referred to in the scientific community as "Katie's Blue Rock"–should be tainted with blood.*'"

"You can be just so emotional some times. Nobody died or suffered permanent injury," Mark says. "There is a positive aspect to all of this. It has definitely focused everyone's attention. There's word that N.A.S.A. will become involved. I have come to accept that the physics are just different from the ones we know about and I'm not alone in this. Remember what I said in the very beginning? We are there now. It no longer is possible to just drop the subject. *The Times* is going to run a feature article next week. They're going to turn the argument around. They'll state definitively that the physics of the fragment don't conform to those of the cosmos and that the scientific community be well advised to look elsewhere. And why do you keep going on about blood?" He takes the paper out of his hands and searches the page. "Here." He shows Toni and hands the paper back. "She has it about right. And you may want to brush up on your knowledge of physics and cosmology a little. It does have a way of crystallizing one's concept of proportionality, to say the least."

Before he starts to read, Toni looks over and squints when seeing the glint in Mark's eyes. "My my, aren't we feeling ever so superior today. I can certainly visualize your students gushing at your feet." He turns his attention back to the article.

"*Now that the debate as to whether it actually is man-made material is all but over, there remains the mystery of how the fragments got to where they were found. The site displays no evidence of any recent impact, and knowledgeable sources consider it impossible for more than one fragment to be found at such close proximity. One hypothesis, originating at Tokyo University, has ancients, having observed a meteor shower, gathering fragments and placing them together.*

And theories about the location, of course, take a back seat to the big question, and the race is on for the answer. If 'Katie's Blue Rock' does not conform to the known physics of our universe, then...!"

"Well," Toni says, "I was right; a bloody mystery. I'm telling you. First, it's missing carbon and now a missing bodyguard. Maybe you'd better go missing too. Hawaii, I say. Were you talking about the picture of Kate and Blue?"

"No. Well, yes, and the columnist, Ruby Sinclair. Something in what she said, when she called, makes me think that her personal involvement with this story goes well beyond the norm. I'll find out when I have dinner with her tomorrow."

Toni folds up the newspaper carefully and pushes it into his overnight bag. "The way she describes the girl, Kate..."

"I noticed that," Mark says. "She seems conflicted about her, even her father, to some extent. As if she can't decide whether they're naïve country bumpkins or not. I can't see her being petty and jealous just because Kate's writings have suddenly started to sell with all that publicity. They've even reprinted a couple of her earlier stories. It's all kid stuff, but she gets some notice for the rapid increase in her level of thoughtful insight. That's likely part of why Sinclair was so insistent about hooking up while I'm in New York, to see what I know."

"Right," Toni says with a last look around for their belongings. "Where did you say our Ruby wants to take us for dinner?"

"She insisted," Mark laughs, "on surprising us."

"Ladies and gentlemen, welcome to the Big Apple."

Cupping his ear, Toni, managing to look concerned, whispers. "Did the captain say 'Big Apple' or 'Big House'?"

– 47 –

The days have come to be just so much colder and shorter now. So many changes. And yet for Blue, with Kate and everyone not expected back before sunset, this day will surely still be a day too long.

After spending most of the morning doing his usual good work keeping his eyes open while staying out of the way in the barn, he had followed Manuel who, shouldering a shovel, had headed for the woods. He had not seemed eager to have him tag along. But Blue, having picked up an unusual scent a day earlier, was not to be denied, though he had kept some distance.

The snow did come, light at first. Manuel had pushed around some dirt at the place where all the troubles began. Probed by many hands and machines, dug up, filled in and leveled, the double fencing now gone, there really wasn't anything left for Manuel to do.

Blue had gone off on his own search and it hadn't taken long for him to be jolted. Having seen only a very small part of the weapon sticking out above the ground, he had felt the hair at the back of his neck stiffen as he remembered that hissing sound and the pain in his side! He had backed away.

It is snowing heavily now and Blue can barely make out Manuel in the distance to his left—he has started to head back. Looking over his shoulder the other direction, he can no longer see the tip of the weapon; the white stuff has covered it. One more glimpse at Manuel. No!

Blue takes a few steps only to hesitate again. Another look back. Kate... maybe Kate...? No. No more. He aggressively shakes the gathering flakes off his coat.

– 48 –

Kate is finding out that driving in a late winter blizzard on a straight highway for a long time is not easy. The snowflakes keep coming at you and after a while they have an almost hypnotic effect. She leans forward and tightens her grip on the steering wheel. You can't be too careful. Kate shakes her head. Stay alert, she tells herself, there are many miles to go.

Kate is driving home by herself. She had been right to anticipate that she might not be her usual level-headed self by the end of the day no matter what the outcome. All three of them had driven to the courthouse for John's sentencing in the morning, Serafina and Leo in one car and she in her own.

The judge had been deliberate and decisive during the sentencing, but had taken a moment to say pointedly to John, "You are extremely fortunate to have realized what you were getting yourself into when you did. Otherwise, the outcome for you might have been quite different." One year and two months with the possibility of parole. It was actually in line with what the lawyers had expected.

That Ely guy—they just can't find. But the small man, whose real name is said to be Anton Dubzak, is next. She heard the lawyers talking this morning. They're puzzled as to how he was able to secure the high-powered legal representation he did. Definitely not legal aid, she'd had heard somebody say.

Marshal Curtis, as of right now, appears to be totally off the hook. Better yet, that man will probably find a way to turn it to his advantage. John had told her that Vincent D'Groth had completely divested himself of his interest in United and that the name had been changed to something she couldn't remember. Kate is not that comfortable admitting this to herself. There had been a time when she would not have cared that much. That is not really the case anymore. Enough has happened to warrant at least some measured consequence to that Curtis.

She had been so pleased when, after the sentencing, Dad had shaken John's hand for the first time. Probably eight months with the probation, is the general consensus.

Kate again shakes her head and rapidly blinks in an effort to stay alert. Perhaps she should slow even more. It's like driving through a tunnel... a narrowing tunnel...

You should have seen the little tyke. The determination. At first, his papa John hadn't paid much attention. But that is only because lately he has become just so preoccupied with Juniors sister Bon-bon.

She had decided that this year she would make it onto the class team for the upcoming spelling bee and that had really captured John's imagination. His patience was endless and they would practice for hours and hours. Little wonder then he hadn't focused on Junior much except when he and Bon-bon had laughed at him.

"It's smooth, Junior," little Bon-bon had said. "Not schmooze."

Easy for her to say—he had trouble with the S's. I have to get it to run more schmoozly, he had said. He said it and then he had done it. All by himself, Junior did. A functional, motorized tractor from a Meccano set with only a single flaw. It was kind of jerky, rolling along the floor, and Junior wasn't happy about that. It was not schmooze. It took him days, but he did it. He studied it, disassembled it, changed it, bent it, filed it, hammered it. And finally... it was smooth. He had found the cause of the problem and the solution by counteracting it. There had been a wheel in the system that was not perfectly round and had created a disturbance. So Junior set about to modify a second wheel in the mechanism and made it also "not round." Now the second square wheel counteracted the disturbance of the first square wheel. That did it—smooth. Papa John was surprised, Grandpa

Leopold clearly pleased and Kate just knew that it had something to do with genes. Yes, yes, she knows genes aren't supposed to work that way, but it's just so uncanny, that kind of thinking. No doubt about it. From Grandpa to Leo—to her—to Junior. People have been wrong before, haven't they? Even really smart people. Both Jacob and Leo, who have become inseparable, have tried to be helpful by gathering material about genetics. Helpful, that is, if not too busy with one of their own 'projects'; not all of them deserving of this description.

No longer involved in manufacturing or engineering, Leo had listened to her suggestion and was considering an investment in a radio or television station. If he did, she had reasoned, they would all benefit. She and Serafina might no longer have to deal with the consequences of his frustrations over the lack of accurate information, and he should be able to put into practice what he had once threatened to do by financing and producing a weekly News Hour to put things right.

It, for good reason, being of considerable importance in Leo's mind whether the world runs out of conventional fossil fuel within the next forty... or two hundred and forty years, and not at all plausible that the United Nations, with respect to the developing world—or any other matter—was either doing everything right or everything wrong, the centerpiece of the programming would be the effort to gather all available opinions, news releases and facts, and extract from them the truth. Recent trends among political leaders of nations shamelessly elevating lying into a new art form and infecting large segments of new generations could likely be slowed, even if not arrested altogether.

"A tall order, daughter. And what would I be growing?" he had fretted.

"Knowledge, Leopold, and truth," she had laughed.

"Hmm," he had said.

Oft times however, Leo and Jacob would just slack off without ever admitting it. They'd amuse themselves endlessly, flipping through the news channels on the small T.V. screen in Leo's study. Jacob stretched out comfortably on the floor, they'd be searching out their least favorite talking heads. Once they found one of those "newscasters" who seemed to know everything and was not shy about conducting U.S. foreign policy for the benefit of the whole world—for free—they would hit the mute button, watch and laugh.

Kate takes a deep breath and starts to hum a melody of sorts when she realizes that her mind has been drifting off. Not a good thing while driving through a blizzard.

She will enjoy her hikes with Blue, especially now that the retreat has been sold to the conservation authority. There is no longer a real urgent need to rush a new cedar fence in area seven and she's come to like walking north, near the lake...no telling what they might find next.

With Leo himself having mentioned the possible reorganization or sale of the business—involving Sam and a group of other employees—she will certainly not be involved in office affairs again. Anyway, her head a little clearer once more, she'll be too busy trying to write. For a while, the pressure from everyone—everyone except Dad—urging her to allow the work to 'mature' had gotten to her. What, leave all her friends behind and risk becoming an egocentric liar? Just give up and learn to exploit for profit the value of shock? Not likely.

Serafina was wrong about Dad, unfortunately. It could be the stress over the last few months, but the signs of his forgetfulness have been increasing. Has his self-diagnosis come to be real now? With Leo, could you ever really know?

He probably should make a change. After all, he has sold businesses before without ever looking back and always seemed to have enjoyed creating and building something much more than managing it. He would no doubt find something new to keep him occupied.

She is certain that she is ahead of Serafina and Dad on the road and that she is going to be home before them.

Serafina had received a text message from Mrs. Eller. "Call, there's news from Reeling." Not until later, all had agreed. Certainly Reeling's view of the importance of her find has evolved over time. He has no longer been so reluctant lately.

They've been too preoccupied to plan anything for the evening, so probably she should do something about dinner. For Dad, anything involving boiled potatoes and gravy would be fine. There's plenty of frozen meat. What kind doesn't matter that much; for him it's all about the perfectly boiled potatoes and gravy. She would have to deal with that same old problem, that's almost certain. She has never really mastered the art of making smooth gravy. Too often it turns out to be lumpy, or the grease will separate from the flour. The age of the universe? No, the age of all? There's a problem for you. It may, appropriately, take forever to be resolved, though the word universe itself has become so limiting in her mind of late. And would any conclusion about her find ever be definitive? And if it was, would it be accepted? Leo thinks not for a long time, if ever. Perhaps Serafina isn't so wrong with her focused concerns over the price of coffee beans. But for herself? She has actually come to be comfortable with the concept of timeless, limitless forever.

Still snowing lightly and a bit windy as she decides to leave her car at the small shed near the entrance and walk down the driveway. Manuel will have his hands full, plowing tonight. There has been quite a bit of snow, she can hear it under her feet. All the fir trees along the side of the driveway have a bright cover on them. Nice if it stays that way for the weekend; she can just imagine what it must look like north, near the lake with those pines.

She sees that orange glow of the sky behind the house. The sun is setting. She will have to check when will be the first opportunity she'll have to visit John. There are no footsteps anywhere, but getting closer to the house she does see a little mound of snow near the front door. She knows what it is. He must have been waiting there a long time.

The little mound moves and Blue's head appears from under the snow and Kate feels her lips begin to quiver.

"Tomorrow, Blue, tomorrow."

Epilogue

"Geez Grandpa, we're talking Madoc, eastern Ontario. A hundred and twenty thousand frigging dollars. When's the last time you heard of anybody around here selling a Mickey Mouse claim for real money?" The kid is eyeing his grandfather's beer while slurping on his Dr. Pepper.

"What's with your damn hurry, Timmy, those big-town losers ain't going nowhere. I can just tell, eh. And watch your language." The old man wets the palm of his right hand with the condensation from the water glass on the table and brushes his white, unruly hair off to the sides of his wrinkled face. "No more rockhounding for this crew, eh boy."

The kid looks out the window of the diner at the parking lot and focuses on the dirty Winnebago. "Hope you're right, would be just in time," he says. "I had trouble sleeping last night. It was cold; we might have a hole at the bottom. Christ, last year you were trying to sell for six thousand and you only paid ... what? Grandpa, a hundred and twenty thousand frigging dollars."

"Timmy!"

He resumes his mission to rescue the two remaining French fries from the mountain of catsup on his plate. "You could think about me for a change, Grandpa. I'm getting on in age now and next you'll have me back in stinking school." His usually bright blue eyes below the long, dirty-blond hair have turned cloudy.

"You ain't got no call to be going that far now—I never said nothing about no school. I still figure we'll wind up in Alaska with a real claim someday soon."

The boy slides the sleeves of his thick grey sweater up his arms and pounds the table with his fist, sending the glasses off on a dance. "Now you're talking. Christ, ain't this our chance? What we got so far? Seventeen ounces of gold, way I figure it. 's all."

"You're not listening, Boy, we'll get what's coming to us. You know it ain't got nothing to do with no gold. Remember that Florida slicker that came to the camp a couple of years ago with all those other people, that Reeling advisor? I'm talking before they dug up all that stuff and started to pay us rent?"

"Kinda. Mark...Mark Reeling."

"He wasn't a bad fellow if you overlooked him being so damn smart. He told me stuff that he probably shouldn't have. That the dark material with those specks they were collecting was alien sure enough and the same as what was found near Orangeville west of—"

"I know all that, Grandpa, everybody does."

"You keep interrupting me and you will wind up with a good education, Kid." The old man's eyes follow the waitress heading back to the counter after bringing Tim his rice pudding. "That's my job," he says when he sees his grandson crank his head.

"Jesus," says the kid.

"Anyway, I didn't pay not much attention then, but that Reeling guy kinda predicted that those official stuck-ups would be around more than we might want. It sorta looks like he knew then what they were going to do now."

The kid lifts the baseball cap off his head to scratch his hair but doesn't say anything.

"Yeah," Grandpa says, "he said because there was so much of that material way down in the ground, they would one day really want to look at how it got there. I think that time is now. And that, Timmy my boy, is how we're gonna cash in."

"I don't get that. They still got the lease and they been screwing around their little shaft all along. What's the damn difference now?"

The old man looks at the kid. "I figure it's our equipment. They need us out of the way. Not just because it's old and patched up. Stop grinning at me... eh! It kinda makes more and more sense and they're not really trying to hide anything. Smart-ass right enough, that Reeling, he said that our panning might interfere with some of the fancy testing they would have to do."

"We best make sure we keep screwing around then 'til we have the deal... right," says Tim.

The Grandfather rubs his left hand across the face but doesn't answer.

Tim sits up straight. "Ain't there Government people in on this too, don't we have to be careful? They can do stuff even if it ain't right, you know... Eh Grandpa, look; here come the suckers."

The old man looks out to the parking lot. "Rusty is a good guy, we can talk to him, eh Kid. The woman? I don't know."

Tim had been fortunate enough to have the better looking of the suckers slide in on his side of the booth when he had gotten up. Rusty Herga, red-faced and big in all directions was a better match opposite at the outside of Grandpa.

"Yaaah David," says Rusty Herga when opening his briefcase to pull out a green folder, "you better know that I'm only here because of my familiarity as the site foreman with so many of the various details and because I've known you for so long. Mrs. Attwater has been given complete authority...by all involved."

"You can call me Rita, Mr. Warren."

"I will, Rita, but you can't, Kid."

Tim chuckles awkwardly when he looks away from "Mr. Warren" to glance at Mrs. Attwater. She's probably about Mom's age, thinks Tim. Maybe about forty and really really fit looking in her black pant-suit with that short, boy-like cut of her brown hair.

"What do I tell my principals, Mr. Warren, are we about there?"

"Was it you who bought them two other claims near us?" David Warren asks.

Rusty Herga looks to Mrs. Attwater for the response but she only nods. "You know we did, David," he says. "Didn't pay that much for them neither. And we did lose some major funding when Marshal Curtis pulled out of the consortium."

"I can't rightly see you as a prospector—Ma'am," Tim is quick to fill the momentary silence, not looking at anyone.

She smiles at David Warren before she punches Tim's arm. "Your grandson has a head on his shoulder." She pauses. "A big one. We all know what this is about; or should. It's been disseminated enough by now in all the papers. It is alien material from somewhere out there and a serious and coordinated effort will be conducted to try and finally determine whether a large chunk of space debris impacted the earth or a craft of some kind crashed to the ground. It's down to these two possibilities. There will be substantial excavation in time, but the initial focus will be on seismic mapping and density analysis of the immediate area. That's thought to have the highest probability of success. And particularly for the seismic tests they cannot tolerate any interference or disturbances. It's your machinery, it's that simple."

David Warren has been following a fly—a big one buzzing the window lacking a discernible plan—with seeming concern. "The first find, 'Katie's Blue Rock'..."

Rita Attwater shakes her head. "I don't think it will ever be determined how that bit of debris got there, right Rusty?"

"Too small, probably some sort of secondary transfer," says Rusty, "or a stray fragment. But big enough to start the whole debate, eh... made the name Kate Walter almost a household name."

"And not just among scientists and readers now with her latest find. Human bones, of all things, near the blue rock site. That girl keeps finding things." Mrs. Attwater has pulled the green folder over to her side but hasn't opened it. She too looks at the confused fly clowning around at the window. "Well, Mr. Warren, do we have a deal?" she asks.

"What were you talking about, Rusty? Curtis... Curtis what?"

"You know, that man. He never lost interest in the rock. The man who was in the fight over the first find. He might well wind up regretting it now, he's been implicated in them finding those bones we were talking about." Rusty Herga laughs. "We had to chase all over South America, Costa Rica finally, just to get some papers signed. Almost like he's hiding... unless he likes to dance the Paso Doble that much."

Rita Attwater waves her hand. "Never mind all that. Mr. Warren, do we have the deal?"

"Right," he says, "ain't nobody ever gonna say David Warren ain't a man of his word. Don't know what we're gonna be doin', Timmy, this claim will be hard to replace, sure 'nough. But... a promise is a promise. Somehow I figures the good Lord will provide. Two hundred thousand and she's all yours."

Rusty Herga stiffens visibly and looks as though he's about to say something when Mrs. Attwater clears her throat. "Uh uh." She has a long look at Timmy on her right who at the moment is concentrating on a Dr. Pepper stain on the table right in front of him. She opens the green folder about an inch and strains to peek inside it for reasons known only to her. "A hundred and eighty," she says.

"Done," says Grandpa Warren.

They're waiting for news from the waitress about the thickness of the available T-bone steaks when they make out Rusty and the Woman in the lightly falling rain outside. They first look at the Winnebago in the parking lot before getting into Rusty's van. As they drive past near the window, Rita Attwater waves at them. David Warren smiles and Tim waves back.

"Christ, Grandpa, what made you so sure it wasn't gonna backfire on us?"

"I wasn't really, in the beginning. But you did get me to thinking, Mr. Bighead; in one way the Government could screw us right enough, but on the other hand they're doing everything with our own damn money anyways. And I think Mrs. Rita kinda liked you."

"Oh Grandpa."

"I said kinda, Boy."

"One hundred and eighty thousand fucking dollars. I wish... I wish there was some way we could find... I could get a hold of Mom."

The old man doesn't say anything.